I was still deep in the wee

As I beeped my car unl

jabbed a gun into my back.

I froze. As a pair of nails dug into my upper arm, a gravel-voiced woman spoke into my ear. "Don't try anything stupid, and you won't get hurt."

Acclaim for the Anastasia Pollack Crafting Mysteries

Assault with a Deadly Glue Gun

"Crafty cozies don't get any better than this hilarious confection...Anastasia is as deadpan droll as Tina Fey's Liz Lemon, and readers can't help cheering as she copes with caring for a host of colorful characters." – *Publishers Weekly* (starred review)

"Winston has hit a homerun with this hilarious, laugh-until-your-sides-hurt tale. Oddball characters, uproariously funny situations, and a heroine with a strong sense of irony will delight fans of Janet Evanovich, Jess Lourey, and Kathleen Bacus. May this be the first of many in Winston's Anastasia Pollack Crafting Mystery series." – *Booklist* (starred review)

"A comic tour de force...Lovers of funny mysteries, outrageous puns, self-deprecating humor, and light romance will all find something here." – *ForeWord Magazine* (Book-of-the-Year nominee)

"North Jersey's more mature answer to Stephanie Plum. Funny, gutsy, and determined, Anastasia has a bright future in the planned series." – *Kirkus Reviews*

"...a delightful romp through the halls of who-done-it." – *The Star-Ledger*

"Make way for Lois Winston's promising new series...I'll be eagerly awaiting the next installment in this thoroughly delightful series." – *Mystery Scene Magazine*

"...once you read the first few pages of Lois Winston's first-in-series whodunit, you're hooked for the duration..." – *Bookpage*

"...madcap but tough-as-nails, no holds barred plot and main character...a step above the usual crafty cozy." – *The Mystery Reader*

"...Anastasia is, above all, a JERSEY girl..., and never, ever mess with one of them. I can't wait 'til the next book in this series..." – *Suspense Magazine*

"Anastasia is as crafty as Martha Stewart, as feisty as Stephanie Plum, and as resourceful as Kinsey Millhone." – Mary Kennedy, author of the Talk Radio Mysteries

"Fans of Stephanie Plum will love Lois Winston's cast of quirky, laughable, and loveable characters. *Assault with a Deadly Glue Gun* is clever and thoroughly entertaining—a must read!" – Brenda Novak, *New York Times* best-selling author

"What a treat—I can't stop laughing! Witty, wise, and delightfully clever, Anastasia is going to be your new best friend. Her mysterious adventures are irresistible—you'll be glued to the page!" – Hank Phillippi Ryan, Agatha, Anthony, and Macavity award-winning author

"You think you've got trouble? Say hello to Anastasia Pollack, who also happens to be queen of the one-liners. Funny, funny, funny—this is a series you don't want to miss!" – Kasey Michaels, *USA Today* best-selling author

Death by Killer Mop Doll
"Anastasia is a crafting Stephanie Plum, surrounded by characters sure to bring chuckles as she careens through the narrative, crossing paths with the detectives assigned to the case and snooping around to solve it." – *Booklist*

"Several crafts projects, oodles of laughs and an older, more centered version of Stephanie Plum." – *Kirkus Reviews*

"In Winston's droll second cozy featuring crafts magazine editor Anastasia Pollack...readers who relish the offbeat will be rewarded." – *Publishers Weekly*

"...a *30 Rock* vibe...Winston turns out another lighthearted amateur sleuth investigation. Laden with one-liners, Anastasia's second outing (after *Assault With a Deadly Glue Gun*) points to another successful series in the works." – *Library Journal*

"Winston...plays for plenty of laughs...while letting Anastasia shine as a risk-taking investigator who doesn't always know when to quit." – *Alfred Hitchcock Mystery Magazine*

Revenge of the Crafty Corpse

"Winston peppers the twisty and slightly edgy plot with humor and plenty of craft patterns. Fans of craft mysteries will like this, of course, but so will those who enjoy the smart and snarky humor of Janet Evanovich, Laura Levine, and Laura DeSilverio." – *Booklist*

"Winston's entertaining third cozy plunges Anastasia into a surprisingly fraught stew of jealousy, greed, and sex..." and a "Sopranos-worthy lineup of eccentric character..." – *Publishers Weekly*

"Winston provides a long-suffering heroine, amusing characters, a...good mystery and a series of crafting projects featuring cloth yo-yos." – *Kirkus Reviews*

"A fun addition to a series that keeps getting stronger." – *Romantic Times Magazine*

"Chuckles begin on page one and the steady humor sustains a comedic crafts cozy, the third (after *Death by Killer Mop Doll*)... Recommend for Chris Grabenstein ("John Ceepak" series) and Jess Lourey readers." – *Library Journal*

"You'll be both surprised and entertained by this terrific mystery. I can't wait to see what happens in the Pollack household next." – *Suspense Magazine*

"The book has what a mystery should...It moves along at a good pace...Like all good sleuths, Anastasia pieces together what others don't...The book has a fun twist...and it's clear that Anastasia, the everyday woman who loves crafts and desserts, and has a complete hottie in pursuit, will return to solve another murder and offer more crafts tips..." – *Star-Ledger*

Decoupage Can Be Deadly

"*Decoupage Can Be Deadly* is the fourth in the Anastasia Pollock Crafting Mysteries by Lois Winston. And it's the best one yet. More, please!" – *Suspense Magazine*

"What a great cozy mystery series. One of the reasons this series stands out for me as a great one is the absolutely great cast of characters. Every single character in these books is awesomely quirky and downright hilarious. This series is a true laugh out loud read!" – Books Are Life–Vita Libri

"This is one of these series that no matter what, I'm going to be laughing my way through a comedy of errors as our reluctant heroine sets a course of action to find a killer while contending with her eccentrically dysfunctional family. This adventure grabs you immediately delivering a fast-paced and action-filled drama that doesn't let up from the first page to the surprising conclusion." – Dru's Book Musings

"Lois Winston's reluctant amateur sleuth Anastasia Pollock is back in another wild romp." – The Book Breeze

A Stitch to Die For

"*A Stitch to Die For* is the fifth in the *Anastasia Pollock Crafting Mysteries* by Lois Winston. If you're a reader who enjoys a well-plotted mystery and loves to laugh, don't miss this one!" – *Suspense Magazine*

Scrapbook of Murder

"This is one of the best books in this delightfully entertaining whodunit and I hope there are more stories in the future." – Dru's Book Musings

"*Scrapbook of Murder* is a perfect example of what mysteries are all about—deft plotting, believable characters, well-written dialogue, and a satisfying, logical ending. I loved it!" – *Suspense Magazine*

"I read an amazing book recently, y'all — *Scrapbook of Murder* by Lois Winston, #6 in the Anastasia Pollack Crafting Mysteries. All six novels and three novellas in the series are Five Star reads." – Jane Reads

"Well written, with interesting characters." – Laura's Interests

"...a quick read, with humour, a good mystery and very interesting characters!" – Verietats

Drop Dead Ornaments

"I always forget how much I love this series until I read the next one and I fall in love all over again..." – Dru's Book Musings

"*Drop Dead Ornaments* is a delightful addition to the Anastasia Pollack Crafting Mystery series. More, please!" – *Suspense Magazine*

"I love protagonist Anastasia Pollack. She's witty and funny, and she can be sarcastic at times...A great whodunit, with riotous twists and turns, *Drop Dead Ornaments* was a fast, exciting read that really kept me on my toes." – Lisa Ks Book reviews

"*Drop Dead Ornaments* is such a fantastic book...I adore

Anastasia! She's clever, likable, fun to read about, and easy to root for." – Jane Reads

"...readers will be laughing continually at the antics of Anastasia and clan in *Drop Dead Ornaments*." – The Avid Reader

"I love this series! Not only is Anastasia a 'crime magnet,' she is hilarious and snarky, a delight to read about and a dedicated friend." – Mallory Heart's Cozies

"It is always a nice surprise when something I am reading has a tie in to actual news or events that are happening in the present moment. I don't want to spoil a major plot secret, but the timing could not have been better...Be prepared for a dysfunctional cast of quirky characters." – Laura's Interests

"This is a Tour de Force of a Murder/Mystery." – A Wytch's Book Review

"Lois Winston's cozy craft mystery *Drop Dead Ornaments* is an enjoyable...roller-coaster ride, with secrets and clues tugging the reader this way and that, and gentle climbs and drops of suspense and revelation to keep them reading." – Here's How It Happened

"...a light-hearted cozy mystery with lots of energy and definitely lots of action and interaction between characters." – Curling Up By the Fire

Handmade Ho-Ho Homicide
"Handmade Ho-Ho Homicide" is a laugh-out-loud, well plotted mystery, from a real pro! A ho-ho hoot!" – *Suspense Magazine*

"Merry *Crises*! Lois Winston has brought back Anastasia's delightful first-person narrative of family, friends, dysfunction, and murder, and made it again very entertaining! Anastasia's clever quips, fun stories, and well-deserved digs kept me smiling, and reading the many funny parts to my husband...does that count as two thumbs up in one?" – *Kings River Life Magazine*

"Once again, the author knows how to tell a story that immediately grabbed my attention and I couldn't put this book down until the last page was read.... This was one of the best books in this delightfully lovable series and I can't wait to see what exciting adventures await Anastasia and her friends." – Dru's Book Musings

"This was such a fun quick read. I can't wait to read more of this series." – A Chick Who Reads

"The story had me on the edge of my seat the entire time." – 5 Stars, Baroness Book Trove

"Christmas, cozy mystery, craft, how can I not love this book? Humor, twists and turns, adorable characters make this story truly engaging from the first to the last page." – LibriAmoriMiei

"Take a murder mystery, add some light-hearted humor and weird characters, sprinkle some snow and what you get is *Handmade Ho-Ho Homicide*—a perfect Christmas Cozy read." –5 stars, The Book Decoder

A Sew Deadly Cruise
"*A Sew Deadly Cruise* is absolutely delightful, and I was sorry when it was over. I devoured every word!" – *Suspense* Magazine
"Engaging Drama! Brilliant! *A Sew Deadly Cruise* earns 5/5 Upgraded Cabins. Winston's witty first-person narrative and banter keeps me a fan. Loved it!" –*Kings River Life* Magazine

"The author knows how to tell a story with great aplomb and when all was said and done, this was one fantastic whodunit that left me craving for more thrilling adventures." – Dru's Book Musings

"The combo of investigating and fun makes for a great read. The author does a good job of keeping the killer a secret. Overall a fun read that cozy fans are sure to enjoy." – Books a Plenty Book Reviews

"Winston has a gift for writing complicated cozy mysteries while entertaining and educating." – Here's How it Happened

Stitch, Bake, Die!

"Lois Winston has crafted another clever tale...with a backdrop of cross stitching, buttercream, bribery, sabotage, rumors, and murder...with vivid descriptions, witty banter, and clever details leading to an exciting and shocking conclusion. All making for a page-turner experience to delight cozy fans." – *Kings River Life* magazine

"...a crème de la crème of a cozy read." – Brianne's Book Reviews

"...a well-plotted mystery that takes the term 'crafty old lady' to new heights." – Mysteries with Character

"This story is fast-paced with wacky characters, a fun resort setting, and a puzzling mystery to solve." – Nancy J. Cohen, author of the Bad Hair Day Mysteries

"Lots of action, a bevy of quirky characters, and a treasure trove of secrets add up to another fine read from Lois Winston." – Maggie Toussaint, author of the Seafood Caper Mysteries, Lindsey & Ike Mysteries, and the Dreamwalker Mysteries

"The mystery was nicely executed, with bits and pieces of clues here and there as well as humorous interludes that enhanced the telling of this tale. This is another great addition to this engagingly entertaining series and I'm patiently waiting for the wedding of the century." – Dru's Book Musings

Books by Lois Winston

Anastasia Pollack Crafting Mystery series
Assault with a Deadly Glue Gun
Death by Killer Mop Doll
Revenge of the Crafty Corpse
Decoupage Can Be Deadly
A Stitch to Die For
Scrapbook of Murder
Drop Dead Ornaments
Handmade Ho-Ho Homicide
A Sew Deadly Cruise
Stitch, Bake, Die!
Guilty as Framed

Anastasia Pollack Crafting Mini-Mysteries
Crewel Intentions
Mosaic Mayhem
Patchwork Peril
Crafty Crimes (all 3 novellas in one volume)

Empty Nest Mystery Series
Definitely Dead
Literally Dead

Romantic Suspense
Love, Lies and a Double Shot of Deception
Lost in Manhattan (writing as Emma Carlyle)
Someone to Watch Over Me (writing as Emma Carlyle)

Romance and Chick Lit
Talk Gertie to Me
Four Uncles and a Wedding (writing as Emma Carlyle)
Hooking Mr. Right (writing as Emma Carlyle)
Finding Hope (Writing as Emma Carlyle)

Novellas and Novelettes
Elementary, My Dear Gertie
Moms in Black, A Mom Squad Caper
Once Upon a Romance
Finding Mr. Right

Children's Chapter Book
The Magic Paintbrush

Nonfiction
Top Ten Reasons Your Novel is Rejected
House Unauthorized
Bake, Love, Write
We'd Rather Be Writing

Guilt as Framed

LOIS WINSTON

Cover design by L. Winston

ISBN:978-1-940795-57-7

DEDICATION

To Collin and Elliot for all those hugs and kisses.

ACKNOWLEDGMENTS

Years ago, while attending my first mystery convention, an auction was held to raise money for a local charity. Several authors donated the chance to name a character in an upcoming book. Bidding was fierce! That's when I learned mystery readers love to have characters named after themselves. Since then, I've donated a character naming, along with a signed copy of the future book, whenever I've attended an event that features a charity auction. I've also periodically run character naming contests through my newsletter and did so as I was writing *Guilty as Framed*. I chose two winners, Jody Tanis and Lournetta (Lori) Smanski. Jody became a news reporter and Lournetta an FBI agent.

Experts are a vital part of an author's research. No author wants to make egregious errors in their books. I'm so grateful to Brook Terpening, P.J. MacLayne, and Karen McCullough for educating me on the technical workings of cloud servers and the large corporations that use them and to Wes Harris and Wally Lind for their law enforcement expertise.

And finally, as always, special thanks to Donnell Bell and Irene Peterson for their superb editorial skills.

ONE

"I know it sounds trite," I said, "but I feel like a kid in a candy shop." Zack and I stood over my dining room table as I ogled three dozen different wall and floor tiles spread across a white sheet being used as a neutral backdrop. Marble. Porcelain. Ceramic. Stone. Glass. Polished versus honed. Solids and patterns. Squares, rectangles, and hexagonals. We had spent the afternoon at a local decorating center, narrowing down thousands of choices to the ones currently spread before us. Now I had to settle on my picks for the two bathrooms and a kitchen backsplash.

My tired nineteen fifties suburban rancher with its peeling linoleum floors and cracked Formica countertops was about to undergo a much-needed facelift. Not that I could afford even a minor update, let alone a major renovation. I'd reluctantly agreed to the costly overhaul that someone else was footing.

Two someones, to be precise. My fiancé Zachary Barnes and my neighbor Jesse Konopka.

Zack was paying for the materials as an early wedding present, even though we still hadn't firmed up a date. Jesse, a contractor, was providing the labor. He insisted as his way of thanking me for figuring out who had tried to kill him a few months ago.

"Any we can eliminate?" asked Zack.

I stacked the half-dozen twelve-inch patterned tiles. "As much as I like these, the designs and colors are not only too trendy, I think they're too busy for such small bathrooms."

When he exhaled what I interpreted as a sigh of relief, I spun to face him. "You hate those! Why didn't you tell me?"

He offered me a sheepish grin. "I didn't want to influence you."

"But you're paying. You should have a say."

"On the contrary. It's why I'm keeping quiet."

From his perch on top of the china cabinet behind us, Ralph squawked. "*To the contrary, I have express commandment. A Winter's Tale*, Act Two, Scene Two."

"That makes no sense."

Zack chuckled. "Are you speaking to Ralph or me?"

At the mention of his name, the Shakespeare-quoting African Grey parrot I'd inherited from my great-aunt Penelope Periwinkle flew to Zack's shoulder and nuzzled his cheek.

I scowled at man and bird. "Both."

Zack reached into his shirt pocket and offered Ralph a sunflower seed. "If I told you which ones I like, you'd choose them whether you like them or not."

Busted. My guilt runneth over. I returned a sheepish grin of my own.

My name is Anastasia Pollack, AKA Clueless Wife. Fifteen months ago, I learned my deceased husband had gambled us into destitution before conveniently dropping dead in a Las Vegas casino. Convenient for him. Not so convenient for me. Instead of a sizable life insurance policy, Karl Marx Pollack left me with the ultimate trifecta—his communist mother, debt equal to the GNP of a Third World nation, *and* his loan shark.

If I allowed him, Zack would wipe out my debt and move us to a new home. I won't let him. My Karl-induced debt is my problem, not his.

Maybe that's why I'm having such difficulty choosing tiles.

But at that moment the doorbell rang, postponing any further conversation on decision-making. I strode from the dining room, through the living room, to the foyer. When I swung open the front door, I came face-to-face with an elderly man dressed in a moth-eaten topcoat and a well-worn dark brown old-fashioned fedora. Deep wrinkles crisscrossed a sallow complexion in need of a razor. At the sight of me, a puzzled expression settled across his face.

"May I help you?"

He spoke around an unlit cigar stub clenched in the corner of his mouth. "I'm looking for Johnnie D."

"You have the wrong house."

"I don't think so."

"No one by that name lives here."

He stared over my shoulder into the hallway and shook his head. "No, this is definitely the house where Johnnie D. lives." Then he turned his attention back to me. "He's got something of mine. I've come to collect it."

"Look," I said, moving to close the door on him, "I don't know any Johnnie D. If he lived here at one time, he's long gone."

He grabbed the door and started to push his way inside. His strength belied his advanced age. Zack came up behind me and grabbed the door to prevent the man from entering. In a forceful tone he asked, "Do I need to call the police?"

Ralph flew off Zack's shoulder, emitted a menacing squawk, and transitioned from mild-mannered pet to protective predator. The guy's eyes grew wide with fear. He dropped his hand and backed away from the entrance. "That won't be necessary."

Then he spun around and made a hasty retreat toward a late model black SUV idling in front of my house. After he jumped into the rear passenger seat, the car sped away. Zack waited until the vehicle had turned the corner before closing the front door.

"What was that all about?"

"Beats me," I said.

"Any chance he was looking for Karl?"

I shuddered. Had Karl used multiple aliases to borrow money from more than one loan shark? How many more of these cockroaches would eventually show up at my door? "I hope not, but from my limited experience with loan sharks, they want their money yesterday. They don't wait a year or more to collect."

Zack nodded. "Valid point. There's another possibility."

"Such as?"

"Someone named Johnnie D. may have lived here decades ago. If this guy suffers from dementia, he might think he's still in the twentieth century."

"Someone else was behind the wheel of that car."

Zack pulled out his phone. "Could be an Uber."

"Uber didn't exist in the twentieth century."

He shrugged. "Time isn't linear for people suffering from dementia."

"Who are you calling?"

"Spader. If the guy has dementia, someone is probably looking for him."

"Spader works homicide."

"I'm aware of that, but after your latest escapade, he asked me to notify him whenever anything odd occurs. That guy showing up strikes me as odd."

"*Whenever?* Not *if?*"

He quirked an eyebrow. "You do have a track record."

"It's not like I go around searching out dead bodies."

"And yet you keep finding them."

"That guy isn't dead."

"But you can't argue that his showing up here wasn't odd."

"Extremely. Call Spader. I'm going back to mulling over tile."

A few minutes later Zack rejoined me in the dining room. "There are no open Silver Alerts anywhere in the tri-state area, but Spader said that could just mean no one has reported the guy missing yet. He asked me to send him a photo from our security camera in case an alert comes in."

He wrapped his arm around my shoulders. "Now it's time to make a commitment."

I smiled and pointed to my engagement ring. "I already did."

"To tile."

I grabbed three samples off the table. "I think we should go classic. Carrera. Basketweave for the bathroom floors. Subway tiles for the showers. Herringbone for the kitchen backsplash."

He squeezed my shoulders. "See, that wasn't so hard, was it?"

"You really like them?"

He grinned. "You know me, I'm a classic kind of guy."

I gave him a once-over. "Indeed, you are." Classic good looks, definitely. After all, the guy's DNA had emerged from the same primordial pool as that of Pierce Brosnan, Antonio Banderas, and George Clooney.

Still, *classic* was not the first adjective to spring to my mind in describing photojournalist Zachary Barnes, unless perhaps *classic* referred to classic spy, completely secretive regarding a side gig he swears is a figment of my overactive imagination. But I bit my tongue. No matter how much I suspected Zack also worked for one of the D.C. alphabet agencies, he'd only deny it, as he had on numerous occasions. This was a can of slimy wrigglers best left unopened. At least for now. I offered him a smile accompanied by a nod.

~*~

As we prepared to sit down for dinner later that evening, the doorbell rang once again. "I'll get it," said Alex.

I stopped him. "Let Zack."

He glanced from me to Zack, then exchanged an odd look with his brother before shrugging. "Sure. Go for it."

"I'll explain later," I whispered as my mother-in-law lumbered into the dining room, scowling as she passed Zack.

"Got it," said Alex. He shot a quick side-eye toward his grandmother, then placed the garlic bread on the dining room table. Nick followed with the green beans as I settled the lasagna onto a trivet.

A moment later Zack returned with Detective Samuel Spader in tow. "Didn't mean to interrupt your dinner," he said, eyeing the spread on the table.

"Would you like to join us, Detective?" Knowing Spader, if he didn't accept, he'd most likely grab a fast-food burger for dinner. He'd never said one way or the other, but I suspected there was no Mrs. Spader or potential Mrs. Spader in his life. "We have plenty," I added.

"You always have plenty," muttered Lucille, "except when I

invite my friends."

I ignored her. Lucille and her friends, all Daughters of the October Revolution, were one-direction communists, always taking without asking. In their eyes, what's mine—or anyone's—was theirs. Which is why we kept everything from office supplies to wine and liquor locked in the apartment above my garage. Although tempted, I hadn't yet padlocked the refrigerator or pantry. Which was why I often arrived home to find both nearly empty.

While Detective Spader debated whether to accept my invitation, Zack headed into the kitchen, momentarily returning with an extra plate, glass, and utensils, and set them at the one available spot at the table. "Have a seat, Detective."

Spader pulled out the chair and sank into it. "Thanks. Been awhile since I've had a home-cooked meal."

I didn't doubt it.

Lucille glared at him from across the table. We were all cognizant of my mother-in-law's disdain of law enforcement, especially local law enforcement, given her constant run-ins with them, and specifically with Detective Samuel Spader. The feelings were mutual.

Spader never just dropped in. Our relationship had improved since we first met last summer when he suspected Lucille of the strangulation murder of her roommate at the Sunnyside of Westfield Assisted Living and Rehabilitation Center. Hence, her overt animosity.

Several dead bodies later, Spader's attitude toward me had moved from antagonistic, to reluctant acceptance, to an admiration of my sleuthing skills. However, our interactions had never crossed over into friendship. Spader never stopped by just to say hello. If he was here, it was because he had information about our earlier visitor.

He held my gaze for a moment, offering me an almost imperceptible nod as I served him a large helping of lasagna. I glanced at Zack. He also nodded slightly, a silent consent among the three of us to postpone our discussion until after dinner when we could adjourn to the apartment for privacy.

~*~

Half an hour later, ignoring her dog's needs, Lucille trundled off to camp out in front of the television in the den. "I guess he's officially my dog now," said Nick, grabbing Devil Dog's leash.

"You've been adopted," said Alex as he loaded the dishwasher.

"If he's my responsibility from now on, I'm officially changing his name."

Lucille, the diehard commie, had dubbed her French bulldog Manifesto after the communist treatise. From Day One we had all refused to use the moniker, opting instead for a name more suitable to the dog's personality. We alternated between Mephisto and Devil Dog. Although in recent months, the pooch had mellowed, turning his back on his mistress, and taking a shine to Nick. Neither Mephisto nor Devil Dog now fit his new personality.

"Have something in mind?" asked Zack.

Nick cocked his head and studied the subject in question. Devil Dog looked up at him with mournful eyes. "I'll think of something. Right now, he's telling me he's really got to go."

"My brother the dog whisperer," said Alex.

"You're just jealous of my talents," said Nick, clipping the leash to the dog's collar.

"Grab a jacket," I said as he headed for the back door.

"It's been spring for weeks, Mom."

"Not according to the thermometer." I pointed toward the mud room. "Jacket. Now."

He pulled a hoodie off a hook and shoved his arms into it. "Happy?"

"Ecstatic. Don't forget a poop bag."

After Alex finished loading the dishwasher and switched it on, he asked the three of us, "So what's going on with you guys? You haven't found another dead body, have you, Mom?"

"No, nothing like that."

"Then what?"

I told him about the stranger who'd come to the door earlier. Then I turned to Spader. "I'm assuming you have some information on him?"

Spader nodded. "Should we talk here?"

We could hear the television blaring from the den. "Once Lucille settles into an evening of *90 Day Fiancé*, the house would have to go up in flames for her to budge."

Spader barked out a laugh. "You're kidding! That old commie bat is a reality TV junkie?"

"As strange as it sounds," said Zack. "You on the clock, Detective, or can we offer you an after-dinner drink?"

Spader checked the time. "I was officially off-duty twenty minutes ago."

When we first met, I was convinced the overweight, middle-aged detective with a fondness for both nicotine and alcohol wouldn't survive to retirement. However, in the last few months Spader had trimmed down, no longer reeked of cigarettes, and had lost the telltale ruddiness often associated with alcoholism. I'd probably never know what had inspired his newfound healthy-living regime, but I no longer viewed him as one beer and a drag away from a massive coronary.

Still, I'm not sure I would have tempted fate by offering him a drink.

Zack handed Alex the apartment key and asked him to retrieve a bottle of brandy. Spader raised an eyebrow. I explained why we didn't keep anything alcoholic in the house. "With the meds she's on, my mother-in-law isn't allowed to drink, but that doesn't stop her."

"She hasn't tried to raid the apartment when you're not home?"

"She can't manage the stairs."

"I've never known an alcoholic to let a flight of stairs stop her," said Spader.

Was he speaking from personal experience?

"She also doesn't have a key," added Zack. "And she never will."

When Alex returned with the brandy, Zack splashed a generous amount into glasses for the adults while my son nuked a hot chocolate for himself, then settled into one of the kitchen chairs. I debated asking him to leave, but depending on what Spader had to say, decided he should probably be made aware of the situation.

Spader took a sip of brandy and smacked his lips. "Smooth."

"Can I assume you've learned the identity of our visitor?" I asked.

"And then some. His name is Cormac Murphy. He was recently released from federal prison after completing most of a twenty-year sentence."

I didn't like the sound of that. "For what?"

"This time? Counterfeiting and forgery. He's a career criminal connected to the Boston mob. The Feds once suspected he had information on the Isabella Stewart Gardner Museum art heist in Boston back in 1990."

"He was a suspect?" I asked.

Spader shook his head. "Not exactly. Turns out he had an ironclad alibi."

"And they believed him?" asked Zack. "We all know alibis can be bought."

"Not this one," said Spader. "He was doing time in Leavenworth. The guy's been in and out of lockup most of his adult life. Back then, he was serving a three-year sentence for armed robbery."

"Then why did they think he had information on a burglary in Boston?" asked Alex.

"They bandied about dozens of theories trying to solve the crime and find the missing artworks. Most centered around Boston's various mobs. One theory suggested members of Murphy's gang pulled off the heist, but Murphy denied any knowledge of the crime."

"Prison sentences have never deterred mob bosses from continuing business as usual," said Zack. "Murphy could have orchestrated the heist from behind bars."

"I'm sure the cops thought along those lines," said Spader, "but neither they nor the Feds could find enough evidence to prove that theory or any of the others."

"I've been to the Gardner Museum," I said. "They display empty frames where the stolen paintings once hung. It's considered history's greatest art theft."

Spader nodded. "Half a billion dollars' worth of masterpieces, and they're all still missing."

Alex whistled under his breath. His eyes bugged out. "You mean they've never found any of the paintings?"

"No," said Spader. "And most of the suspects are now dead. The case is still open, but it's going nowhere for obvious reasons."

"Why would Murphy show up here?" I asked. "Do you have any information on this Johnnie D. he claims lived here?"

"Maybe. Johnnie D. could be John Doyle. One of the prevailing theories is that Murphy's mob stole the artworks to leverage his release. His driver was Robert "Bobby" Doyle, one of the FBI's prime suspects in the heist. They believe he hid the artworks until the manhunt for the thieves waned and he could negotiate Murphy's release."

"Which obviously didn't happen," I said. "What went wrong?"

"Doyle was brutally murdered about a year and a half after the heist."

"Who killed him?" asked Alex.

"No one knows," said Spader.

"Had Doyle begun negotiations?" asked Zack.

Spader shrugged. "Your guess is as good as mine. According to my sources, the Feds remain mum on the subject."

"John Doyle is a common Irish name," I said, "but if Johnnie D. is John Doyle, how does he fit into all of this?"

"Bobby Doyle had a cousin named John Doyle," said Spader.

"I'm willing to bet there are dozens of Robert Doyles throughout the Boston area," said Zack, "and many of them probably have a cousin named John."

"Agreed," said Spader.

"Besides," I said, "we're nowhere near Boston. Why would Murphy think he'd find the guy he's looking for here?"

"Do you know the name of the family who owned this house before you?" asked Spader.

"Not offhand. It wasn't Doyle, though. I'm sure of that. I'd have to look through our records."

"I'll save you the trouble," said Spader. "It was Gallagher. Kellen and Shauna Gallagher."

"That sounds about right. We never met them. They had moved before we made an offer on the house. Their attorney handled settlement for them."

"If I were a betting man," said Spader, "I'd put money on the Gallaghers and their young son having entered Witness Protection."

"What makes you think that?" asked Zack.

"Because there's no trace of them since Murphy's conviction, and Shauna Gallagher was Johnnie Doyle's sister."

TWO

"Another *was*?" asked Zack.

"Or is," said Spader. "Of course, there's no way of knowing for sure if the Gallaghers entered WITSEC. The U.S. Marshals don't divulge that information."

"Ever?" asked Alex.

"I've never heard of it happening," said Spader. "But I'm a county detective with no skin in this game. No way would anyone give me information on whether someone entered WITSEC, let alone offer me current details about them."

I locked eyes with Zack. He reached for my hand and gave it a reassuring squeeze as I asked Spader, "Do you think Murphy showed up here to take revenge on the Gallaghers for something Johnnie D. did?"

"Doubtful. He could have orchestrated that years ago from prison. These guys don't wait decades to settle scores. More likely, he thinks Johnnie D. knows where his cousin stashed the artworks."

"Assuming Bobby Doyle was involved in the heist," I added. "But even if Johnnie knows where the artworks are hidden, why would he tell Murphy?"

Spader quirked his mouth. "Come on, Mrs. Pollack. You know the answer to that."

"I don't," said Alex.

I nodded toward Spader. "Because Murphy would make him an offer he couldn't refuse."

"What kind of—" Alex's jaw dropped, and his eyes grew wide. "Oh!"

"I don't think we need to worry," Zack assured him.

Famous last words. My track record of late proved otherwise. "Wouldn't Boston PD and the FBI have questioned all of Bobby Doyle's associates and relatives years ago?"

"I'm sure they did," said Spader. "Were they truthful?" He shrugged. "In my experience, people in the mob and those connected to them by blood or marriage are rarely truthful. They have too much to lose. If it's one thing organized crime hates more than anything, it's a rat. But whatever information the Feds did glean through interviews, none of it ever resulted in arrests or recovery of the artworks."

"However," he continued, "as far as I can tell, there's never been any definitive evidence linking Bobby Doyle to the artworks, either for the theft or afterwards. Just loose connections to various other suspects and lots of speculation."

"His murder had nothing to do with the art theft?" asked Zack.

"No one knows. Or if they do, they're not saying. Doyle was a loser trying to worm his way into the upper echelons of the mob," said Spader. "Over the years he'd made lots of enemies. Any one of them might have had a big enough beef with the guy to kill him.

One theory speculates he was killed in retaliation for a plot against a rival crime boss. Another suggests his bragging about a non-existent connection to the Gardner heist led to his demise."

"Why would someone brag about a crime he didn't commit?" asked Alex.

"Street cred," said Spader. "Happens all the time with mobster wannabes."

At that point Nick returned with the dog formerly known as Mephisto/Devil Dog. "Leonard," he announced as he stomped into the kitchen.

"Leonard who?" I asked.

Nick stooped to unhook the leash. "That's his new name."

"Why?" asked Alex.

"Because," said Nick, "we're studying World War Two in U.S. History, and he looks like the pictures of Winston Churchill I've seen in my history book. Minus the cigar."

"Then why not call him Winston or Churchill?" asked Alex.

Nick rolled his eyes at his brother. "Too obvious. Leonard was one of Churchill's middle names. Winston Leonard Spencer Churchill. Besides, you have any idea how many bulldogs are named Winston or Churchill?"

"Can't say I've ever been curious enough to look it up," said Alex, "but do you realize Devil Dog—"

"Leonard."

"Whatever. *Leonard* is a *French* bulldog, not an English bulldog?"

"I don't care," said Nick. "He still reminds me of Winston Churchill."

Spader cleared his throat and stood. "I'm having flashbacks to my youth," he said.

"You had a dog named Leonard?" asked Nick.

"No, I had a brother." He turned to me. "I should get going. Mrs. Pollack, my compliments on a delicious meal."

"All the credit goes to Zack," I said. "Cooking is one of his many talents."

Spader doffed an imaginary cap toward Zack. "I may have to show up uninvited more often."

"You're always welcome," said Zack. He tilted his head in my direction. "Just as long as no dead bodies are involved."

Spader glanced in my direction. "That would make my life much easier."

"Mine, too," I agreed as we walked Spader to the door. But before he left, I asked him one more question. "Whatever happened to Johnnie D.?"

"No one's saying," said Spader, "but Johnnie had been working as a bagman for Murphy, and he disappeared around the same time as his sister and her family."

"Could he have entered Witness Protection as well?"

Spader nodded. "Or he's dead. He testified against Murphy at his last trial."

Which explained why the Gallaghers might be in WITSEC. I glared at Spader. "Nothing like burying the lede, Detective."

Once again, he shrugged. "It's nothing but speculation, Mrs. Pollack. All I can tell you is, if Doyle is dead, his body has never been recovered. Same for the Gallaghers."

"Which means nothing," I said. "We're talking about mobsters. They *disappear* bodies all the time." Especially in New Jersey, home to many an unmarked final resting place, thanks to the Atlantic Ocean and the swamps of the Meadowlands.

"I'm not privy to information that would provide us with any facts one way or the other," said Spader. "There's no open case, missing persons or otherwise. Even if there were, it wouldn't fall to my department to investigate unless Doyle or one of the Gallaghers turns up dead in Union County. That hasn't happened, and for all concerned, I hope it never does."

I nodded. "Ditto to that, Detective."

After Spader departed, Zack and I pulled Alex aside. "Not a word of what you heard to anyone, understand?"

"Not even Sophie?"

"Especially not Sophie."

"Why?"

"She's dealt with enough lately," said Zack.

Alex's girlfriend had recently lived through the murder of her estranged mother, an attempt on her father's life, and her own near kidnapping, which I'd thwarted only because I was in the right place at the right time. "Don't give her something else to worry about."

"Okay." He then glanced back toward the kitchen where Nick was busy filling Leonard's water and food bowls. "What about Nick?"

What about Nick? His maturity level had not yet caught up with that of his older brother. I turned to Zack. "What do you think?"

"Bare-bones," he said. "And we make it clear he's not to say a word to anyone."

After Alex headed to his room, Zack and I joined Nick in the kitchen. He shrugged off the Cormac Murphy episode as uninteresting, unimportant, and unworthy of repeating to anyone. Fine by me.

Once we were alone, Zack said, "At least we've ruled out

Cormac Murphy having a connection to Karl."

"Cold comfort," I grumbled. "Too much of what happened today makes no sense."

"Like?"

"If Murphy suspected Bobby Doyle knew where the Gardner artworks were hidden, why didn't he strongarm him into telling once he got out of prison years ago?"

"Maybe Bobby was dead by then."

"Point taken but if so, why wait so long to pressure Johnnie into telling him?"

"We don't know that he did wait. If, as Spader suggested, Bobby lied about his connection to the burglary, Johnnie wouldn't know anything about the whereabouts of the paintings."

"And Murphy would believe Johnnie?"

Zack nodded. "He'd have no reason not to, especially if he figured out Bobby didn't have the smarts to pull off such a heist and was lying about his connection to the crime."

"Maybe the Feds suspected Murphy had information about the artworks because Bobby told them Murphy had planned the heist. If Murphy found out Bobby had squealed to the Feds, he would have retaliated against him."

"That's certainly a possibility, but if Bobby had lots of enemies, as Spader indicated, it's all a guessing game."

"Then what changed Murphy's mind? Why come looking for Johnnie now?"

"Maybe nothing. He might want other information from Johnnie."

"Something that means more to Murphy than putting out a contract on Johnnie for sending him to prison for nearly twenty years?"

"Makes sense," said Zack.

"Unless Murphy lied to me, and Johnnie didn't have anything that belonged to Murphy. Maybe he just wanted the pleasure of personally killing Johnnie and was willing to wait until he was released from prison. If he didn't have Johnnie killed, he may not have known that he'd disappeared years ago."

Zack shook his head. "Unlikely. Mob bosses stay connected, even in prison. Besides, you know as well as I do, guys like that don't get their hands dirty. They have people who perform those tasks for them."

I sighed. "There is that." But it didn't explain why Murphy would come looking for a man he knew disappeared years ago, whether he had had him killed or not.

Before I could voice that thought, Zack dropped a bombshell. "I suspect Doyle and the Gallaghers never entered Witness Protection."

"Then what happened to them?"

"I think Murphy had them eliminated before you and Karl purchased this house."

"But we bought the house from them."

"Did you? Or did you buy it from their estate?"

I pondered that for a moment. "Wouldn't we have known if it was an estate sale?"

"Normally, but what if the Feds had a reason for keeping that information to themselves?"

"What would be their motive?"

Zack threw his arms up. "Beats me. I'm just tossing out theories."

"Then why would Murphy show up here today?"

"For one thing, we don't know that he's not suffering from

dementia. If he's been in prison all these years, he may not have any living relatives who would report him missing. Or care that he's missing."

If that was meant to ease my mind, it didn't.

~*~

The next morning as I made my way toward the kitchen, I noticed an older model black SUV driving slowly down our street. When it stopped in front of our house, I raced into the kitchen where Zack was flipping pancakes. "I think Cormac Murphy is back."

He transferred a batch of pancakes from the griddle to a plate in the microwave, switched off the burners, and followed me back into the living room. The two of us stood off to the side of the bay window to avoid notice as we spied on the vehicle and waited for the occupant to step from his car. "Can you tell if that's the SUV from yesterday?" I asked, not knowing one late model black SUV from the dozens of others on the road.

"Same make, model, and color," said Zack, "but there are thousands of those in New Jersey."

"How many with recently released mob bosses who showed up at our front door yesterday?"

He draped his arm over my shoulders and pulled me closer to him. "In all likelihood, the driver stopped to answer his cell phone or check directions."

"Really?" I craned my neck and scoffed. "In my experience, many drivers either use hands-free devices or ignore state law and talk on their phones while driving. They don't pull over."

We continued to watch, waiting for the driver to turn off the ignition and exit the vehicle, but after a few seconds, he pulled away from the curb and continued down the street.

"Do you think he noticed us?"

"No, and I don't think it was Murphy."

"What makes you so sure?"

Zack pointed across the street. "Read the sign."

Back in December, a construction crew had razed the house directly across the street from us. After her untimely death, Betty Bentworth's estranged children had sold the property to a developer. Given what had occurred inside that house, not to mention my involvement, I wasn't upset about the first tear-down on our street. I didn't need a constant reminder of Betty's murder every time I looked out my windows or exited my home.

However, the three-story garish McMansion the builder had erected was completely out of place on our street of mid-century ranchers, split-levels, and Cape Cods. I feared it was the first of many to come as more of my elderly neighbors either passed away or moved into assisted living facilities. The tear-down trend had already taken over many Westfield neighborhoods, as well as countless other towns throughout New Jersey.

The bright red sign with white lettering that had popped up on the freshly sodded front lawn announced the home would soon be on the market with an open house scheduled a week from today. As I stared at the sign, two additional cars slowly drove down the street from opposite directions, one stopping in front of the McMansion, the other in front of our house.

Zack squeezed my shoulders. "Relieved?"

"About the SUV? Definitely." Not so much for what the future held for my neighborhood.

As we stood at the window, we heard the unmistakable sounds of the rest of the household coming awake. "KP duty calls," said Zack, leading me toward the kitchen. While he returned to flipping additional pancakes, I set the dining room table.

Minutes later Nick arrived in the kitchen, his new best friend at his heels. The dog settled his rump directly in front of the stove. Doggie drool collected at the corners of his mouth, his tongue hanging to one side, as he stared at the bacon crisping inside the oven.

Nick snapped his fingers. "Peeing and pooping before bacon, Leonard."

The dog formerly known as Mephisto/Devil Dog glanced up at Nick, then emitted a doggy sigh, before standing and waddling toward the mud room.

I stared after him, then at my son. Never had I observed the dog respond to commands from Lucille the way he did to Nick. "He already answers to his new name?"

"He's smarter than we realized," said Nick.

"Who would have guessed?"

"He really is the dog whisperer," said Alex, entering the kitchen. "You should have heard him last night."

"Nick or the dog?" asked Zack.

Alex directed a thumb toward his brother. "He spent an hour performing a pet psychoanalysis and concluded Devil Dog—"

"Leonard," said Nick.

Alex sneered at him. "*Leonard* exhibited passive-aggressive tendencies stemming from his years with Grandmother Lucille."

Nick clipped the leash on Leonard. "At least one of us has a superpower."

"I have heard that pets often take on the personalities of their owners," I said. If my mother-in-law didn't hold the title for the most passive-aggressive person on the planet, she ran a close second.

Speaking of the devil—not the former Devil Dog—at that

moment the commie in question entered the dining room. In a demanding voice she bellowed, "I'm ready for my breakfast, Anastasia."

I glanced over at Nick and Leonard. At the sound of Lucille's voice, the dog had cowered behind my son. As I bit down on my tongue and began a mental count to a hundred, because anything less no longer worked, Nick and his four-legged pal escaped the house. Alex rolled his eyes. Zack yelled into the dining room, "Breakfast isn't ready for you, Lucille."

"I wasn't speaking to you," she barked back.

"That does it," I said, giving up on the calming mental recitation that I knew had little chance of working anyway. I stepped into the dining room to confront my mother-in-law. "Lucille, if you can't be civil toward Zack, you can take care of your own meals from now on."

She glared at me. "That usurper doesn't deserve any civility."

"Usurper?"

"For all I know, you were having an affair with him before my dear Karl died. Have you ever considered he may have had something to do with my son's death?"

"Of all the asinine conspiracy theories—"

At that moment Zack entered the dining room. He carried a tray filled with breakfast for one and headed toward the bedrooms. He returned shortly, sans tray, and said, "Your breakfast is in your room, Lucille. From now on, you can join us for meals only if you treat the members of this family with the respect they deserve."

"How dare you!"

"I dare, and I did."

A staring standoff commenced, but Lucille's stomach quickly

took precedence. After one final eye dagger hurled at Zack, then me, she pushed back from the table. As she lumbered toward her bedroom, pounding her cane with each step, she muttered, "I should have the police investigate both of you."

I couldn't stifle the snort or the retort that followed. "I'm sure they'd be happy to waste taxpayer money on a wild goose chase for you, Lucille. After all, you have such a great relationship with Westfield law enforcement."

At that moment Ralph flew in from the kitchen and squawked, "...*thou has more of the wild-goose in one of thy wits....* *Romeo and Juliet*, Act Two, Scene Four."

Ralph has always had impeccable timing. He settled on Zack's shoulder to await his sunflower seed accolade for another spot-on performance.

THREE

A week later, Zack and I returned from a trip to the supermarket to find traffic backed up in both directions on our street and every available curbside parking spot taken. "Good thing we have a driveway," I said as we inched our way toward the house.

"Too bad someone's parked in it," said Zack.

Sure enough, a Mercedes SUV with New York plates had pulled into our driveway. "The nerve! Now what?"

"I see only one choice," said Zack. He parked my Jetta perpendicular to the driveway, blocking the SUV from leaving.

"And what if he decides to drive across the lawn? With all the rain we've had recently, he'll cause major landscaping damage."

"With all the rain we've had recently, he'll wind up stuck up to his running boards in mud."

"And exactly how does that solve our problem?"

Zack winked at me. "I'll pull the Jersey card and make him an offer he can't refuse."

"Meaning?"

"He pays to repair the lawn in exchange for us not pressing charges for trespassing and property damage."

"I suppose that's a plan." Not a very good one but a plan, nonetheless. "Or we leave a note on his car telling him to ring the doorbell."

"That was Option Two."

"I vote for that one."

Today was the open house for the new McMansion across the street. As we began to unload groceries, I eyed the circus that had taken over our neighborhood. Two hours before the start, a queue of men, women, and children had formed, snaking from the McMansion's front door, down the block, and around the corner. "Some enterprising kid could make a fortune with a hot cocoa stand," I said.

"Preferably spiked," said Zack, his breath forming a miniature cloud as he spoke. "Feels more like December than two weeks into April."

"In more ways than one. The street looks like a mall parking lot right before the stores close on Christmas Eve." Except for the occasional outlier, all the vehicles, both parked and cruising for spots, were mostly black high-end SUVs.

Even though Cormac Murphy hadn't made a return visit, a sense of unwanted déjà vu wormed its way inside me. Attempting to rid myself of lingering trepidation, I changed the subject. "Why do so many people drive black SUVs?"

"Because black is slimming?" Zack chuckled at his own joke.

I tossed him a side-eye. "Black turtlenecks and jeans are slimming, not behemoth gas guzzlers."

"Some of those gas guzzlers are actually electrics and hybrids."

Green black cars? There was a joke hidden somewhere within those three words, but my Quip-o-Meter had deserted me. I cast a scowl at the line of people, the parked cars, the traffic, and the McMansion, then landed my ire on the oversized Mercedes SUV taking up half my driveway—the middle half—not only preventing us from parking on my own property but also blocking in Zack's Boxster. Luckily, Alex and Nick had left for their jobs at Starbucks and Trader Joe's before the Mercedes SUV arrived.

As I made my way toward the kitchen door, I stopped alongside the Mercedes SUV and tried to peer inside, but the vehicle's tinted windows obstructed my view of the interior. In a fit of pique, I kicked one of the tires.

Zack squinted at me, his silence conveying he couldn't believe what he'd just seen.

"Okay, I admit that was childish, but I feel like we're stuck in the middle of a funeral. Or a convention of drug dealers."

"I have no idea why people gravitate toward black vehicles," he said. "You could ask Ira."

"I'd rather continue living in ignorance." Ira Pollack, Karl's previously unknown half-brother, had entered our lives last summer. He owned a string of car dealerships across the state and was father to three extremely spoiled brats, thanks to his questionable parenting skills.

"There's always Google," said Zack.

"Do you realize we were supposed to have blush and baby blue cars on the road by now?"

"You're kidding."

"I'm serious." I explained how after the Color Council had deemed blush and baby blue *au courant* a few years ago, interior decorators and clothing designers had embraced the color palette. Sadly, the automotive industry had not.

Once inside, Zack set the grocery bags on the kitchen table and turned to face me, his arms crossed over his chest. "Out with it."

"Out with what?"

"Whatever is really bothering you. Non sequitur rants about SUVs and Color Council choices? I'm not buying it."

"I rant all the time."

He stepped closer and placed his hands on my shoulders. "About things that matter. You can't fool me. I know you too well. Car colors don't rate so much as a miniscule blip in the greater scheme of things that bother Anastasia Pollack."

I sighed. Busted again. "You're right. All those black SUVs out there. How do we know one of them doesn't belong to Cormac Murphy? What if he's hiding in plain sight, waiting to strike?"

"To do what?"

I threw my arms up in the air. "I don't know. That's what freaks me out the most. Even though it's been a week, I don't think we've seen the last of him, and I can't shake this feeling that something bad is going to happen."

"Would you feel better if we keep the alarm set twenty-four/seven?"

"And have Lucille trip it hourly?"

He grimaced. "Good point."

"I can't believe I'm about to say this, but maybe you should start wearing your gun."

Zack's eyes widened. He knew I was no fan of deadly weaponry, even though I owed my life to his Sig Sauer. Call it a love/hate relationship, heavy on the hate.

"You really are scared," he said.

I nodded, fighting back the tears threatening to spill down my cheeks as he drew me into his arms. "After everything that's happened this past year, maybe Cormac Murphy is the straw that finally breaks this reluctant amateur sleuth's back."

"I won't let that happen," he said.

I desperately wanted to believe in my fiancé's superpowers, not to mention his superior marksmanship. I inhaled a few calming breaths and tried to shake off the uneasiness that had settled over me since Cormac Murphy first appeared at my door. "Okay," I said. "I'll start putting the groceries away while you stick a note on that Mercedes."

Neither of us got very far before the squealing of brakes, followed by a loud crash sent us racing from the kitchen. Zack flung open the door in time for us to witness two drivers exit their crumpled vehicles and quickly progress from hurling insults to throwing punches. As traffic backed up in both directions, car horns blaring, two women emerged from the passenger sides of the fender-bender vehicles and joined in the melee.

None of the people waiting in line for the open house interceded, but those with an unobstructed view of the fight had whipped out their phones and began recording. "Just what the world needs," I said, watching both men draw blood as the women fought to gouge each other's eyes out.

"What's that?"

"Another Humans Behaving Badly video posted all over social media."

Zack shook his head. "Never underestimate the stupidity of the human race." He then pulled out his own phone, not to record the fracas but to called 911.

In less than two minutes we heard the approaching sirens, but with cars parked on both sides of the street and others clogging the roadway, the police were forced to abandon their patrol cars at the end of the block and hoof it the remainder of the way to the brawling adults.

Officers Harley and Fogarty were the first to arrive. As they attempted to pull the two men apart, one of them hauled off and landed a right hook to Harley's nose.

Fogarty zapped him with his taser, and while the guy writhed on the ground, Harley cuffed his assailant. The second guy was too stunned to offer any resistance, and he, too, was swiftly cuffed.

Meanwhile, the two women continued to brawl, yanking out fistfuls of hair from each other's heads until another pair of Westfield's finest arrived to separate and cuff them. All four were then marched down the street and locked into waiting patrol cars.

While Fogarty began taking statements from the nearby crowd, Harley headed in our direction. He held a wad of tissues under his nose to stanch the bleeding, but from the small amount of red staining I saw, his injury appeared minor. Still, he'd probably soon have a robust shiner. "Want some ice?" I asked as he drew near.

"If you don't mind, Mrs. Pollack." He gingerly touched the bridge of his nose and winced.

"Looks like it's broken," said Zack.

"Occupational hazard. Not the first time. Probably won't be the last."

I headed into the house to grab an ice pack for him and additional tissues. When I returned, he placed the ice across the bridge of his nose. The bleeding had subsided. "I'm beginning to think it's safer dealing with drug gangs than these crazy house hunters," he said. "Third weekend in a row we've had to break up one of these fights."

Westfield and every other town within a short commute into

Manhattan had always been prime real estate, but lately the demand had grown exponentially as even the outer boroughs became out of reach for many families. Few suburban houses remained on the market more than a day or two and often sold for tens of thousands of dollars above asking price. I could get a king's ransom for my house, but I'd have to spend a king's ransom times three to buy something else. Besides, thanks to Karl, I still owed a king's ransom of debt.

One of the other officers jogged up the walk and spoke to Harley, "I've got two guys clearing the traffic. We've radioed in for two tow trucks. Anything else you need?"

"Help Fogarty take statements and see if any of those people will share the videos they took."

"Too bad we can't have that Mercedes SUV towed," I said.

Harley glanced toward the driveway. "That's not someone visiting you?"

"We came home to find it parked there," said Zack. "Probably belongs to someone waiting in line across the street."

"Trespassing on private property?" Harley lowered the ice pack and held it out to Zack. "Mind holding this for a moment?"

He dropped the ice pack into Zack's outstretched hand. Then he strode toward the SUV, pulled a pad from his inside jacket pocket, and wrote up a ticket, which he slipped under the windshield wiper. When he returned, he said, "Hopefully, I didn't just ticket your new neighbor."

"Hopefully, the ticket will keep the inconsiderate reprobate from becoming our new neighbor," I said.

Before Harley left to join the other cops canvassing the line of house hunters, he said, "I heard you had an unwelcome visit from a member of the Boston mob last week."

"Was I this week's topic of gossip around the coffee pot?" I asked.

He offered me a guilty grin. "Given your track record, Mrs. Pollack, we have to stay on our toes."

"That didn't sound like a compliment," I grumbled to Zack as we watched Harley dart across the street.

"It wasn't."

"The Westfield Police must think I'm the Typhoid Mary of murder and mayhem."

He raised an eyebrow. "Can you blame them?"

No, I suppose I couldn't. I blamed Karl, the Dead Louse of a Spouse, for my recent reputation. Before he dropped dead in that Las Vegas casino, I'd led a normal life as a happily married suburban working mom. No members of organized crime had ever shown up on my doorstep. Not a single dead body had crossed my path. No one had ever tried to kidnap me. Or kill me. Those were the days....

Of course, my supposedly happy life had also been built on an enormous lie and had collapsed around me once the liar rolled snake eyes and crapped out—permanently.

However, had Karl lived and continued to fool me into thinking everything was hunky-dory, I wouldn't now have Zack in my life. Given a choice between continuing to live in blissful ignorance with a louse or being blissfully happy with Zack was a no-brainer. Even if it meant having become a reluctant amateur sleuth who dealt with murder and mayhem on a regular basis.

~*~

An hour after the open house had ended and the street had cleared of all house hunters, the black Mercedes SUV remained parked in our driveway. If the owner hadn't attended the open house, where was he? I stepped outside and scanned the other houses on our street.

"What are you doing?" asked Zack, coming up behind me.

"Checking to see if one of our neighbors is hosting a party. The Mercedes might belong to an inconsiderate guest."

"Doesn't look like it," he said.

I had to agree. Now that the open house had ended, I recognized the few cars parked on the street and those in neighboring driveways. I heaved a sigh. "I suppose it's time to place a call to the police." Given my frequent interactions with local law enforcement, I should request installation of a hotline.

A short time later Officers Harley and Fogarty arrived at my front door. "My apologies," Mrs. Pollack, said Harley.

"For what?"

He cocked his head toward the SUV and scowled. "I figured we were just dealing with some inconsiderate jerk when I wrote up the ticket."

"We're not?"

"We just ran the plates. That SUV was reported carjacked out of a Walmart parking lot on Staten Island early this morning."

The needle on my Uh-oh-Meter swung into the red zone. "And it wound up in my driveway? What are the odds of that?"

"For anyone else," said Fogarty, "about one in a billion. For you?" He shrugged, not bothering to finish his statement.

Not what I wanted to hear. "What happens now?"

"We've called for a tow truck," said Harley.

"Do you think this could be connected to Cormac Murphy showing up last week?"

The two officers exchanged a quick glance before Fogarty said, "Hard to say. Since he's never had any dealings in New Jersey—"

"That we know of," added Harley.

Fogarty nodded. "Right. Anyway, he's not on our radar. Detective Spader might know more."

"Spader's Homicide, not Organized Crime," I reminded them.

"They often go hand-in-hand," said Harley. "Anyway, we'll let him know about this."

Zack had pulled out his phone while the officers spoke. After a few taps, he accessed video from our security system. It clearly showed the Mercedes SUV pulling into our driveway soon after we'd left to go shopping. A man dressed in black and wearing a ski mask exited the Mercedes. He jumped into a second SUV that had pulled up to the curb, then sped away.

Zack pulled up a second video, the one from last Sunday when Murphy rang my doorbell. The four of us compared the images. "Looks like the same vehicle," said Harley. "Or at least the same make and model."

"Nissan Pathfinder," added Fogarty. "Definitely the same vehicle. Check the scratch behind the back passenger door."

I squinted at the screen. "What scratch?"

Fogarty pointed to an extremely faint line behind the rear wheel directly under where the taillight wrapped around the SUV from the rear end to the side. Sure enough, the scratch appeared on the vehicles in both videos. "Too bad the camera didn't capture the plate," he added.

We never saw the SUV driver last week. It may have been the same man who ditched the Mercedes in my driveway. Or he could have been driving the SUV that picked up the Mercedes driver. Either way, my Uh-oh-Meter had skyrocketed beyond the red zone. Cormac Murphy definitely had something to do with a stolen vehicle winding up on my property. But why?

~*~

I continued to ponder that unsettling thought throughout the day as Zack and I packed up the kitchen. Ralph perched on the back of one of the kitchen chairs, and Leonard sprawled in front of a heating vent, both silently keeping eyes on us as we worked.

Jesse Konopka and his crew were scheduled to start demo first thing tomorrow morning. After breakfast the boys and Zack had moved the refrigerator and microwave into the dining room. I'd set up a coffee station on a card table in the corner of the room. Nonperishables filled cartons lining the floor under the dining room windows and the bump-out of the living room bay window. We'd use the apartment kitchen for cooking, and we'd wash dishes in one of the bathrooms or the basement slop sink.

Once the kitchen renovation was complete, the crew would move on to the master bathroom, then the bathroom shared by Lucille and the boys. Jesse had already discovered oak hardwood in pristine condition under all the wall-to-wall carpeting throughout the house. He assured me he'd have no trouble matching new wood to replace the tile in the foyer and the linoleum in the kitchen.

If Jesse said I'd never be able to tell where the old wood ended and the new wood began, I believed him. I'd seen the renovations he'd done on his own home, and I knew I was leaving mine in capable hands.

Besides, if I wasn't happy with the results, Robyn, his wife, would never let him hear the end of it. Not that I'd ever tell either of them. I had enough guilt knowing that Jesse refused to accept any payment for the job beyond the cost of materials.

As if thoughts of a Boston mob boss and the upcoming turmoil of a renovation weren't enough, at that moment I heard my mother-in-law and Harriet Kleinhample, her nasty sidekick, trudge into the house. Harriet is the spitting image of Estelle Getty, the actress who played Sophia on *The Golden Girls*. However, even though she also embodies all the crabbiness of that character, her personality is devoid of Sophia's few charms.

"What's going on here?" asked Harriet.

"Instead of paying for the apartment my son promised me, Anastasia is spending Karl's money on a new kitchen and bathrooms," said Lucille.

"Typical," said Harriet. "Frankly, Lucille, I don't know how you put up with her selfishness. You deserve better."

Zack and I were in the kitchen when we overheard this exchange coming from the living room. He placed his arm around my shoulders and drew me close. "Count to ten," he whispered in my ear.

"Ten?" I cocked my head to look up at him. "Ten thousand wouldn't be long enough." Inwardly, I seethed, but I made no attempt to leave the kitchen and confront my mother-in-law and her vicious cohort. What was the point? Lucille refused to accept that her son was ever anything but perfect.

Karl had been perfect, all right. A perfect con man. According to Ricardo, his loan shark, Karl had tried to kill his mother to get his hands on her life's savings. Being an old-time commie, Lucille didn't trust banks and kept all her money in a shoebox under her bed.

After a failed hit-and-run that left her injured instead of pushing up daisies, Karl decided to steal her money and torch the apartment to cover up the theft. However, instead of paying off his debt to Ricardo, he hopped a plane to Las Vegas and gambled away his ill-gotten gains before dropping dead. Now I'm permanently stuck with Lucille.

I never revealed any of this to my mother-in-law because I knew she wouldn't believe me. With a twisted logic I'll never understand, she blames me for Karl's death. She also believes I received an enormous life insurance payout which I've refused to share with her. The truth is, had Karl left me money instead of debt, I would have immediately bought her an apartment—as far away from me as possible.

A moment later we heard *The Real Housewives of Beverly Hills* blaring from the den. Leonard placed his paws over his ears and emitted a sorrowful howl. Ralph flapped his wings and let loose an earsplitting squawk.

I grabbed Leonard's leash and clipped it onto his collar while Zack tucked Ralph into the crook of his arm to keep him warm. Then the four of us escaped to the peace and quiet of the apartment above the garage.

We were nibbling on cheese and sipping wine when we heard someone climb the steps and knock on the door. "Mrs. Pollack? You in there?"

Zack opened the door to Detective Sam Spader.

"No one answered at the house," he said, as Zack led him inside. "I thought you might be up here."

"We're hiding," I said.

"I thought as much. I could hear the TV as I made my way around back. You two don't strike me as *Real Housewives* enthusiasts." He eyed the food and open bottle of wine on the coffee table.

"Care to join us?" asked Zack.

"Wish I could. I'm here on official business."

I didn't like the sound of that. "About the Mercedes?"

Spader scowled as he nodded. "We found something locked inside."

I stared at him, he stared back at me, and I knew what he was going to say before he said it. Still, I kept hoping he'd reveal they found a gun. Or drugs. Or a suitcase filled with gold bullion.

But he didn't. Spader uttered the one word I absolutely, positively did not want to hear. "A body."

FOUR

"The Mercedes owner?" I asked.

"No, the driver was a woman. She was pulled from the vehicle during the carjacking. The victim is an older male. Mid-to-late sixties or early seventies."

"No ID?" asked Zack.

"Not on him," said Spader, withdrawing his phone from his inside jacket pocket. "We're working to identify him." He tapped the screen a few times before turning the phone toward us. "Either of you recognize this guy?"

The photo showed the face of a man with his eyes closed, but his gray pallor was a dead giveaway that he wasn't sleeping. That and the bullet hole in the middle of his forehead. An unkempt beard and deep wrinkles did little to disguise the acne scars of his youth. Both the beard and his shoulder-length hair were dyed an unnatural jet black that drew attention to his age rather than disguising it.

"If I'd seen this man," I said. "I would have remembered him."

"Why is that?" asked Spader.

"He looks like a bad caricature. He stands out for all the wrong reasons."

Zack agreed. "It looks like a botched attempt to disguise himself. One look at that guy, and you'd know he's trying to hide something."

As Spader pocketed his phone, I asked, "Detective, are you suggesting the carjacker deliberately killed someone, placed him in the stolen Mercedes SUV, and parked the vehicle in my driveway?"

"It's a theory," he said.

"Why?"

"To send a message?" offered Zack.

Spader nodded toward Zack. "Sure looks that way." He then turned his attention back to me. "Made any new enemies lately, Mrs. Pollack?"

I was having difficulty processing this unwelcome news, and I could certainly do without sarcastic cop humor. "Like Cormac Murphy? Why? We have no history. He came looking for someone who lived here years ago. End of story."

"Is it?"

Wasn't it? Murphy is Boston mob. My previous mob dealings had involved New Jersey loan sharks and hitmen, like Ricardo Ferrara and my mother's ex-husband Lawrence Tuttnauer. But Ricardo was serving a life sentence, and Lawrence recently died in maximum security, which ironically, had turned out to be not at all secure for him.

Was there some connection between Murphy and Lawrence? Knowing Murphy was scheduled for release, had Lawrence secured his services before he met his untimely fate?

Lawrence was a sadistic monster. He wouldn't kill me or my kids because he knew that would kill my mother, and in his own warped way, he had still loved her. It hadn't stopped him from trying to kill Zack, though. And he wouldn't think twice about paying someone to make my life a living hell, especially since I was responsible for his arrest and conviction.

The thought broke the needle of my Uh-oh-Meter. "Was Murphy doing time at the same prison as Lawrence Tuttnauer?"

Spader shook his head. "Not even in the same state. Murphy's last sentence was served in Massachusetts."

"That leaves Ricardo."

"Ricardo?" asked Spader.

"Ricardo Ferrara, my deceased husband's loan shark. He tried to kill me nearly a year and a half ago, before you and I met."

"I'm glad he didn't succeed," said Spader.

"That makes two of us. The same can't be said for some of his other victims, though. He's locked away for life with no chance of parole."

"But not in Massachusetts," added Zack.

Spader shook his head as he eyed me. "I made that lateral move from Essex County to Union County to reduce the stress in my life. Thanks to you, that hasn't happened."

The nerve of the man! My voice rose. "I didn't ask for any of this, Detective. I don't go looking to stick my nose in police business."

"Not saying you do," he muttered, "but still...." He let his words trail off, then added, "The murder rate in Union County has increased substantially over the last year."

"Right around the time you arrived, if I'm not mistaken, Detective."

We stared at each other for a beat before he broke the tension with a belly laugh. "Touché, Mrs. Pollack." He then whipped out his spiral pocket pad, flipped it open, and jotted a few notations. "I'll see if Murphy had any connection to either Tuttnauer or Ferrara."

"Check out Emerson Dawes while you're at it," said Zack, referring to the man who provided him with half his genes and who had killed his mother. "He never served any time in Massachusetts, though."

"I'll add him to the list," said Spader, "but these are probably longshots."

"Why is that?" I asked.

"From what I've learned about Cormac Murphy, the guy is a vindictive brute. Intimidation is the least of his sins."

"Are you saying this is his way of retaliating because we didn't allow him inside the house to prove Johnnie D. doesn't live here?"

"He's done far worse."

"Worse than having his goons kill some random stranger and park him in my driveway?"

"Our vic might not be a random stranger," said Spader. "He may have been killed for some other reason. Your run-in with Murphy gave him a sadistic way of dumping the body and killing two birds with one stone, so to speak."

I shuddered. "Really, Detective?"

He shrugged. "My bad. At any rate, whether the vic was a random killing or a planned hit, it appears Murphy is taking out his frustration at not finding Johnnie D. on you."

"That's bat-bleep crazy!"

"He's a mobster, Mrs. Pollack. You should know by now they're all bat-bleep crazy."

Unfortunately, I couldn't argue with that. And here I'd thought that after a week of no further Cormac Murphy appearances, I could file last Sunday's episode away as a one-time non-event. Who was I kidding? In the space of little more than a year, I'd transformed from your average suburban working mom into a Mafia magnet, attracting bottom feeders not only throughout New Jersey but now mobsters as far away as Boston.

"Maybe we should consider entering Witness Protection and moving to some remote cabin in the woods," I said.

"Let's hope it doesn't come to that," said Spader, completely missing my attempt at humor. Or was he deliberately ignoring what might wind up as the only viable solution for keeping us all safe?

Zack laced his fingers through mine and gave me a reassuring squeeze. "Any suggestions?" he asked Spader.

"I'll keep you posted. Meanwhile, watch your backs. There's no telling what this guy's endgame is."

And that was the problem in a nutshell. Or as Ralph might say, "Ay, there's the rub." Even though no one gave voice to the thought, we all knew the body in the Mercedes was not the finale of this episode but merely the opening gambit to whatever game Cormac Murphy had decided to play.

After Spader left, Zack said, "I'm taking you and the boys out to dinner tonight."

"You won't get any argument from me, but what made you decide that now?"

"The *Real Housewives* fan club camped out in the den. You know Lucille will demand Harriet stay for dinner."

"Nothing new there." Using my standard excuse of not having enough food prepared to feed an extra person always resulted in a huge fight with my mother-in-law. Allowing Harriet to join us, meant I'd suffer through a meal peppered with her snide barbs. Whether I chose the rock or the hard place, the decision would result in both indigestion and adding additional stress to an already stressful day.

"I refuse to cook dinner for either of them tonight," added Zack, "not after the conversation we overheard earlier. They can fend for themselves."

"As long as they don't set the kitchen on fire." Lucille had a lousy track record around major appliances. As for Harriet, if her driving skills—or lack of them—were any indication of her other abilities, I wouldn't trust her with so much as a rubber spatula.

Zack shrugged. "What if they do? The security system will immediately alert the fire department. Besides, the kitchen is being gutted tomorrow anyway."

I laughed. "Now that's a once-in-a-lifetime rationale."

He offered a knowing grin and winked. "You go with what you've got."

~*~

I left for work the next day before Jesse Konopka and his crew arrived to begin demolishing my kitchen. Zack was in-between assignments—either photography or the duties he claimed sprang from my imagination—which often took him out of town for anywhere from a few hours to several weeks. Along with making sure Lucille didn't annoy the workmen, he intended to spend the day fleshing out a book proposal for his publisher.

After arriving at work, I headed for the break room where I found food editor and bestie Cloris McWerther, the woman responsible for, among other things, keeping my sweet tooth satisfied. She'd also played Watson to my Sherlock on more than one occasion, even saving my life last year when a crazy morning television producer had tried to kill me.

As I helped myself to a cup of coffee and one of the lemon blueberry muffins she'd brought from home, she asked about my weekend. Although Cloris already knew about Cormac Murphy showing up last week, I wasn't quite ready to talk about the body in the Mercedes. That would take at least a second cup of coffee and an additional muffin. Maybe more.

Instead, I opened with the kitchen renovation. "Demo is probably starting as we speak. Zack has taken on the task of keeping Lucille from causing any problems."

"He's not itching to take a sledgehammer to your countertops and cabinets?" she asked.

"You better believe I challenged him on that."

"And?"

"He said women aren't the only ones capable of multitasking."

Cloris snorted. "I'll believe that when I see it."

"I told him if he does pick up a sledgehammer, he'd better tamp down the urge to use it on Lucille. I suspect she's going to be one pain in the patootie during this renovation. I want him to enjoy cooking in that new kitchen once it's finished, not reduced to seeing photos of it from behind prison bars."

"What did he say to that?"

"He said it's the one incentive that keeps him from killing her."

Cloris cocked an eyebrow. "And what's your incentive to keep from killing your mother-in-law?"

"You know I can't lie with a straight face. I'd never get away with murder."

She popped the last bite of muffin into her mouth and washed it down with a swig of coffee before commenting. "I'm glad you realize that. I'd hate to have to bake a cake with a file hidden inside it."

"I'm not worth it?"

"Of course, you're worth it," she said, reaching for a second muffin, "but I have no idea how I'd get that cake through prison security without setting off the metal detectors."

"There is that." I gazed longingly at the remaining nine muffins before turning toward the coffee maker to refill my cup. I had probably gained a pound with that one glance. Not for the first time, I envied the metabolism of my Size Two friend.

"You only live once," said Cloris.

"But I don't want to look like a house on my wedding day."

"Which is?"

I shrugged. "We still haven't agreed on a date."

"*You* still haven't agreed on a date. If it were up to Zack, you'd be married already." She shoved the box in my direction. "Take the muffin, Anastasia. Heck, take all nine. At the rate you're going, you'll have plenty of time to work off all those calories."

I pushed the box back towards her. "Don't tempt me. As much as I could use a sugar high today, I'm going to exercise self-control or die trying."

"More Lucille problems over the weekend?"

"Lucille problems are a constant in my life. This was much worse."

"Does it involve your visitor from last week?"

"Oh, yeah." I stood and glanced out into the hall to make sure no one was headed our way, then closed the break room door before returning to my seat. After taking a deep breath, I told Cloris the tale of the body in the Mercedes.

"I don't get it," she said when I'd finished.

"Get what?"

"Most people live their entire lives without ever encountering a murder victim. I'll bet the odds are greater for being struck by lightning. What is going on with you?"

Cloris's concern was justified. Only weeks ago, she and I had stumbled across two murder victims while presenting workshops at a conference for retired women executives. At one point, we feared becoming the third and fourth victims. A harrowing nighttime ride home at the end of the conference confirmed our suspicions were justified.

I shrugged, forcing a levity I didn't feel to lighten the moment. "Some people have all the luck?"

"Not funny."

"Believe me, I know."

"So now what?"

"That, I don't know. Depends on what Detective Spader finds as he investigates."

"Well, he'd better hurry before your luck finally runs out." When Cloris realized what she had said, she turned the shade of one of her red velvet cakes, stared into her coffee mug, and stammered, "Oh... I didn't mean...I...I'm...sorry...I...."

I reached across the table and placed my hand over hers. "I know. Believe me, I'm just as worried."

She raised her head and met my eyes. "How do you deal with it, Anastasia? I'm still having nightmares over what happened at Beckwith Chateau."

"I find it helps to blame everything on Karl."

Her eyes bugged out. "Karl is dead. He's been dead for more than a year."

"I'm well aware of that. But I also know that not only did he leave me in debt up the wazoo, ever since he died, dead bodies keep piling up around me. At this point I've stopped believing it's all coincidence."

"You think it's some kind of cosmic curse?"

I flipped my hands palms up. "Hey, it's a theory. Maybe a warped one, but then again, the universe is warped. So, who knows?"

Cloris released a nervous laugh. "You're pulling my leg, right?"

"What do you think?"

She tilted her head to one side and eyed me. "You're pulling my leg."

"Of course, I am." I stood and opened the break room door. "We'd better get to work." But as Cloris and I headed toward our cubicles, I said, "Who knows? Maybe there really is some sadistic cosmic puppet master pulling my strings."

"Woo-woo doesn't become you. Let's just blame it on Karl and leave it at that, okay?"

I nodded. "Agreed. The simplest explanation is usually the best." Still, I had to wonder. Aside from homicide detectives, serial killers, and fictional sleuths, how many people have encountered the number of murder victims I have over the course of their lives, let alone in less than two years?

FIVE

I arrived home from work that night to discover a Dumpster in my driveway, my kitchen stripped down to the studs, and my mother camped out in my living room. Catherine the Great, her more-than-pleasingly-plump white Persian cat sat purring on her lap.

Mama lived by herself in a nearby condo, mortgage-free, thanks to Ira Pollack's generosity, ever since the government sent her latest husband to Club Fed. A well-meaning but misguided assassin had recently dispatched Lawrence Tuttnauer to a more permanent resting place.

Mama never brought Catherine the Great with her when she dropped in unannounced for a visit, which occurred, more often than not, around mealtime, unless....

"Oh, good. You're home, dear," she said. Catherine the Great yowled her annoyance as my mother stood, thus eliminating the cat's comfy resting spot. "We can go now."

"Go?"

"Out to dinner, of course. I'm famished."

I quickly embraced my mother, planting a peck on her cheek, before making my way into the dining room. Zack closed his laptop and rose to greet me. While still in his embrace, he whispered in my ear, "We have a slight problem."

"I can see that," I whispered back. "Why?"

"The hot water heater in the apartment above hers sprang a leak."

Which explained the presence of Catherine the Great. This was no mere popping in to mooch dinner visit. I sighed. "The timing sucks."

"Tell me about it."

I plastered a sympathetic smile onto my face and turned back to my mother. "Sorry to hear about your apartment, Mama. Was there much damage?"

"Enough to cause a massive inconvenience but nothing that can't be repaired."

Inconvenience for whom? "How long will the repairs take?"

"Several weeks at least, and that's assuming the contractor doesn't run into supply problems."

I stifled a groan. I knew better than to ask why her insurance wasn't springing for a hotel room. Mama would consider the question insulting and lecture me on family duty. Of course, that argument didn't go both ways. When I'd used it to explain why Lucille still lived with us, she had said, "That horrible woman is not your family, Anastasia. You owe her nothing." According to Mama, "'til death do us part" extended to all surviving in-laws of a communist persuasion.

However, the last thing I needed was another person in the

house now that I had no kitchen, especially a person who would have to share a bedroom with her arch nemesis. And if Mama wasn't back in her own place before Jesse started on the bathroom renovations, we'd have six people sharing one bathroom every morning.

"I'm sorry for crashing," said Mama. She waved her hand in the direction of the gutted kitchen. "However, I'd much rather stay here, even under the current situation, than have to move into the bedbug-ridden extended-stay motel the insurance company offered me."

I shuddered. "Bedbugs? You saw them?" Did I now have to worry about her or Catherine the Great having brought some into my home?

"Of course not. I refused to step foot in that awful place."

"Then how do you know they have bedbugs?"

She sniffed. "Don't they all? It's not like they offered to put me up at the Ritz or Waldorf."

I thought better of uttering the retort on the tip of my tongue, instead forcing another sympathetic smile. "We'll make the best of it, Mama. I'm going to change out of my work clothes. Then we can leave for dinner."

Zack followed me into the bedroom. "I offered to let her stay in the apartment above the garage."

"And?"

"She refused. Said she was afraid of falling down the steps in the dark. What if we stay in the apartment?"

I shook my head. "Not knowing what Cormac Murphy is up to, I don't feel comfortable leaving the boys alone at night with my mother and Lucille."

I thought for a moment. "Why don't we let the boys stay in the apartment? One of them can take the bed, the other the pull-out sofa. They won't have to share a bathroom with their grandmothers, plus they'll have a kitchen at their disposal. I think they'll jump at the chance."

Zack nodded. "I certainly trust your sons more than I trust your mother and her cat."

As soon as I had changed into jeans and a sweater, we headed for the boys' room. They greeted our suggestion with a resounding whoop.

"We'll help you move your things into the apartment when we get back from dinner," said Zack.

"No need," said Alex. "We can handle it."

"Right," said Nick.

Zack handed them both keys. "Keep the apartment door locked at all times."

"Even if we're just going back and forth to the house?" asked Nick.

"Even then," I said. "Zack has all his camera equipment up there."

"Understood," said Alex, pocketing his key.

"Ditto," said Nick.

"All right," I said. "Let's go to dinner." It was then that I realized we were shy one family member. "Where's the cantankerous commie?"

"She called Harriet to pick her up the moment Grandma arrived and announced she was staying for a few weeks," said Alex.

"I don't suppose she packed a suitcase."

Nick snorted. "Really, Mom? When has your luck been that good?"

"Thanks for pointing that out, Nick. However, on the bright

side, at least I'll have a meal free of mother vs. mother-in-law bickering."

Zack wrapped his arm around my shoulders and gave me a squeeze, "Spoken like a true Pollyanna."

"Hey," I said, "sarcasm is my forte. Get your own schtick."

"What's keeping all of you?" yelled my mother from the front hallway.

Zack, the boys, and I exchanged eye rolls. "We're coming, Mama."

"It's about time," she said as we grabbed jackets from the hall closet and joined her. "I'm getting overheated standing around with my coat on."

I bit back another retort. Two and counting so far this evening. I loved my mother, but her Blanche DuBois sense of entitlement grew exponentially with each passing year. If I didn't know better, I'd wonder if Tennessee Williams wrote the character in *A Streetcar Named Desire* with Mama in mind. Part of me wished that Flora Sudberry Periwinkle Ramirez Scoffield Goldberg O'Keefe Tuttnauer would find herself a seventh husband— preferably one who would support her in the style she believed she deserved. I could use the break.

Zack opened the front door and ushered us outside. As we walked toward the driveway, I noticed a dark SUV parked in front of the house next door. I froze. Zack grabbed my hand and urged me toward my Jetta. "It's not the same car," he whispered in my ear.

But Nick's words echoed in my head as I slipped into the passenger seat. *When had my luck been that good?*

Once Mama and the boys had piled into the backseat and buckled up, Zack started the car. As he pulled out of the driveway, the SUV's headlights turned on. I glanced into the sideview mirror and watched as the vehicle pulled away from the curb, made a U-turn, and began to follow behind us.

From the corner of my eye, I noticed Zack glance at the rearview mirror. At the intersection, he turned left. The SUV followed.

"Déjà vu," I mumbled as an unwelcome recent memory flashed through my brain. Cloris and I had been in a similar position two weeks earlier. The harrowing experience might have turned deadly if not for my driving skills and some quick thinking on the part of Detective Spader.

Zack reached for my hand and gave me a reassuring squeeze. I squeezed back.

"I thought we were going to that new Vietnamese restaurant downtown," said Mama.

"We need to stop for gas first," said Zack.

Good thing Mama couldn't see the gas gauge from where she sat. My tank was three-quarters full. We continued driving down Central Avenue. When Zack pulled into the gas station at Raritan Road, the SUV never slowed down. Instead, the vehicle continued through the intersection. While Zack topped off the tank, I watched as the SUV switched into the access lane for the Garden State Parkway.

I exhaled a sigh of relief. False alarm.

~*~

I waited until we had arrived home to tell Mama about the sleeping arrangements Zack and I had decided. She immediately voiced her objection. "I thought you'd give me your room this time, dear. I much prefer sleeping in a large bed."

Don't we all. "You have your choice, Mama, take the boys'

room or bunk with Lucille."

She snorted. "I've had my fill of sharing with that commie witch, but I don't see why you and Zack can't move into the apartment instead of the boys."

"It's complicated, Mama."

Her eyes grew wide. "What's that supposed to mean? Don't tell me you've gotten yourself mixed up in more trouble."

Zack stepped in to rescue me. "Flora, take it or leave it. You declined the apartment. Your only other option is the hotel if the accommodations at Chez Pollack aren't up to your standards."

Mama placed her hands on her hips, screwed her face into a scowl, and sniffed. "Well, I never! And to think, I used to like you, Zachary."

Zack placed his hand over his heart. "You wound me, Flora."

Ralph, who sat perched on his favorite human's shoulder, squawked his two cents worth of Elizabethan wisdom. *"I have some wounds upon me, and they smart." Coriolanus.* Act Two, Scene One."

Mama glared first at Ralph, then Zack. "You deserve it. I'm not getting any younger. I need my beauty rest."

My mother, who routinely shaved years off her age, had used countless ploys over the decades to manipulate situations to her benefit. However, I'd never heard her play the age card. The woman, a dead ringer for Ellen Burstyn back when she starred in *Same Time Next Year*, looked and acted much younger than her actual age. Her sex life rivaled that of the average twenty-something. Every one of her former husbands could have attested to that—had any of them survived.

Zack wasn't buying it. "Your daughter and I are the two working members of this family, Flora. You have the luxury of sleeping in every morning. We don't."

Mama folded her arms across her chest. "Fine. I'll stay in Alex and Nick's room." Channeling Blanche DuBois, she placed the back of her hand on her forehead, closed her eyes, and said, "I've had such a difficult day."

When that performance didn't solicit a reaction from any of us, other than sideways glances she couldn't see, she opened her eyes and turned to the boys. "Would the two of you be dears and bring me my suitcases? Zachary deposited them in the Bolshevik's bedroom. I'm going to soak in a hot tub while you move your things to the apartment."

The boys headed toward Lucille's room, returning a minute later with two enormous suitcases and a cosmetics case which they deposited on the beds. "The Uber driver only had room for these in his trunk," said Mama. "I'll need you to fetch my other luggage tomorrow, Anastasia."

Mama's two suitcases qualified as mini steamer trunks. I could have packed my entire wardrobe in them. "You need more than this for a two-week stay?" I asked.

"Of course, dear. You can't possibly expect me to decide what to wear days or weeks in advance."

Before I could say another word, Zack slipped his hand into mine and said, "Why don't you and I take Leonard for his evening walk while Alex and Nick clear out their room for your mother?"

Without answering beyond a nod, I allowed Zack to lead me from the bedroom. We grabbed our coats, and once out of earshot of my mother, I asked him, "Was that your way of keeping me from saying something I'd regret?"

"I sensed you were about to blow."

I sighed. "That obvious, huh?"

He chuckled. "Oh, yeah."

As I rounded up Leonard and attached his leash, I said, "I'll admit, I've found both my patience and my fuse growing shorter lately."

Zack placed Ralph in his cage and grabbed the leash from me. "I've noticed," he said as we left the house. "You've been dealing with more than your share of problems lately, but I have a solution."

"What's that?"

"A vacation."

I shot him a side-eye. "We recently took a vacation. It didn't end well."

"That doesn't mean we'll encounter murder and mayhem on every vacation we take."

"We're two for two." Besides the murders on our recent cruise, I had been kidnapped a few months ago when I'd accompanied Zack on assignment in Barcelona.

"That only means the odds are now in our favor."

Once again, Nick's words regarding my luck—or more precisely, my lack of luck—rang in my ears. "What are you proposing?"

"I think it's time we got married and I take you on a relaxing honeymoon."

"In the middle of renovations and with a Boston mob boss up to no good?"

"The renovations will only take a few weeks, and by then I have complete faith that Detective Spader will have dealt with Cormac Murphy."

"I love your optimism. On both counts."

"So, what do you say?"

I held up my hand and pointed to my ring finger. "I've already said yes."

"But you still haven't said 'I do.'"

"I will."

"When?"

"How about as soon as the renovations are completed and I'm no longer on Cormac Murphy's radar?"

He held up his little finger. "Pinky swear?"

I hooked my finger with his. "Pinky swear."

"I'm going to hold you to that. The Law of the Pinky Swear makes this a binding agreement."

Leonard chose that moment to stop to do his business. Zack took the opportunity to wrap me in his arms and capture my lips with his.

"I really do need a vacation," I said once we'd placed some air between us.

He laughed. "Tell me something I don't know."

With Leonard having finished, after Zack scooped the doo-doo into a plastic bag, we turned around, and hand in hand, Zack and I headed back to the house.

We stopped short when we turned the corner. An SUV idled at the curb in front of the house. I clutched Zack's hand tighter.

"It's probably just someone copying down the realtor's phone number," he said.

Except at that moment Leonard strained on the leash, his attention riveted on the Dumpster, and began growling. "Something is in the Dumpster," I said.

"Not something," said Zack. "Someone." He handed me the leash, dropped the doggie poop bag, and withdrew his gun. "Stay here."

SIX

I watched from the shadows as Zack silently crept down the street. Either he was channeling the heroes of every action movie he'd ever watched, or he knew exactly what he was doing because he really did work for one of the alphabet agencies.

Even so, instead of pulling out his gun, he should have pulled out his phone and called the police. To my way of thinking, that's the difference between those of us with double-X chromosomes and those with an X and a Y. I would have opted for a safer, more sensible course of action—like hiding behind a tree and dialing 911.

As I held my breath, my emotions ricocheted between fear for Zack's safety and anger over his Macho Man decision. Would I wind up regretting asking him to carry his gun? At the same time, I prayed the guy in the Dumpster hadn't come armed with his own deadly weapon.

Then it hit me. If he had, I was standing directly in the line of fire.

I tugged on Leonard's leash, dragging him behind the nearest parked car, and crouched beside him. He kept up a steady, low growl that I hoped was drowned out by the constant stream of traffic along Central Avenue.

"Shh." I whispered as I stroked his fur. But the dog had sensed danger and was having nothing to do with my efforts to calm him into silence.

As the seconds ticked by, each one feeling more like an hour, I wondered what the Dumpster diver hoped to find in the broken remains of a kitchen built around the time of my mother's birth. The Dumpster contained nothing of value. The kitchen was builder's grade when it was cobbled together more than sixty years ago, and unlike fine antiques, it hadn't aged well throughout the decades. The only thing the scavenger could possibly come away with was a case of tetanus from stepping on a rusty nail, and given my luck, he'd sue me.

Zack had finally snaked his way to within a few yards of the Dumpster. I could barely make out his shadowy figure, but I saw him stoop, then stand and pitch something at the Dumpster. A moment later a loud clang reverberated down the street.

The SUV blared its horn. Leonard stopped growling and began barking.

"Climb out," shouted Zack. "Slowly. Try anything, and I'll shoot."

A moment later, someone leaped from the opposite side of the Dumpster from where Zack stood and raced toward the idling SUV. The driver peeled away from the curb as Dumpster Guy dove into the car.

I raced down the street to Zack. By the time I got to him, he was already on his phone, rattling off make, model, and license plate number to the 911 dispatcher.

"Why didn't you just call the police to begin with?" I demanded after he'd hung up. "What if that guy or his accomplice had a weapon?"

"Because he was most likely only scavenging for copper wire."

"That's a huge assumption. How can you possibly know that?"

"Copper has become a cash crop. Unscrupulous scrap metal dealers pay well for it—in cash, no questions asked. Enterprising thieves have been targeting construction sites, both commercial and residential, going so far as to rip out newly installed copper pipes in unoccupied buildings. It's a growing problem."

I didn't bother asking how he knew so much about copper thefts. I directed my ire toward a more pressing issue. "What if you'd been wrong? What if that guy was connected to Cormac Murphy?"

"Why would Cormac Murphy order someone to hunt around in a Dumpster in our driveway? Besides," He pointed to the gun he had holstered. "Just in case, I had backup."

Zack's explanation made sense. I could think of no plausible explanation for a Boston mob boss wanting one of his underlings to search through the broken remains of my New Jersey kitchen. It seemed highly unlikely Murphy had decided to go into the scrap metal business. No matter how high the price of copper, it wouldn't come anywhere close to the street value of a pound of fentanyl, cocaine, or meth.

Murphy had claimed that Johnnie D. had something belonging to him. Whatever that "something" was, it certainly wasn't going to be found in a construction Dumpster among the detritus of my kitchen.

Although I wanted to believe Zack, doubts continued to ping-pong around in my brain. Unless the cops located the Dumpster diver and he admitted to searching for discarded copper wiring, we'd never know for certain.

Zack slipped Leonard's leash from my grasp. His other hand reached for mine. After returning to retrieve the doggie poop bag, we strolled silently toward the back door.

We met Alex and Nick as they were leaving the house. Alex carried his laptop and a load of textbooks. Nick balanced Leonard's dog bed, food and water bowls, a bag of kibble, and a box of dog biscuits in his arms.

"Last load," said Nick.

"You're taking Leonard?" I asked.

"He insisted," said Alex, nodding toward his brother and sounding not at all happy about having to share the apartment with Nick's new best friend.

"He'll be lonely without me," said Nick. "I'll come get him once I dump all his stuff."

"You think Lucille will even notice her dog is missing?" asked Zack as we headed into the house.

We were immediately bombarded with a blaring rendition of Mama singing along to "Just You Wait, Henry Higgins" from *My Fair Lady*. Mama had adopted the song as her anthem ever since the demise of her short-lived marriage to Lawrence Tuttnauer.

I opened my mouth to answer Zack's question, but he held up a finger. "Hold that thought."

I followed him as he strode across the demoed kitchen, through the dining room and living room, and down the hall, stopping in front of the bathroom door. He rapped sharply and yelled, "Mind turning that down, Flora?"

A moment later, Eliza Doolittle's decibel level had reduced

slightly. "A little more," yelled Zack.

"Oh, for Heaven's sake!" said Mama, lowering the volume another few decibels.

Zack turned back to me. "You were about to say?"

I slipped off my coat, hung it in the hall closet, and handed Zack a hanger for his coat. "Leonard is Nick's dog now. Lucille abdicated all responsibility. And although I don't purport to have Nick's dog whisperer talents, I'm certain Leonard prefers it that way."

"Just prepare yourself for a confrontation at some point."

I laughed. "Haven't you noticed by now? When it comes to Lucille, confrontations are a daily occurrence. I'm always on guard for the next one."

He frowned. "You shouldn't have to be."

I shrugged. "Not much I can do about that particular albatross. I'm stuck with her."

He took my hands in his. "*We're* stuck with her."

"At least you had a choice."

"That's right," he said. Releasing one hand, he tipped my chin up and planting a kiss on my lips. "And I chose you."

At that moment Nick returned to claim Leonard, interrupting the romantic interlude. As soon as we heard the back door close behind Nick and the dog, Zack asked, "Where were we?"

I knew where I wanted to be, but with Mama camped out in the bathroom and the boys now occupying the apartment, a romantic evening wasn't in the cards. Instead, we settled for watching TV in the den, turning the volume up enough to drown out Eliza and Mama. With a parrot chaperone perched on Zack's shoulder, we cuddled until the doorbell rang.

"Lucille probably forgot her key," I said.

"I'll get it," said Zack. He left the den, and a moment later I heard Detective Spader say, "I never would have expected Mrs. Pollack's mother-in-law was someone who listened to show tunes."

"She isn't," I said, rising to greet him as he and Zack entered the den. "That's my mother. Lucille is more into Shostakovich."

Spader nodded. "That I'd believe. Sorry to barge in on you this evening, Mrs. Pollack."

"I take it this isn't a social call?"

"Wish it were. I thought it best to deliver this news in person."

I glanced at Zack. "That sounds ominous, Detective. What's going on?"

He cleared his throat, and I held my breath. "Looks like Cormac Murphy finally caught up with Johnnie D."

"That's a good thing, right? Murphy found the guy he was looking for and will leave us alone now."

"Not necessarily," said Spader.

"What do you mean?"

"We identified the body in the Mercedes SUV. It was John Doyle."

I fell back onto the sofa. "I don't understand. If Murphy was only looking for Doyle to kill him, why leave the body here?"

"He's sending a message," said Spader.

"That's obvious, but what message? What do we have to do with any of this, other than having bought the house that Doyle's sister and brother-in-law once owned years ago?"

"That's what we don't know," said Spader. "Yet."

"Doyle was never placed in Witness Protection?" asked Zack.

"He was," said Spader. "For a time. Since he's dead, the Feds were willing to give up some information once we got a positive match on the vic's prints. Doyle was kicked out of the program for violating WITSEC terms. Seems he gave up his identity when he entered the program, but he never gave up his life of crime. He was eventually caught fencing stolen property. He jumped bail while awaiting trial and vanished."

"They never caught him?" I asked.

Spader shook his head. "He was probably living under various assumed names, never staying in any one place for very long."

"And he wound up back here?" asked Zack.

"We don't know," said Spader. "I'm guessing he got wind of Murphy's release and planned to get to Murphy before Murphy got to him."

"That still doesn't explain why two Boston thugs showed up here," I said.

"It's possible Doyle was tailing Murphy ever since he got out of prison," said Spader.

"Or the other way around," said Zack. "With Murphy's connections, he may have found out where Doyle was."

"Another possibility," said Spader. "Doyle could have been killed anywhere."

"But why leave his body where it could be found?" I asked. "Why not dispose of it?"

"Because Murphy *wanted* Doyle's body found."

"Why?" I asked.

"To announce no one messes with Cormac Murphy and gets away with it."

"But why choose my driveway?"

"Convenience?" said Spader. "Because you didn't invite him in for a cup of tea?" He shrugged. "Who knows? Cormac Murphy is a psychopath. He doesn't need a reason to act crazy. Hopefully, he got what he wanted from Doyle before he killed him, and he's back in Boston by now."

"Are you suggesting his message was meant for the Boston mob and not for us?"

"Most likely."

Most likely? "I would have preferred a *definitely*, Detective."

"You know I can't give you a definitely, Mrs. Pollack."

"But won't law enforcement now pick Murphy up for questioning?"

"Of course," said Spader. "But Murphy's gotten the band back together. He'll have an ironclad alibi with plenty of witnesses to back him up."

"Where does that leave you and your investigation?" asked Zack.

"Out of it," said Spader. "The moment Johnnie D.'s body was identified, the Feds took over the case."

SEVEN

The next morning in the break room, I quickly caught Cloris up on my unexpected house guest, the curious incident of the guy in the Dumpster, and Spader's revelation about the body in the Mercedes.

"Your mother always picks the most inopportune times to descend on you," she said. "But look on the bright side. Maybe Lucille will stay away until Flora returns to her condo."

"I should be so lucky."

Then, as she filled two coffee mugs, she pivoted back to my previous Dumpster diver news. "Zack's right about the copper thefts, though. I saw a news account about them the other night. The cops think there's a gang operating in the area."

"I'm glad to hear he didn't make up the story to keep me from worrying that Cormac Murphy was somehow involved."

Cloris handed me one of the mugs. "Why would you think that?"

"Wouldn't you?" I added a splash of half and half to my coffee and handed her the container. "Given what's happened lately?"

"I suppose so. But now that he's settled the score with Doyle, you don't need to worry about him showing up again, right?"

I reached for a chocolate-dipped almond biscotti from the box Cloris had deposited on the table and dipped it into my coffee. "I hope so," I said before taking a bite.

She eyed me over the rim of her coffee mug. "You don't sound convinced."

"That's because I don't know what Murphy was looking for and whether or not he found it."

"You have no idea what it was?"

"None. Could have been anything from information to stolen property. Or he lied."

"About Doyle having something of his? Why?"

I shrugged. "As an excuse to get inside my house? Maybe he thought we were hiding Doyle."

"That makes no sense. Why would he think you were hiding someone you didn't know existed?"

"Who knows?" I parroted Detective Spader's explanation. "He's a crazy mob boss. He doesn't need a reason or an excuse for anything he does."

Cloris frowned as she grabbed another biscotti before we headed to our cubicles. "I see what you mean."

Then, most likely to quell my fears, she changed the subject again and asked, "How's the reno going?"

I pulled out my phone and showed her a photo of my demolished kitchen.

"I like what you've done with the place," she said. "Very cutting edge. Totally minimalist."

"Maybe you should stick to baking and leave the snark to me."

She proffered the biscotti she'd been holding. "Take it. You need it more than I do."

Not that I needed the extra calories, but I grabbed the biscotti anyway before she changed her mind and ducked into my shoebox of an office. Cloris makes the best almond biscotti, and when she finishes it off by dipping it in chocolate? Pure heaven!

I settled at my desk and booted up my computer to start my day. While I waited, I closed my eyes and savored the added shot of caffeine and sugar until Cloris yanked me out of my gastronomic trance, shouting from across the hall. "What the heck?"

My eyes flew open. "What?"

"Is your computer working?"

I glanced at my monitor. "All I'm seeing is a blank screen. What's going on?"

"Beats me. We have power. The lights are on."

I picked up my office phone and heard a dial tone. "Phone works."

A buzz of voices grew around the office. I stepped out into the hallway as others did the same.

"Anyone know what's going on?" asked Janice Kerr, our health editor. "My computer just died."

"Mine, too," answered decorating editor Jeanie Sims.

"We can't get any work done without our computers," said fashion editor Tessa Lisbon, stating the obvious. "We might as well all go home."

She ducked into her office, stepping out a moment later wearing her coat, her purse slung over her shoulder. As she made her way to the elevator, she raised her arm over her head and said, "See you all tomorrow."

"Hold up a minute, Tessa."

We turned to find Kim O'Hara, our editorial director's assistant, racing down the hallway, her Jimmy Choo four-inch stilettos tapping a staccato rhythm on the Terrazzo floor.

Tessa stopped short and turned around. Hands on hips, she pulled a face and huffed out her annoyance, remaining where she stood rather than returning to join the rest of us.

"Do you think fashion majors are required to take Diva 101 in college?" I whispered.

"Definitely," said Janice. "Have you ever worked with a fashion editor who wasn't a diva?"

"Although Tessa is certainly an improvement over her predecessor," said Jeanie, referring to Marlys Vandenburg, *American Woman's* former fashion editor, who met a shocking demise shortly after Karl died. Marlys was the first dead body to cross my path in what has become a never-ending stream of dead bodies.

Kim cleared her throat, and we turned toward her, but she was focused on Tessa. After a staring competition that lasted at least thirty seconds, Tessa gave in and walked back to where we stood. "Well?" she said, crossing her arms, a scowl on her face.

"As you're all probably aware by now," said Kim, "we're having major computer problems this morning."

"Were we hacked?" I asked.

"Unlikely," said Kim. "IT had performed scheduled maintenance last night. Something apparently went wrong."

"No duh!" said Tessa.

"So mature," muttered Cloris, her words dripping with sarcasm.

Nepotism, not experience or talent, had played a role in Tessa's hiring. The twenty-something, born with a platinum spoon in her mouth, landed her position at the magazine thanks to an uncle who sat on the Trimedia board.

Kim ignored Tessa and continued, "They expect to have the issue resolved in a few hours. You're all welcome to leave but be prepared to return this afternoon. We'll keep you posted."

As the gaggle of editors dispersed, Cloris asked, "Are you staying or leaving?"

"I'm debating. Do I really want to drive forty minutes only to have to turn around and drive back a short time later?"

"Assuming the repairs only take a few hours," she said. "What are the chances of that?"

"I suppose it depends on the problem."

"We're not talking one computer," she said. "Or even one department. If the Trimedia server is down, the entire corporation is impacted, not just our magazine."

"True. By the time everything is up and running again, it will probably be too late to return."

"Exactly. And that's assuming they not only identify the problem quickly, but that it's an easy fix. I wouldn't count on it. We may still be down tomorrow."

"You've convinced me," I said. "Let's get out of here."

~*~

When I arrived home, Jesse Konopka's truck was parked in my driveway. I expected to hear hammering, sawing, and drilling but stepped into an empty house. No Jesse. No work crews. No Zack or Mama. No Lucille. Empty and silent. Or so I thought until I heard what I hoped weren't mice or squirrels scampering around in the attic.

I walked through the house to the hallway and found the

overhead ladder stairs to the attic pulled down. "Hello?" I called.

A moment later Jesse peered down at me. "Hey, there!"

"What's going on?"

"I need to rough in the new electrical before we Sheetrock the kitchen. I'm running the wires for the overhead lights right now."

"Have you seen Zack or my mother?"

"Zack's working in the apartment. I saw your mother hop into an Uber earlier."

"With her cat?"

He tilted his head toward the closed door of the boys' bedroom. "The cat's in there."

"Thanks, I'll leave you to your wires."

"Hold on a sec. I have something to show you."

A moment later Jesse climbed down the ladder stairs. He carried a wooden box and held it out to me. "I found this buried under a pile of insulation under the eaves in the corner of the attic."

"What's in it?"

"It's not yours?"

"I've never seen it before."

"Maybe it belonged to Karl."

As far as I knew, Karl had gambled away all our savings. Was it possible he'd stashed some of his winnings in the attic? Or was this the fifty thousand dollars he'd stolen from his mother to repay Riccardo, his bookie?

Both Riccardo and I had assumed Karl gambled away that money in Las Vegas before he died. But what if he hadn't? What if it had been hidden in my attic all this time?

I stared at the box. A combination of rudimentary carving and woodburning, it reminded me of a Cub Scout project. A slightly off-center oval border surrounding the initials CDQ decorated the top. A rusty metal hasp with a small lock through the loop secured the lid in place. I gave the box a shake. The contents rattling around inside sounded metallic. Definitely not a wad of Benjamins.

"I don't think this belonged to Karl," I said. "Not with those initials."

"Well, it belongs to you now," said Jesse. "Whatever it is. I'm going back upstairs to finish the electrical work."

I headed for the apartment above the garage.

I found Zack at his computer, Ralph on his shoulder, Leonard curled up under the coffee table. "You're home early," he said, greeting me with a kiss.

I told him about the computers. "Cloris thinks the repairs might take more than today. At least everything is stored on the cloud, and we can work remotely until then."

"What's that?" he asked pointing to the box.

"A mystery. Jesse found it hidden in the attic." I pointed to the hasp. "It's locked."

"I'll get my tools."

Zack stepped into the bedroom and returned a moment later with a toolkit. It took him no time to pry off the nails holding the hasp to the box. "Do you want to do the honors?" he asked.

I removed the lid and stared at the contents, an assortment of garish vintage jewelry. "Do you think any of it is real?"

He lifted a pearl-encrusted gold brooch from the box and flipped it over. His eyes widened. "This is stamped eighteen karat gold."

I removed a cocktail ring, squinted around the interior rim, and stared back at him. "I don't see any markings on this one."

Zack spilled the jewelry onto the coffee table, and we began to sort the pieces into two piles. Approximately half were real gold, some containing diamonds and other precious gems. The rest consisted of extremely hideous costume jewelry.

I pointed to the gold items. "What do you think they're worth?"

"Hard to say. We can take the real pieces to a jeweler for appraisal."

"Someone had lousy taste." I screwed up my face. "I wouldn't wear any of this."

"Then we'll sell it and buy you something you would wear."

"Better yet, I'll use the proceeds to pay down more of my debt. But shouldn't we first try to track down the owner?"

"How do you plan to do that?" asked Zack. "The initials don't match the people you and Karl bought the house from, even if we knew how to contact them. The jewelry probably belonged to the original owners of the house."

"I'm sure they passed away years ago."

"Besides," Zack said. "Anything left in a home after the sale of a house belongs to the new owners."

"Why would anyone hide jewelry in an attic?"

"It's not uncommon for people to hide their valuables when they travel."

"And forget about them?"

He shrugged. "I suppose it happens. Every so often you hear of someone discovering something of value hidden away in an attic or basement. Years ago, someone discovered an original copy of the Declaration of Independence hidden behind a framed picture they bought at a flea market."

"I remember hearing about that."

"Maybe the person who placed the box in the attic thought all the jewelry was fake."

"Then why hide it under the eaves beneath a pile of insulation?"

"What if the person who hid the box suffered from dementia?"

I considered this for a moment. "That would also explain why the box was forgotten in the attic."

Zack gathered up the jewelry and deposited everything back in the box. "I'll stick this in one of the cabinets in the dark room. We can deal with it after the renovation is finished."

"Good idea. I'll change out of my work clothes and return shortly to sojourn into the cloud. We've got an issue deadline looming, and I don't want to be the editor who throws a monkey wrench into the schedule."

He raised an eyebrow. "You? Have you ever missed a deadline?"

"No, and I don't intend to start now." I gave him a quick lip peck and darted back to the house.

Jesse's drywall crew had arrived and started to cut and nail Sheetrock in place. I waved a hello to them as I made my way through the kitchen. As I entered the dining room, I overheard Jesse speaking to someone. Walking through the living room, I found him standing at the open front door.

"I'm afraid I don't have any openings right now," he said.

"Can I leave my references and contact info with you in case something turns up?"

I stepped into the foyer and saw a muscular man of about thirty-five with a soul patch and long shaggy brown hair tied back in a ponytail standing on the other side of the door. A snarling tiger tattoo wrapped around his neck, the tail winding up his left cheekbone. When he saw me, he smiled, nodded, and said, "Ma'am."

Jesse accepted the white business envelope the man had extended toward him. "I'll let you know if I have an opening." He offered his right hand to the man. "Thanks for stopping by."

"Thank you," said the man, shaking Jesse's hand. He turned and walked down the path to a black pickup truck parked at the curb. At least it wasn't a black SUV.

"Who was that?" I asked when Jesse closed the front door.

"Some guy new to the area. He's looking for construction work."

"Is it common for workers to drop by home renovation projects to ask for jobs?"

"It happens occasionally. Usually when a mutual acquaintance has recommended them, though. This guy says he's just moved here from New Mexico."

"Looking for work?"

Jesse nodded. "Construction is booming here, not so much in New Mexico. Lots of construction workers are itinerant. They go where the jobs are."

"Where do you usually get your crews?"

"Since I went out on my own, I haven't had a need to hire anyone. All my guys worked with me at Parthenon."

Jesse had been Parthenon Construction's general contractor until the owner, Paul Leonides, tried to kill him. And me. And my mother. Luckily, all three attempts had failed. Unfortunately, Paul had had more success eliminating his brother Dion.

"Electrical is all roughed in now," said Jesse, changing the subject. "You'll now have plenty of light in the kitchen and can say goodbye to playing musical plugs with all your small appliances."

"That will go a long way toward making the kitchen more efficient," I said.

Prior to Jesse upgrading the electrical, the kitchen had one overhead light and two outlets. Back when the house was built, the only small appliance most people owned was a toaster. Coffee was percolated on the stove. The myriad of electrical gadgets we'd come to rely on didn't exist.

I thanked Jesse and headed down the hall to the bedroom as he strode toward the kitchen. I was walking back down the hall after changing my clothes when someone pounded on the front door. I checked the peephole and found my mother-in-law standing in the entry. A purple bruise covered her right cheek, the eye above it swollen shut.

EIGHT

I swung open the front door. "What happened?"

"I was mugged by some hooligan." She pushed me aside and clomped into the house. "I need twenty dollars," she said. "Now."

"What for?"

"To pay the cab driver. Not that he deserves a cent, given how long it took for him to show up."

I glanced over her shoulder and saw a taxi idling at the curb. "Why didn't Harriet drive you home?"

"She can't drive."

"Was she also hurt?"

"No, some Goody Two Shoes called the cops. When they showed up, they arrested Harriet for driving with a revoked license."

I sent up a silent Halleluiah. Harriet Kleinhample was a menace on the road and had lost her license after her latest accident, the one that had resulted in the death of Lucille's would-be assassin. However, the revocation hadn't kept Harriet from getting behind the wheel after she'd recovered from her injuries, and unfortunately, it also wouldn't stop her from driving again once she was released from jail. Harriet believed driving was her God-given right—or bestowed by whoever gives rights to godless commies.

"I'll get my wallet," I said. "You should put some ice on your cheek and eye."

With a grunt, Lucille hobbled toward the dining room. I grabbed my wallet and a jacket and walked out to the cab. "How much do I owe you?"

"Nineteen seventy-five."

I executed a virtual eyeroll. Had I handed Comrade Lucille a twenty-dollar bill, she would have given the cabbie a twenty-five-cent tip. So much for being a champion of the working class, Yet so typically Lucille. I gave the driver a twenty-dollar bill and four ones, thanked him, and returned to the house.

I found Lucille stretched out on her bed, an icepack held against her cheek, her eyes closed. Both legs of her emerald, orange, and purple plaid polyester pantsuit were ripped, her knees scraped. "Did you hit your head?"

"No, I didn't hit my head." She sounded like a petulant teenager. Strike that. My own teenagers have never behaved as belligerently as their grandmother.

"Then how did you get that bruise on your face?"

"Not that it's any of your business but he grabbed my purse and walloped me across my face with it."

"Didn't the police offer to bring you to the hospital?"

"I don't need to go to the hospital. I'll be fine once the swelling goes down."

The swelling wasn't going down. It had grown worse, and a

shiner had sprouted around her eye. I bit my tongue, knowing any further suggestions on my part would be unwelcome. I was surprised she had taken my advice and grabbed an icepack from the freezer.

Instead, I changed the subject. "Why didn't the police drive you home?"

She lowered the icepack, opened her good eye, and glared at me. "I refuse to accept charity from those people."

"It's not charity, Lucille. Our taxes pay for local law enforcement to protect and serve us."

She responded with one of her classic harrumphs, closed her eye, and returned the icepack to her face. I had been dismissed. I gave up and left the room without offering to clean and bandage her knees.

When my friendly neighborhood crime fighting duo of Officers Harley and Fogarty arrived an hour later with Lucille's purse, I learned more about the mugging.

"Looks like they grabbed her cash, credit cards, and ID before tossing her pocketbook in the nearest trash can," said Harley. "Left her keys, though. At least you won't need to change your locks."

"She refused to file a report," added Fogarty. "She really needs to do that, along with contacting the credit bureaus, canceling her credit cards, and contacting Motor Vehicle."

"No need," I said. "Lucille doesn't have any credit cards, and she's never had a driver's license. As for the keys, she's so paranoid about the government spying on her that she never carries any form of ID."

Harley laughed. "We've already got a huge file on that rabblerouser. I'm sure the Feds do, too, given her latest antics, whether she carries ID or not."

"You know that, and I know that," I said, "but we also both know Lucille lives in a world of communist-inspired conspiracies and delusions."

"You have any idea how much money she was carrying?" asked Fogarty.

"No more than a few dollars," I said. "My mother-in-law may appear to be an easy mark, but the mugger struck out when he targeted her."

Officer Harley then filled me in about Harriet. Along with locking her up, the police had impounded her latest VW minibus. "Turns out, the vehicle wasn't registered."

"No surprise there." By my count, this was Harriet's second vehicle purchased after losing her license this year. I didn't want to know what sort of shady connections she had in the used car world. Were there commie car dealers who supplied vehicles to Bolsheviks, no questions asked?

At least the citizens of Westfield and the surrounding communities were a little safer on the roads—for now. At some point, a misguided judge would feel sorry for Harriet and order her release. It wouldn't be the first time. Harriet could turn on the charm—or the waterworks—whenever it suited her.

And then she'd buy herself another VW minibus from a questionable dealer.

Mama arrived shortly after Harley and Fogarty departed, her arms laden with shopping bags from a day spending money at the mall. When she learned Lucille had returned, her reaction would have made her fellow Daughters of the American Revolution reach for their smelling salts.

~*~

As Cloris had predicted, the Trimedia server problems were not resolved by the end of the day nor the next morning. We were all instructed to work from home. Kim's email indicated IT promised a fix by the end of the day. "I'm not holding my breath," I said to Zack over breakfast. That's what they said yesterday."

"They should hire Tino," he suggested.

"If Trimedia offered Tino the sun, the moon, and the stars, I doubt he'd accept."

Zack grinned. "Good point."

Tino Martinez, ex-special forces, tech genius, and hacker extraordinaire, had briefly worked as a bodyguard for Trimedia's now disgraced and former CEO Alfred Gruenwald. I once thought Tino was out to kill me. I was wrong. He's since saved my life on several occasions and become a good friend—in more ways than one—to both me and Zack.

His latest challenge has been to transform Ira's spoiled brats into model citizens, for which he's so far received mixed reviews. Unfortunately, we've learned even Tino's superpowers have their limits.

With the boys having gone into school early to prepare for this evening's annual science fair, and with both Mama and Lucille sleeping in this morning, Zack and I enjoyed a peaceful breakfast free of mother versus mother-in-law contentious bickering, a rare occurrence at Casa Pollack, no matter the meal. The Daughter of the American Revolution and the Daughter of the October Revolution could both fend for themselves whenever they decided to rise and shine.

"Time to start my workday," I said, gathering my dirty dishes.

"Leave those," said Zack. "I'll clean up and join you once Jesse and his crew arrive."

That deserved a kiss, after which I grabbed a jacket and headed for the apartment above the garage.

Our monthly staff meeting would take place in five days. Along with presenting a status report on other magazine issues in various stages of production, the editorial staff would plan the issue five months down the road. I needed to come up with a craft idea for that issue.

An hour later, after a research trip down the rabbit hole otherwise known as the Internet, I'd come up with plenty of ideas but none that sparked my creative juices. If I couldn't get excited about a project, I knew my readers wouldn't, either.

I had a devoted following among *American Woman* subscribers and those who routinely purchased our monthly issues at the supermarket checkout. They expected a certain level of design and functionality from the crafts I presented in each issue, but at the same time, the projects had to be both relatively easy to make and budget-friendly.

Zack still hadn't joined me in the apartment, and I wondered what was keeping him. Since I'd wasted the last sixty minutes, I decided to take a break and find out. Perhaps I was trying too hard. A bit of procrastination and a cup of coffee might stimulate the creative side of my brain.

I walked into the kitchen to find Zack hard at work—sanding spackle. My heart executed a little pitter-pat at the image. Forget the HGTV twins from Canada or the former boy band pop star. My guy ran circles around them and could easily star in his own DIY show. I smiled and quirked an eyebrow. "Midlife crisis career change?"

"Jesse is short a guy this morning. Roscoe and Wendel had a blowout on Rt. 22 on their way here."

"Are they okay?"

Zack shook his head. "Wendel is. He called from the hospital. Roscoe's being admitted. Jesse ran over to the hospital to check on his condition and pick up Wendel. I decided to lend a hand to keep the job on schedule."

"I hope Roscoe's injuries aren't too severe."

"That makes all of us. Jesse said Roscoe's wife is expecting their first child in a few months."

Ever since Karl died suddenly and I discovered how he'd screwed me and our kids, I've fought to maintain a positive attitude, no matter how often I'd wanted to curl up into a ball of self-pity. Then I'd realize how lucky I am. Yes, I still have massive Karl-induced debt, and I'm stuck with the commie mother-in-law from Hades, but I have two great kids, and I now have Zack. We're all healthy, and we're not living out of a cardboard box on the street. I'm slowly digging my way out of the financial mess I inherited. Things could be worse. A lot worse. Hopefully, they wouldn't be for Roscoe, his wife, and their soon-to-be new baby.

I left Zack to his sanding and walked into the dining room to make two cups of coffee. As Ralph kept an eye on me from his perch atop the china cabinet, I heard bickering coming from the other side of the house. Coward that I am, I worked as quietly and quickly as possible to avoid getting swept up in Mama and Lucille's latest squabble.

"Let me know when you hear about Roscoe," I said as I handed Zack a steaming mug.

"Will do." He gave me a quick kiss. Then I slipped out of the house and headed back to the apartment before either Mama or Lucille ambushed me.

When Zack texted a short time later to say Jesse had returned,

I raced to the house. Zack and Wendel turned as I entered the kitchen. "How's Roscoe?" I asked.

"Lucky to be alive," said Wendel. "I gotta give him props. When that tire blew, he fought with everything he had to maintain control, but a vehicle behind us couldn't stop in time and clipped us. The truck flipped several times as it slid down an embankment, finally landing on the driver's side. Roscoe's got a concussion, a pierced lung, a compound fracture of his left leg, and a dislocated shoulder." Wendel grimaced. "I walked away with only a few bruises."

"Still, you should go home," I said. "Your body has probably sustained more trauma than you realize."

"That's what Zack was trying to convince me," he said. "But I'd rather get back to work than sit at home and think about Roscoe laid up in the hospital."

"You're going to be really sore tomorrow," said Zack.

Wendel shrugged. "I was in combat. I've been through much worse."

I heard Jesse on the phone in the dining room. "Is he speaking with Roscoe's wife?"

Wendel shook his head. "Nah, some guy who stopped by yesterday looking for work. With Roscoe out for several weeks, Jesse's now shorthanded. We've got multiple jobs running. He can't afford to lose one of us even for a few days."

"Weird how that works out," said Zack. "One person's misfortune becomes another person's lucky break."

From the dining room we heard Ralph ruffle his feathers, then offer up an appropriate Shakespearean quote. "*And in this thought they find a kind of ease, bearing their own misfortunes on the back of such as have before endured the like.*" He squawked once before adding, "*Richard the Second*. Act Five, Scene Five."

~*~

A few hours later when I returned to the house to make lunch, the man I saw speaking with Jesse yesterday was hard at work in my kitchen, applying a second coat of spackling to the drywall. His arm muscles and abs strained the fabric of a black T-shirt that showcased a good deal more of his tiger neck tattoo than what I'd previously noticed.

He tipped his head and greeted me with, "Good afternoon, ma'am," then introduced himself as Dennis Clancy. "But I go by Denny."

I smiled and said, "Nice to meet you, Denny. You recently moved to the area?"

"That's right, ma'am. Not much construction work going on in New Mexico. I heard New Jersey was booming with renos and teardowns and thought I'd give the northeast a shot." He glanced out the window at the dreary day. An icy wind whipped around the yard, threatening the newly emerged spring flowers. "Can't say I expected such cold weather the end of April, though."

"Welcome to Spring in New Jersey. Come tomorrow, temperatures might soar into the eighties, then plummet into the thirties a day later. You never know this time of year."

"I'm learning that."

"Do you have a family you brought with you?"

"No, ma'am. Just me."

"Well, I hope you'll enjoy living in the Garden State. I promise, it will warm up and stay warm eventually, at which point everyone will complain about the heat and humidity."

He laughed as I moved into the dining room and grabbed a few sandwich fixings from the refrigerator to bring back to the apartment.

I hadn't heard any further verbal sparring coming from the bedroom area, but I wasn't taking any chances. My goal was to run in and out before either Mama or Lucille became aware of my presence.

I'd nearly made my escape when my mother came up behind me. "What are you doing home? And why didn't you tell me you were here?" she demanded.

I inhaled a deep breath, slowly exhaling before turning around to face her. "I'm working from home today, Mama. We're having computer problems at work."

She clapped her hands together. "Wonderful!"

"Wonderful?"

"We can spend the afternoon together, do lunch and a bit of shopping." She eyed the bread, condiments, cheese, and deli meats in my arm. "Put those away and grab your coat and purse."

I raised an eyebrow. "Shopping? Didn't you clean the stores out yesterday?"

"Really, Anastasia! Sarcasm is not becoming."

"I told you I'm working, Mama."

"Who's going to know if you take a few hours off?"

"My editorial director when I don't meet my deadline."

She dismissed my excuse with a wave of her hand. "I won't tell if you don't. You can finish up this evening if necessary."

"I'm sorry, Mama. I can't. In case you've forgotten, we're having dinner with Shane and Sophie this evening, then going to the science fair at the high school. Both Alex and Nick have exhibits, as does Sophie."

Mama blushed. "I did forget. I'm sorry. Thanks for reminding me." Then she perked up, clapped her hands together again, and said, "What a perfect opportunity to wear the new dress I bought yesterday."

"Just make sure you're ready to leave by five o'clock."

"Why so early?"

"The science fair opens at seven and runs until nine-thirty."

"Then what's the rush?"

"The kids need to arrive by six-thirty to set up. Shane is serving an early dinner so they can eat before they have to leave."

"I'll remember, dear."

"Good." Cradling the lunch items against my chest, I carefully leaned toward her and pecked her cheek. "I'm going back to work. I'll see you later." With that I pivoted and darted into the kitchen and out the back door.

NINE

Not surprisingly, Lucille expressed no interest in attending the science fair, even though both of her grandsons stood a good chance of winning in their respective categories, Alex in Chemistry and Nick in Earth Science. Since I no longer had a working stove, I didn't worry about her burning down the house while we were gone. I left a dinner platter for her in the refrigerator. All she had to do was zap it in the microwave for two minutes.

Of course, Lucille being Lucille, there was the possibility she'd ignore my directions and set the timer long enough to explode her dinner. But since Zack had insisted on purchasing new appliances as part of the kitchen remodel, I decided not to worry. If my mother-in-law detonated her dinner in the microwave, she could fix herself a peanut butter and jelly sandwich.

Shortly after five o'clock, we bundled up in our winter coats and headed across town to the Lambert home, Alex driving Nick in his Jeep. Zack, Mama, and I followed in my Jetta.

We'd met Shane Lambert back in December after Alex had begun dating his daughter Sophie. A subsequent murder, followed by my thwarting of an attempt to kidnap Sophie, had bonded the two families together.

Shane and Sophie had prepared a buffet dinner of assorted salads and sandwich fixings, perfect for an eat-and-run meal—which is exactly what the teens did. Once they headed off to the high school, the adults relaxed over coffee until shortly before the science fair opened.

We arrived at the high school in plenty of time to tour the various booths before the awards ceremony. Then we watched as both Alex and Nick took first place in their categories, as did Sophie, who won in the Environmental Science category. Afterwards the seven of us celebrated over ice cream sundaes.

~*~

We pulled into the driveway shortly before eleven o'clock. As soon as we made our way to the front door, we heard *Dancing with the Stars* blaring from the den television. "Is that commie going deaf?" asked Mama, raising her voice and covering her ears.

"She will if she keeps this up," said Zack. He unlocked the door and allowed us to enter ahead of him. As Mama and I hung up our coats, Zack strode toward the den. A moment later silence reigned. Total silence.

"That's odd," I said.

"What's that, dear?" asked Mama.

"Not a peep of complaint from Lucille."

"Completely out of character for the old bat," agreed Mama. "Maybe she fell asleep."

"Or something's wrong," I said.

As I headed down the hall, Zack stepped out of the den. "She's not in there," he said.

I flipped on the bathroom light and peered inside. No Lucille. Although it seemed unlikely, given the darkened room, I even checked the bathtub. Still no Lucille.

I exited the bathroom, made my way to Lucille's bedroom, and pushed aside the curtain that had replaced the bedroom door after she had locked Mama out of the room one time too many. Lucille wasn't on her bed nor was she lying unconscious on the floor. We hadn't seen her in either the living room or dining room when we entered the house.

"She's not in the master bedroom or bathroom," said Zack after checking both.

"Not in here," said Mama, stepping out of Alex and Nick's bedroom.

"That leaves the kitchen and basement," I said. Although I couldn't imagine why my mother-in-law would enter a construction zone or head down to the basement for any reason. The world would come to an end if Lucille Pollack took it upon herself to do her own laundry.

"I'll check," said Zack. But a few moments later he reappeared, shaking his head.

"This is bizarre," I said.

"What's bizarre?" asked Alex as he and Nick entered the house.

"The commie," answered Mama. "This is so typical of that thoughtless Bolshevik. She probably went out without bothering to turn off the television, let alone leave a note."

With Harriet still locked up, Lucille had no wheels. Leonard was in the apartment, so Lucille wasn't taking him for a walk. Besides, she'd previously abdicated all responsibility for her dog.

Mama yawned theatrically. "I don't know about the rest of

you, but I need my beauty rest. Wherever she is, it's not our problem. She's a grown woman." She then spun on her heels and with a backward wave said, "Goodnight, all," as she entered the boys' bedroom, closing the door behind her.

A moment later Mama let loose an ear-piercing shriek.

Zack, Alex, Nick, and I raced into the room. We found Mama standing in front of the open closet door, her mouth agape, her eyes wide, one arm outstretched. A shaky index finger pointed to something within.

"B..b...b," she stuttered, unable to force out any words, let alone a coherent syllable.

The four of us crowded around Mama and stared into the closet. I expected to find a giant bug freaking her out. Mama hated bugs, but this was no bug. It was a body. My mother-in-law's body. Inside the closet, partially hidden under a pile of clothes and shoes.

I moved Mama aside as Zack stepped closer. He bent down and removed some of the garments covering Lucille's trussed-up body.

"Is she alive?" I asked.

Zack placed his fingers alongside her neck. "I'm getting a pulse, but she's got a huge gash on the side of her head."

I whipped out my phone and called 911. After explaining the situation to the dispatcher and being told to remain on the line, I told Zack, "An ambulance is on its way."

Lucille began to stir as Zack worked to loosen the electrical cords binding her arms and legs. She forced open her previously uninjured eye, which now matched the injured one, took one look at Zack, and tried to jerk away. "Get your hands off me!"

"Don't move," he said. "We don't know the extent of your injuries."

She stared up at us, and in a raspy voice, demanded, "What did you do to me?"

"How dare you!" said Mama, her horror-stricken demeanor having segued into indignation. "*We* certainly didn't do this. You nearly gave me a heart attack. You should be grateful I found you when I did."

I shot a glance at Zack, then muttered, "Not helping, Mama."

My mother screwed her face into a pout and fisted her hands on her hips. "Well, we didn't, and I resent the accusation."

I glanced over at my sons who took the silent hint. Alex reached for Mama's arm and said, "Come on, Grandma. I'll make you a cup of tea while Nick takes Leonard for a walk."

"Manifesto!" shouted Lucille, regaining her voice enough to chastise my son. "His name is Manifesto."

"Not anymore," said Nick.

Mama and her grandsons left the room to the sounds of Lucille's accusations. "This is all your fault, Anastasia. Those boys of yours have no respect."

I bit my tongue. I was itching to tell her respect is earned, but we currently had more pressing matters. Like, who assaulted her. And why? "What's the last thing you remember?" I asked her.

She scowled at me and refused to answer. Whether her silence stemmed from petulance or a lack of memory of the attack, I had no idea.

Zack had removed the electrical cord around her wrists and feet. She tried to stand, but he placed a hand on her shoulder to prevent her from rising. "It's best to wait until the ambulance arrives."

She swatted away his hand. "I don't need an ambulance. You'd love to lock me up in that horrible place again, wouldn't you?

Well, I won't have it. Get out. Leave me alone."

Lucille grabbed the doorjamb and tried to hoist herself to her feet but immediately gasped before sliding back onto the floor. The pile of scattered clothing cushioned her rump but did little to prevent her head from slamming into the closet wall. She let out a loud moan before losing consciousness again.

I stared down at my mother-in-law. "We can't force her into an ambulance if she refuses to go."

"She won't have that choice if she doesn't regain consciousness."

One could only hope. Getting Lucille into an ambulance and to the hospital would go much smoother if she remained unconscious. "Do you think she broke something?"

Zack shrugged. "Hard to say. Her reaction when she tried to stand may indicate a broken bone. Or worse."

"Do you think Murphy's behind this?"

"I'll check the security cameras. Someone got into the house, whether by force or because she let him in. I don't see Lucille allowing a stranger into the house, do you?"

"Definitely not."

"He either broke in or forced his way inside when she opened the door. We'll know more shortly." He whipped out his phone and started scanning video from the time we left the house earlier that evening.

I stood alongside him as he fast-forwarded through the security videos, but we saw nothing suspicious. As we continued to scan the security feed, we heard a siren growing louder.

"Sounds like the ambulance is almost here," said Zack. He paused the video. "This will have to wait until we deal with Lucille."

Not that it mattered. "Whoever attacked her is probably long gone. I doubt he's lurking in the bushes. And he was probably smart enough to hide his face."

"Most likely. But the video will show how he got in and when."

"But not who he is or what he wanted."

"Not unless he's really dumb," said Zack.

We left my mother-in-law sprawled in the closet and made our way to the front door.

Zack glanced around the living room. "There are no signs of anyone having ransacked the house. This could be personal."

"Someone deliberately wanted to hurt Lucille?"

"She certainly has a knack for pissing off people," said Mama, adding her two cents from the living room. She sat alone on the sofa, except for Catherine the Great, who was curled up alongside her. Steam rose from the mug Mama cupped between her hands. "Maybe she finally mouthed off to the wrong person," she added.

I ignored her comment, no matter how much I agreed with her. When it came to Lucille, anything was possible. The only people I knew who tolerated her were her fellow Daughters of the October Revolution. Her own son had liked her best when two rivers and an hour's drive separated them.

Instead, I asked, "Where's Alex?"

"He went up to the apartment as soon as he nuked my tea."

"And Nick?"

"Also in the apartment."

"You're sure?"

"He darted into the house to say goodnight before going up."

By now the ambulance and an accompanying patrol car had pulled up to the curb. Zack swung the door open as the EMTs, followed by Officers Harley and Fogarty, made their way up the front path. Zack directed the EMTs to the bedroom. While they worked to stabilize Lucille, Zack and I filled Harley and Fogarty in on the little we knew.

"I was checking the security footage before you arrived," said Zack.

"Did you see anything suspicious?" asked Harley.

"Not so far, but we were gone more than five hours. I'll keep looking." He opened his phone and accessed the feed.

As the EMTs were about to roll my still unconscious mother-in-law out of the house, Zack said, "This is disturbing."

"What?" I asked.

"Lucille's assailant had a key to the house."

TEN

Mama bounded off the sofa, toppling Catherine the Great onto the floor, as she hurried to where Harley, Fogarty, Zack, and I stood in the foyer. Zack turned the phone screen toward us.

At seven-thirty-five this evening someone dressed entirely in black and wearing a ski mask had walked up to our front door and let himself into the house. Except for the ski mask, nothing about the intruder stood out, but considering the moonless and overcast night, anyone who happened to be on the street at the time would only have seen the back of a head wearing a ski cap, not a masked man.

He was of average height with no distinguishing gait, his posture erect. He didn't slouch nor hunch his back. He had walked purposefully up to the front door, neither hurrying nor acting in a suspicious manner. A three-quarter length puffer coat hid a build somewhere between slight and extremely muscular. We had no way to tell.

The ski mask prevented us from seeing any facial features once he stood close enough to the camera except for two dark eyes peering out from the holes in the mask. It was impossible to ascertain whether he was bald, had a full head of hair, sported a beard, or was clean-shaven.

"How in the world did he get a key to the house?" asked Mama. "And what if he comes back? He could kill us all in our sleep!"

Not that any of us would sleep tonight with the crime scene unit on the way and an assailant on the loose. As if that weren't enough, I needed to deal with Lucille, which meant a trip to the hospital. A battle royale would ensue if she had regained consciousness and the hospital wanted to admit her for observation and tests. If she insisted on leaving, we were powerless to force her to remain.

"We'll post a detail outside the house," said Harley.

"For how long?" demanded Mama. "And if your answer isn't until you catch the creep, think again."

Harley huffed out a sigh. "Until the locks are changed, ma'am." He pulled out his phone, turned his back on Mama, and spoke directly to Zack and me. "There's a twenty-four-hour service we use. I'm texting them to get someone out here tonight."

"Much appreciated," said Zack.

"But how did he get a key in the first place?" asked Mama.

I could think of only one way. Lucille's mugger hadn't ditched her purse immediately after stealing her money. He'd first made a copy of the key.

"Must have been the guy who stole her purse," said Fogarty.

Mama's eyes widened as she zeroed in on Fogarty. "When was this?"

"Yesterday," said Fogarty. "When she was mugged."

Mama splayed her fingers on her hips and turned to direct her ire at me. "Why am I first hearing about this now?"

"You didn't notice her black eye and the bruises on her face?" I asked.

She waved a dismissive hand. "I figured she'd walked into a door or a wall. If this happened yesterday, why didn't you change the locks immediately?"

"Because we found her pocketbook," said Harley, "shortly after the incident. The keys were still inside."

"I suppose, in hindsight," said Fogarty, "we should have realized the mugger had time to make a duplicate key."

"Seriously?" Mama waved her arms widely as she raised her voice several decibels. "What if he had killed us all!"

She had a point. Tonight could have ended with all of us in body bags. I shuddered at the thought.

"Since we were assured she never carried any ID," said Harley, "we all decided he wouldn't have known where she lived."

"*All* of you decided this?" Mama focused in on Zack and me. "You both went along with this decision? With your recent track record, Anastasia? Where are your brains? And you," she said turning on Zack. "Mr. Observant Photojournalist or possible spy? Where did you park your common sense?"

Another point in her favor. "You're right, Mama. We jumped to a wrong conclusion. Maybe we should have changed the locks immediately."

Mama offered us a Lucille-like harrumph. "I don't think there's any *maybe* about it, dear."

I hung my head like a kid caught with her hand in the cookie jar. At this point, I could only draw one conclusion. Someone had targeted Lucille, either following her once she left the house yesterday or when she took the cab home. That someone then made a copy of her key before disposing of her purse. But who? And why? Had he only wanted to harm Lucille, or was she collateral damage? What was his endgame?

With Mama so upset and still fearful about being murdered in her sleep, Zack offered to book a room for her for the night. She gladly accepted. "As long as you make a reservation at a hotel that allows pets," she said. "I'm not leaving Catherine the Great here tonight."

"No problem, Flora." Zack performed a quick search on his phone. A few taps of his screen later, he told Mama, "You're all set. You've got a room at the Holiday Inn. An Uber will pick you up in ten minutes."

Mama's eyes grew wide. "Ten minutes? That's impossible!"

"How so?" asked Zack.

"That's too soon. I need time to pack."

"The bedroom is a crime scene, ma'am," said Harley. "I can't allow you in there until the Crime Scene Unit has processed the room."

"But I need my things!" said Mama, getting up in Officer Harley's face. "You can't possibly expect me to sleep in my brand-new dress. Do you have any idea how much I paid for this?"

Probably nothing. For some time now, I'd suspected Ira of footing all of Mama's bills, not just her condo. I placed a hand around her shoulders and gently nudged her to step back from Harley's personal space. "You can borrow some of my clothes, Mama."

"I suppose that will have to do," she said. "At least all my toiletries are in the bathroom." She glared at Harley. "Unless that's off-limits, too."

"No, ma'am. You can get your things from the bathroom."

Mama turned back to me. "I'll also need Catherine the Great's food bowl and her food."

"I'll get those," said Zack.

Ten minutes later, we loaded Mama into the Uber. As soon as the car pulled away from the curb, the Crime Scene Unit arrived, followed by Detective Spader.

A short time later, the hospital called to say they were keeping Lucille overnight.

"Is she still unconscious?" I asked.

"She's semi-conscious," said the doctor who had admitted her, "but showing steady improvement. I expect she'll gain full consciousness within a few hours. We'll continue to observe her overnight and run some tests in the morning."

Good luck with that, I thought, but didn't say anything other than thanking her for the update.

Zack and I finally tumbled into bed at half-past two. I had heard no word from the office regarding the computer system. Since I had some comp time coming to me, I shot off an email to Naomi, copying Human Resources, that I'd be using one of those days tomorrow. "Don't wake me in the morning," I told Zack. "I'm sleeping in."

He laughed. "Sure you are."

~*~

I lay awake for hours, forcing myself not to toss and turn. I didn't want to disturb Zack who had fallen asleep the moment his head hit the pillow. No sense both of us enduring a sleepless night.

Along with the worry of last night's incident, I still couldn't get Cormac Murphy out of my head. The man he'd been looking for had turned up dead in my driveway. No one could convince me Murphy wasn't behind his murder. Was Murphy also responsible for the attack on Lucille?

The more I thought about it, the more convinced I became that Lucille's assault wasn't a random mugging but orchestrated specifically to get her housekey. But why? Nothing in the house was missing. Nothing even disturbed. The intruder hadn't been startled and fled before he got what he came for. We didn't arrive home for hours after he had entered the house.

Maybe he hadn't been after anything. Maybe he'd come to kill Lucille. He may have thought he had killed her. Or had inflicted severe enough wounds that she'd ultimately die from them. Was this all about revenge? And if so, for what?

Every time I thought about revenge, my brain circled back to Cormac Murphy. But he'd already taken his revenge on Johnnie D.

Was it possible that Lucille and Murphy had crossed paths sometime in the past? Had he seen her leave the house one day while hiding nearby and decided to eliminate her as well? That sounded too preposterous to consider, and yet I couldn't shake the thought.

I finally drifted off to sleep around five-fifteen. At least, that was the last time I remembered glancing at the alarm clock.

Minutes later—or so it seemed—the sounds of construction startled me awake. Prying open one eye, I tried to focus on the blurry alarm clock numbers. A jumble of eights and zeros bounced around in front of my eyes. I moaned and buried my head under the quilt. Unfortunately, my bladder had other ideas. I dragged myself out of bed and into the bathroom, did the necessary, then hopped in the shower.

By the time I emerged from the steamy bathroom, Zack had arrived with a cup of coffee. "You forgot the toothpicks," I mumbled after nearly draining the mug in one long gulp.

"Toothpicks?"

"To keep my eyelids pried open today."

"We're all out," he said, "but I did fix you breakfast."

"I'd prefer the toothpicks."

"I'll see if I can get Jesse to whittle a few for you from the leftover scraps of two-by-four studs."

I mustered enough strength to kiss him. "My hero."

"After breakfast, you should go back to sleep in the apartment," he said.

I yawned. "Good idea. Except I should probably go to the hospital to check on Lucille."

"Lucille can wait. If anything changes, the hospital will call you."

"True." I yawned again. "A morning nap sounds lovely."

However, once I had finished eating breakfast and entered the apartment, I found myself wide awake, my mind once again racing and fixated on Cormac Murphy.

I was convinced either the universe or my subconscious was sending me a signal. Instead of crawling into bed and burrowing under the quilt, I made myself another cup of coffee and settled onto the sofa, my feet propped on the coffee table, my laptop perched on my thighs. I was determined to learn as much as I could about Boston mob boss Cormac Murphy.

A search of the man brought up thousands of hits. I narrowed my search to add Robert Doyle and found dozens of articles about the Gardner heist. As Detective Spader had mentioned, Doyle had been a member of Murphy's gang and was suspected of orchestrating the museum burglary as leverage for bargaining down Murphy's prison sentence.

However, even though Doyle had bragged about his involvement, most of the people interviewed by the FBI insisted Doyle didn't have the smarts to pull off such an audacious theft. This included Connor Myles, Boston's most famous art thief. Myles claimed Doyle was his accomplice in the theft of five Andrew and N.C. Wyeth paintings from an estate in Maine years before the Gardner heist.

According to Myles, Doyle had accompanied him to the Isabella Stewart Gardner Museum on several occasions. Once there, they'd stand in front of various masterpieces, whispering as if discussing the merits of each painting. In reality, they were musing over various strategies for robbing the museum.

But Myles claimed Doyle was the classic all-brawn, no-brains low-level gangster. He insisted Doyle was incapable of planning, executing, and getting away with a theft of such magnitude.

In one of the articles regarding the connection between Connor Myles and Robert Doyle, Myles mentioned Garrett Quinn, one of Doyle's close friends. He suggested if Doyle was involved in the Gardner heist, Quinn may have been the brains behind the theft.

Three men had executed the heist at the Gardner Museum. Two had entered the museum. A third had remained outside as both a lookout and getaway driver.

Robert Doyle had been Cormac Murphy's driver. Did he also drive the getaway car the night of the burglary? The FBI must have suspected as much. They'd had Doyle under surveillance days before his murder.

Of course, none of this gave me any further insight into why Cormac Murphy had shown up at my home or whether he was somehow connected to Lucille's assault. Besides, except for

Murphy, most of the suspected players in the Gardner heist were now dead.

I was hooked, though. The more I read, the more there was to read, each article linking to dozens of others. I kept clicking away, once again tumbling deeper and deeper down the Internet rabbit hole.

Except this time my research had nothing to do with coming up with a craft for a future issue. I rationalized my obsession by remembering I had taken a comp day. I didn't have to work at being a crafts editor today. My time was my own.

And on my own time I finally stumbled upon something that sucked the air from my lungs and sent my heart racing and my entire body trembling.

I don't know how long I stared at the words on my computer screen, reading and rereading them. I didn't hear Zack climb the steps up to the apartment or enter. I didn't even notice him standing in front of me until he finally cleared his throat and I looked up to find concern written across his face.

"What?" I asked, afraid I'd hear additional bad news.

"You tell me. I expected to find you luxuriating in bed. Thought I might even join you."

I ignored his invitation and instead said, "I found something."

The corners of Zack's mouth curved down, and the worry lines on his forehead deepened. "From the looks of it, I don't think you're pleased with whatever it is you found."

"We need to look through that box of old jewelry Jesse found in the attic."

Without questioning me further, Zack nodded and entered the darkroom. He emerged a minute later with the carved wooden box and handed it to me. "Anything special we're looking for?"

I rooted through the box until I found the locket. "This." Then I opened the rectangular case and gasped.

ELEVEN

"Is that who I think it is?" asked Zack, staring at the image inside the locket, a tiny etching of what appeared to be a portrait of a young Rembrandt van Rijn.

"It's definitely Rembrandt," I said. Having majored in art in college and taken four years of art history classes, I absolutely, positively, without a shadow of doubt knew Rembrandt when I saw him—whether portrayed in his youth or as an older man. "Meet *Portrait of the Artist as a Young Man* or *Rembrandt Aux Trois Moustaches* as the etching is often dubbed."

Zack squinted at the etching. "*Three* mustaches?"

"Weird, huh? For some reason the sobriquet is a reference not only to the hair on his lip but also the hair on his chin and the fact that his cap appears to sport a mustache."

"In which course did you learn that nugget of trivia?"

"None. I found a copy of the original hand-written bill of sale when the etching was purchased for Isabella Stewart Gardner." I shrugged. "Maybe the art dealer had a strange sense of humor."

"Whether one mustache or three, it's got to be a copy, right?"

Rather than agree, I said, "I'm not so sure. We need to measure it."

Zack strode across the room and pulled a small ruler from his desk drawer, handing it to me when he returned to the sofa. I gently opened the hinged glass that held the etching inside the locket and measured, taking care not to touch the actual artwork. "Exactly one and three-quarters inches by one and fifteen-sixteenths inches."

I replaced the glass and locked eyes with Zack. "Exactly the size of the miniature etching stolen from the Gardner Museum during the burglary in 1990."

Zack let loose a low whistle. "Do you suppose this is what Murphy wanted from Johnnie Doyle?"

"This and probably some of the other pieces." I filled him in on what I'd read.

"After Murphy's release from Leavenworth, he was suspected of burglarizing a jewelry store in the Beacon Hill section of Boston. His partner-in-crime was named Garrett Quinn, one of the men the FBI suspected of pulling off the Gardner heist."

"Were they arrested?"

"They were brought in for questioning but never charged due to a lack of evidence."

"And I'm sure neither talked."

"Of course not. But get this: Garrett Quinn's wife is Colleen *Doyle* Quinn. She's Johnnie Doyle and Shauna Doyle Gallagher's sister."

"Interesting coincidence."

I offered him a catbird smile. "Oh, but it gets better. At one point the FBI executed a search of the Quinn's farm in New

Hampshire in conjunction with a drug investigation. They came up empty in their search for drugs but found a cache of weapons. At that point, Colleen Doyle Quinn, who was recently widowed, volunteered that her husband Garrett had been in possession of two of the stolen paintings from the Gardner Museum. When the Feds asked her where the paintings were, she claimed that prior to his death, Garrett had turned them over to another mob associate, Lochlin Fitzgerald."

"She was probably worried she'd be charged for illegal possession of the weapons," said Zack. "She dangled information about the Gardner paintings as a carrot in case she needed to cut a deal."

"If so, she wasn't very smart."

Zack agreed. "She should have called her lawyer before offering up any knowledge of the paintings."

"Anyway, when the Feds picked up Lochlin Fitzgerald for questioning, he told them he never saw any paintings, that Colleen had lied. The Feds didn't believe him until he dropped a bombshell—Colleen wore the miniature Rembrandt etching in a locket around her neck. He claimed she showed it to him."

"Whoa!"

I held up a finger. "I told you it gets better. The Feds got a second search warrant, but my guess is that Colleen had freaked out after their first visit and mailed her jewelry, or at least whatever she knew was stolen property, to her sister Shauna Doyle Gallagher for safekeeping.

"When the Feds showed up at the farm the second time, they failed to find the locket. Colleen wasn't wearing it, and it was nowhere on the property. When questioned, she said she'd never owned any locket and never met Lochlin Fitzgerald."

"Then how did Colleen know her husband gave Fitzgerald the paintings?"

"She said he told her."

"Which may or may not be what happened to the paintings—if Quinn ever had any of them in the first place. Or the Rembrandt etching."

"True, but Lochlin Fitzgerald stuck to his story about the Rembrandt in the locket. He claimed Colleen Quinn was crazy and had been for years. Said it was common knowledge and the Feds could ask around. Remarkably, cocky mobster that he was, he offered to take a polygraph."

"Did he pass?" asked Zack.

"That's yet another strange chapter in this story. He failed. Miserably."

"He probably thought by offering, the Feds would believe his version of the story and wouldn't go ahead with the test."

"But they called his bluff. When presented with the results, Fitzgerald admitted he'd made up the entire story."

Zack studied the locket. "Or not. Maybe he got cold feet and decided he shouldn't have told the Feds anything in the first place."

"You think he backpedaled and said he lied?"

"Makes sense. How else would the locket wind up here?"

"What do we do now?"

Zack pulled out his phone. "I'm calling Ledbetter."

FBI Special Agent Aloysius Ledbetter was the cousin of Zack's ex-wife Patricia. I'd previously met him under less than pleasant circumstances, but he'd immediately earned my respect.

When Ledbetter answered, Zack explained the situation. He then listened for a few seconds before saying, "See you soon," and ended the call.

"Sounds like he was interested," I said.

"Extremely. By the way, do you know there's a ten-million-dollar reward for information leading to the return of the Gardner artworks?"

"That did come up in my online research." I sighed dreamily. "Imagine being able to pay off Karl's debts by finding one of the stolen pieces of art. With plenty leftover."

"If the etching is the original."

I shrugged. "That's a question for the experts. Eight semesters of art history didn't provide me with anywhere near the expertise I'd need to determine an original from a forgery. That's an entirely different field." At best, I might be able to determine if the etching was a modern-day print of the original, but I knew better than to remove the piece from the locket to examine it closer.

"This etching isn't signed," I said. "I don't know if the one stolen from the Gardner Museum was signed and numbered or not, but I suspect it wasn't."

"Why is that?"

"None of the images I found on the Internet showed a signature, date, or print number. What are the chances the museum would frame an original Rembrandt in such a way as to hide those details?"

"None. But we both know not all artworks are signed."

"True, especially preliminary sketches and etching proofs. Rembrandt may have seen this self-portrait as no more than an exercise."

"Or something that didn't rise to the high standards he set for himself," added Zack. "Could have been the mustache on the cap. Maybe Rembrandt himself named the piece."

"I suppose it depends on whether he had a sense of humor. If this was a work-in-progress, he may never have gotten back to it for any number of reasons. Given the tiny size, he may have lost or misplaced the etching plate. Nothing I came across in my reading offered any additional details about the work."

~*~

Agent Ledbetter arrived an hour later with a second agent, a woman of about fifty with light brown hair pulled back into a no-nonsense bun at the nape of her neck. He introduced her as Special Agent Lournetta Smanski. "Agent Smanski is a member of our Art Crime Team," he said. "She deals with fakes and forgeries."

"Would you also be able to determine if the jewelry was stolen?" I asked.

Agent Smanski shook her head. "Normally, no. That would be our Jewelry and Gem Theft division. However, when Agent Ledbetter told me what you had found, I talked to one of their agents. A spate of robberies occurred at jewelry stores in and around Boston shortly after Murphy's release from prison back in the early two-thousands. Not all were solved." She opened an attaché case and removed an iPad and a piece of heavy white felt as she continued to speak. "I have photos of the pieces that are still missing."

She unrolled the felt onto the coffee table. Ledbetter pulled a pair of rubber gloves from his pocket and began to assemble the jewelry on the felt. I glanced at Zack. Neither of us had thought to wear gloves when we handled the pieces.

"If you're going to dust those for prints," he said, "you'll find both mine and Anastasia's on them."

Ledbetter frowned. "Thought you both knew better."

"At the time," said Zack, "we didn't suspect we'd discovered stolen property, especially since half the pieces appear to be costume jewelry. They have no markings."

"What about the locket?" asked Agent Smanski.

"We never opened it until today when I read about Colleen Quinn."

Zack and I began to explain the events of the last week and what I'd discovered about the Rembrandt. When we'd finished, Agent Ledbetter said, "I don't know why I was called in, Mrs. Pollack. The way you solved my last case, you'll probably have this wrapped up on your own by the end of the week." He winked and added, "My offer still stands. You'd be a huge asset to the agency."

"Thanks," I said, knowing his offer wasn't serious, "but murder and mayhem have given me too many gray hairs lately."

Agent Smanski paused from examining the locket and cast a questioning eye toward Ledbetter.

"I'll tell you all about it later," he said.

Zack slipped an arm around my waist. "And I'm turning gray from worrying about her, Ledbetter. So stop asking."

Ledbetter shrugged. "I tried."

Agent Smanski closed the locket. "I won't remove the etching here. I need to look at this back at the lab to run some tests."

"I expected as much," I said.

She snapped a photo of the locket, both opened and closed. Then she set about photographing the other pieces of jewelry. "I'm uploading them to the database," she said. "We should know if we have any hits shortly."

Within seconds, her iPad chimed. The three of us hovered around her as she tapped her screen. When she had finished, she looked up at me. "Congratulations, Mrs. Pollack. You've uncovered a treasure trove of stolen jewelry."

"All of it?" I asked.

"Only the pieces that are stamped." She nodded toward Zack. "The remainder, as you and Mr. Barnes suspected, are costume jewelry, gold-plated and paste. They have no value."

I wondered if there was a reward offered for the jewelry but contained myself. Asking seemed tacky. I'm sure I'd learn soon enough. Instead, I asked, "Were they all from the same burglary?"

"Since that's not my division," Agent Smanski said, "I don't have that information. It makes sense, though. If not from the same burglary, then most likely the same thief."

Ledbetter began placing the stolen jewelry in evidence bags. He also bagged the non-valuable pieces. "Why are you taking those?" I asked.

"We'll dust them for prints as well. You never know what forensics will reveal."

"And DNA?" I asked.

Agent Smanski raised an eyebrow. "What exactly do you do for a living, Mrs. Pollack, if you don't mind my asking?"

"I'm the crafts editor at a women's magazine."

"But in her spare time, she catches killers," added Ledbetter.

Agent Smanski eyed me for a long moment, then turned to Agent Ledbetter. "Sounds like I'm going to hear quite an intriguing story on the way back to headquarters."

"You have no idea," he said, shooting me another wink as he and Agent Smanski prepared to leave.

"Now what?" asked Zack after the two FBI agents had departed.

My stomach answered with a loud rumble. "Lunchtime?"

Zack opened the refrigerator and began pulling out an assortment of meats and cheeses and two apples. I grabbed a box of crackers from one of the cabinets and started a fresh pot of coffee. As we set about fixing two plates of food, I said, "I think I'll visit Rosalie this afternoon."

"Any special reason?"

"Just being neighborly."

"Or perhaps you want to ask her what she knows about the Gallaghers?"

No fooling that man. I offered him a self-incriminating grin. "That, too."

~*~

Rosalie Schneider had lived in the Cape Cod behind our rancher most of her adult life. A row of azalea bushes, rather than a fence, separated our yards. The back walls of our garages stood a mere three feet apart.

She and her husband had purchased the home shortly after their marriage, but not long afterwards, he'd run off with her sister. Rosalie had remained in the house by herself ever since.

We'd bonded years ago over a shared love of crafts after I saw her award-winning quilts hanging on her clothesline one day and introduced myself. Now in her mid-eighties, she still had the eyesight and nimble fingers of a quilter half her age.

I knew Rosalie didn't get along with the neighbors on either side of her. One had a dog that barked incessantly. The other came and went at all hours of the night on a Hog you could hear half a mile away. I wondered what she'd have to say about the previous owners of my home.

Not having any homemade baked goods to bring with me, I raided my craft stash in the basement and found several yards of cotton print fabric samples sent to me by one of the magazine's advertisers. Knowing Rosalie, she'd drool over the fabric the way

I'd drool over freshly baked brownies or cookies.

She greeted me at the back door. "Anastasia! What a pleasant surprise."

I handed her the fabric. "I thought you'd like these."

She cradled the pieces in one arm, her other hand caressing the sample cuts as if she held a newborn kitten. "What gorgeous patterns and colors. How thoughtful of you. Come in, dear. I was just about to have a cup of tea and a slice of lemon poppyseed cake. You'll join me, won't you? I've got a loaf fresh from the oven."

"Rosalie, I'd never pass up freshly baked anything from you." Rosalie's talents in the kitchen were second only to her talent with a needle and thread, her baking prowess running neck-and-neck with Cloris.

As we sipped our tea and feasted on the lemon poppyseed cake, I asked her about the Gallagher family.

She glanced up, as if she could pluck some memories from the ceiling. "Haven't thought about Shauna and Kellen Gallagher in years," she said. "They pretty much kept to themselves, but when the weather was nice and the windows open, I often heard Shauna and Kellen fighting like cats and dogs."

"Any idea over what?"

Rosalie nodded. "Shauna once confided in me. I saw her out in the backyard one day. She looked like she was crying. I walked over and asked if she was okay. At first, she seemed embarrassed, said she was fine, but then it all came tumbling out in a flood of words."

Rosalie paused to take a sip of her tea. "Her brother Johnnie used to stay with them for extended periods of time. He was a troublemaker, but Shauna made excuses for him."

"What sort of excuses?"

She waved her hand dismissively. "The usual. 'You can't blame him. He had a rough childhood.' Yada, yada, yada. Shauna didn't come right out and say it, but I got the sense drugs were involved and perhaps some run-ins with the law. Kellen thought the brother was a bad influence on their son. What was his name?" she muttered to herself. Pausing, she stared off into the distance for a moment, then said, "Aiden? Yes, I'm sure his name was Aiden. Anyway, that's what they fought about mostly. That and money, of course."

"Was her husband often out of work?"

"Not that I'm aware. It was the money she gave her brother and what she spent on the kid. That boy was spoiled rotten. I think Kellen worried he'd turn out like Johnnie."

"Did he?"

Rosalie shrugged. "I have no idea. One day they were gone. Then you moved in."

She rose to steep a second pot of tea. "Why the sudden interest in the Gallaghers?"

"Our contractor found something in the attic that we're assuming belonged to them."

"The jewelry?"

I nearly choked on a mouthful of cake. "You know about that?"

Rosalie returned to the table with the teapot. "After she unburdened herself that day, Shauna and I occasionally got together for tea or coffee. I don't think she had any close friends. I felt sorry for her."

She cut two more slices of cake for us. "One day Shauna told me she'd received a box of jewelry from her sister Claire." Rosalie paused, pursed her lips, and shook her head. "No, that's not right. Some other common Irish name." She thought for another few seconds, then smacked her hand on the table and said, "Colleen. Colleen Quinn. And Colleen's husband was Garrett Quinn."

Rosalie smiled at me as she tapped her temple with an index finger. "The old girl's still got it, Anastasia."

"I don't doubt that for a second, Rosalie."

"Anyway," she continued, "Shauna said Colleen asked her to keep the jewelry for her, but Shauna suspected the pieces were from a burglary."

"Why would she think that?"

"Shauna said Garrett had a record and was in and out of prison over the years."

"If Shauna suspected the jewelry was stolen, why didn't she notify the police?"

"I urged her to do so, but she was afraid her sister would be charged." Rosalie sneered. "For some people, dear, no matter what a relative does to you, blood is thicker than water."

I wondered if that was a reference to Rosalie's own past. "What did she do?"

"The box was only half-full. She filled the remainder of the box with costume jewelry that had belonged to her mother."

That explained why the box contained both valuable and worthless pieces of jewelry. "And hid the box under the eaves in the attic?"

Rosalie finished her tea, then said, "To my knowledge, she never told anyone but me, not even her husband. I suspect she deliberately left the box in the attic when they moved. Or maybe she forgot it was there."

She refilled our cups with the freshly steeped tea. "Out of curiosity, I'd love to see that jewelry," she said. "Shauna was too spooked to show any of it to me."

"I'm afraid I no longer have the pieces," I said.

Rosalie's eyebrows arched. "Oh? What did you do with them?"

I decided to keep my explanation as vague and simple as possible. "We suspected one of the items was connected to a high-profile burglary from 1990. Zack called someone he knows in the FBI. We turned everything over to him."

Her brow creased. "1990? Unlikely, dear."

"How so?"

"I'm a little fuzzy on the dates, but I'm sure Shauna didn't receive the jewelry from her sister until at least ten years later, maybe a few years before you and Karl moved into the house."

I didn't see the point of explaining all that I'd learned from my hours of research earlier that morning. Instead, I said, "I'm sure the FBI will sort it all out."

"No doubt. You will let me know what happens, won't you?" She clasped her hands together. "I do love a good mystery. I've read every Agatha Christie book multiple times."

I thanked Rosalie for her hospitality and rose to leave. "If I hear anything, I'll let you know."

TWELVE

As I crossed Rosalie's backyard on my way home, my phone rang. The display indicated the call was from the hospital. Before answering, I inhaled a deep breath, bracing myself for whatever news I'd receive. "Hello?"

"Mrs. Pollack?"

"Yes."

"This is Dr. Pavlochek at Overlook Hospital."

Dr. Pavlochek was the neurosurgeon on call when Lucille suffered a minor stroke last year. Tests had discovered a small brain tumor, which had required surgery but when biopsied afterwards, proved benign. "Is Lucille conscious?" I asked.

"Conscious and feisty as ever. All her tests came back negative. She's free to leave."

"For home or rehab?"

"Rehab isn't indicated."

"Really?" Not that I had hoped Lucille's injuries were more severe, but the last thing I needed was dealing with a demanding semi-invalid during a major home renovation, not to mention a killer on the loose. Lucille was enough of a challenge when free from wounds or illness. "Are you sure she wouldn't be better off in rehab for a few days?"

"Medicare won't cover it," said the doctor. "Aside from the gash on her head, which required several stitches, and a few bruised ribs, her injuries are relatively minor. She's already up, walking around, and demanding we release her. Just don't let her attempt anything strenuous for a few days."

"That won't be a problem," I said. Except for carrying around her dog, Lucille had never lifted a finger to do anything since moving in with me. However, she'd even given up stooping to scoop the former Devil Dog into her arms or onto her lap ever since he'd made it clear he preferred Nick over his rightful owner.

"I can pick her up in half an hour," I said, then thanked the doctor before disconnecting the call.

"I guess sometimes it pays to have a thick skull," said Zack after I informed him about Lucille. Then he added, "I'll go to the hospital with you. If she's in one of her moods, she might be a handful."

"Is she ever not in one of her moods?" Still, I appreciated the offer. I graciously and gratefully accepted, giving him a kiss because *handful* was my mother-in-law's middle name.

When we arrived at the hospital, we were surprised to find her sitting in a wheelchair parked under the portico at the entrance. A blanket was draped across her lap and tucked under her legs. She clung to a second blanket wrapped like a shawl around her shoulders. Behind her, a frowning orderly held fast to the wheelchair handles.

My jaw dropped open. "Why would the hospital make her wait

outside in this weather?" Another cold front had moved in overnight, and the addition of wind gusts made the day feel more like November than late April.

"My guess?" said Zack. "She insisted." He pulled up in front of her.

I opened the passenger door and jumped out of the car. "Lucille, why didn't you wait inside? I brought you a change of clothes and your coat."

She ignored my question, and as I opened the back passenger door, instead demanded, "What took you so long, Anastasia? I've been waiting out here for hours."

I stared in shock at the orderly. "Hours? Dr. Pavlochek called me thirty minutes ago."

The orderly checked his watch. "We've been standing out here exactly three minutes, ma'am." His frown grew into a scowl as he tucked his chin and glared at the top of Lucille's head. "And only because the patient insisted. I tried to keep her in the lobby until you arrived, but she demanded I wheel her outside."

"Why couldn't she wait in her room?"

The orderly raised his head, locked eyes with me, and seethed, "Because she refused."

He undid the wheelchair brake, rolled her closer to the back passenger door, and muttered under his breath, "I don't get paid nearly enough to put up with patients like her."

"I'm sorry," I mouthed as Zack exited the Jetta and grabbed Lucille's cane from the trunk.

The orderly shrugged. "Not your fault. We all have our burdens to bear."

Zack assisted the orderly in getting Lucille into the car. Even then, both men struggled. As much as Lucille wanted to put distance between herself and the hospital, she certainly wasn't cooperating with the transition from wheelchair to backseat.

When Zack and the orderly finally got her settled and buckled in, I closed the door and thanked the orderly. "I don't envy you," he said.

Under the circumstances, I couldn't blame the man for his unprofessional comments. Orderlies didn't have the easiest of jobs, even without having to deal with the likes of Lucille Pollack, a straw that would break the strongest camel's back. I offered him a smile of commiseration and said, "I don't envy me, either."

Most people with bruised ribs would find it hard to keep up a nonstop diatribe. Not Lucille. She started haranguing me the moment we pulled away from the hospital entrance. I closed my eyes, trying to tune her out, but attaining my inner Zen proved futile. Even Buddha would find my mother-in-law a near-impossible challenge.

Making matters worse, our timing sucked. Schools had let out for the day. When we weren't stopped by crossing guards directing traffic at schools or allowing pedestrians to cross streets, we were stuck behind school buses dropping off kids. The trip back to Westfield took nearly twice as long as the drive to the hospital. And through it all, Lucille's incessant complaints sucked the air from the car.

As we sat in traffic, Zack removed one hand from the steering wheel and settled it on my thigh. "Deep breaths," he whispered.

~*~

When we finally arrived home, we were greeted with hammering, drilling, friendly chatter, and rock music coming from the kitchen. Before we'd had a chance to remove and hang up our coats, Lucille added the noise level to her litany of complaints. "I need my rest," she said. "Tell those men to come back another day."

"That's not going to happen," said Zack.

"How dare you!" She raised her cane at him. "This is my son's house, not yours."

"No, Lucille, this is my house," I said, stepping between the two of them. "Mine and Alex's and Nick's and Zack's. Karl is dead. You're here as my guest. If you don't like the accommodations, you're more than welcome to find another place to live."

"I can offer you a pair of noise-cancelling headphones," said Zack, his voice much calmer than mine. When Lucille answered with a dagger-eyed glare, he added, "Or arrange for you to stay at Sunnyside until the renovation is finished."

"You're not locking me up in that hellhole again," she said. "They tried to kill me. I'll have you arrested for elder abuse."

No one had tried to kill my mother-in-law during her stay at one of the most upscale rehab and senior living facilities in the state. Someone had tried to kill me. However, in typical Lucille fashion, she'd usurped the narrative and made the story her own.

"Your choice," said Zack, helping me out of my coat before removing his own. He strode down the hall to the coat closet. When he returned moments later, he said, "Let me know if you want those headphones, Lucille." Then he headed toward the kitchen.

"That man is a charlatan," my mother-in-law said, sneering at Zack's back. "You're too stupid to realize he's only interested in you as a way to get his hands on what you inherited from my son."

I laughed. "That man is one of the highest paid photojournalists in the world. He doesn't need my non-existent inheritance."

"Believe what you want to believe," she said. "I know the truth.

You'll be sorry you ever took up with him and sullied my son's good name."

Karl had sullied his own good name when he took up with Lady Luck, a fact Lucille adamantly deemed fiction. I bit my tongue and walked away. Her injuries notwithstanding, if Lucille had sufficient lung capacity to verbally abuse us, she had the strength to shuffle herself off down the hall to her bedroom.

Nick arrived home while Zack and I stood admiring the progress Jesse and his crew had made so far in the kitchen. After dropping his bookbag in the mudroom and gracing me with a perfunctory peck on the cheek, he asked, "Computers still down at work?"

"As far as I know. I haven't heard otherwise. No after-school practice today?"

"Coach has the flu."

"Where's your brother?"

"He and Sophie stayed to work on something in the library. Did anyone walk Leonard?"

"Not yet. Zack and I only returned a few minutes ago from picking up your grandmother at the hospital."

"Really? She sure didn't look okay last night."

"I wouldn't call her okay, but she isn't in bad enough shape to take up a hospital bed."

"Is she refusing to go to Sunnyside again?"

"According to the doctor, her injuries aren't severe enough to warrant rehab."

He scowled. "Too bad."

I shot him a Mom Look. "Really, Nick?"

His cheeks grew red. "I only mean it would be nice to have a break from her. She's not the easiest person to be around."

"Tell me something I don't know."

He smirked. "Really, Mom?"

"Touché, Nick."

"I'm going to walk Leonard, then toss the Frisbee around to give him some exercise."

"Isn't it too cold and windy?"

"We won't stay out long."

I watched from the kitchen window as Nick bounded up the stairs to the apartment, then made his way back down with Leonard. But something was wrong. Barking and growling menacingly, Leonard nearly dragged Nick down the staircase. Nick struggled to hold onto the railing and keep from losing his footing. Once they reached the bottom of the stairs, Leonard refused Nick's efforts to steer him toward the driveway. Instead, Leonard yanked Nick toward the backyard.

"What's going on with Leonard?" asked Zack, breaking off his conversation with Jesse and coming up behind me.

"I'm not sure, but something has him riled."

Leonard broke free from Nick and raced along the side of the garage. Nick chased after him. "Leonard, stop!"

The dog darted behind the garage. Nick followed, then suddenly screamed, Mom! Zack! Come quick!"

But we were already on our way, not even bothering to grab our coats.

We found Leonard digging through a fresh mound of dirt where a narrow strip of groundcover had separated my garage from Rosalie's garage. Nick stared in horror at what Leonard had uncovered.

Zack grabbed Leonard's collar and yanked the dog away. Leonard snarled in protest. I grabbed the leash and handed it to

Nick. "Get him out of here."

"Where should I take him?"

"Go for a walk to calm him down. If that doesn't work, lock him in the basement."

Nick managed to drag the dog out of the backyard. A moment later, the barking subsided.

I turned back to find Zack already on his phone speaking with the 911 dispatcher. "Yes, a body," he said. "Buried behind the garage."

~*~

I ran into the house to grab our coats while Zack stood guard over Leonard's find. As soon as I returned, we began to hear sirens, growing louder as they neared us. Within minutes, law enforcement vehicles, both marked and unmarked, their lights flashing, had arrived. While uniformed officers worked to cordon off the crime scene, others held back a gathering gaggle of curious neighbors.

After Agent Ledbetter's admonition about handling the stolen jewelry, except for my mad dash coat retrieval, Zack and I remained frozen in place. We were too afraid to disturb any possible evidence that might lurk among the freshly emerging blades of grass and residual winter muck.

Detective Spader arrived and shook his head as he lumbered toward us. Apparently, he was less concerned about disturbing the crabgrass. "Another body, Mrs. Pollack?"

"Not funny, Detective."

"On some days, macabre humor is the only way to get through this job." He removed his notepad and a pencil from his coat pocket and flipped to a blank page. "How'd you discover the body this time?"

"I didn't. Leonard did."

He squinted at me for a moment before recognition dawned. "Oh, the dog."

I explained how Leonard had pulled away from Nick and raced behind the garage. "Nick yelled for us when Leonard uncovered a foot."

Spader looked past us to where crime scene techs were already carefully removing dirt from the body. "Was that pile of dirt there previously?"

"No," said Zack. "The ground was flat, planted with pachysandra to keep down the weeds."

Jesse and his crew had stopped work and gathered on the patio. A uniformed officer prevented them from moving closer. "What's going on?" he called to us.

"Say nothing for now," said Detective Spader. "We're going to have to question him and his crew."

"Surely, you don't think they're responsible?" I asked.

"No, but one of them may have seen or heard something. Anyone else in the house? The boys?"

"Nick is walking Leonard," I said. "Alex is still at school."

"Lucille," said Zack.

Spader paused from scrawling something on his notepad and glanced up. "She's out of the hospital already?"

I nodded.

"Do you think this is somehow connected to the attack on her?" ask Zack.

Spader answered with a question of his own. "Don't you? Seems awfully coincidental otherwise."

"But how do you connect the dots?" I asked. "Why would Lucille's attacker leave her tied up in the closet but risk getting caught by taking the time to bury a body behind the garage?"

"Hopefully, we'll connect some of those dots when we identify the victim," said Spader.

Zack had pulled out his phone. "What are you looking for?" I asked.

"Last night I stopped watching the security feed once we saw the intruder had used a key to enter the house. I never checked any of the other cameras around the house."

"Better late than never," said Spader. "Now would be a good time to take a look because at least one other person was on your property last night."

Zack glanced up from his phone. He wasn't happy, but I could tell his grim expression had little to do with Spader's comment. Zack was annoyed with himself.

"Don't kick yourself," I said. "It was a crazy night. Besides, didn't the crime scene unit check the property last night? Why didn't they see a freshly dug grave between the garages?"

"Valid point," said Zack. We both stared at Spader.

"I have no answer for that," he said. "If they'd done a thorough search of the property, they should have noticed this." He called over one of the officers. "Eastman, who searched the property last night?"

"I did, sir, along with Officer Temple."

"Did you check behind the garage?"

"Of course, sir."

"You didn't see a fresh mound of dirt?"

"We did, sir."

Spader's voice grew threatening. "You didn't think that was worth mentioning?"

Officer Eastman stared at his superior. "Should we have, sir?

We were in search of a perp possibly hiding on the property, not a dead body."

"And a mound the size of a grave didn't seem odd to you?"

Eastman shrugged. "Not really, sir."

Spader gritted his teeth. "And why is that?"

"It's spring, sir. Everyone is getting topsoil deliveries to freshen up their planting beds."

Spader sighed. "Thank you, Officer Eastman. Carry on."

"Yes, sir." With relief written across his face, he scurried back to his position.

After he left, Spader said, "Under the circumstances, I suppose I might have jumped to the same conclusion."

"Except that this is the second dead body found on our property in less than a week," I said.

"There is that," said Spader. "On second thought, maybe I wouldn't have jumped to the same conclusion as Officer Eastman."

"I would hope not, Detective."

"I appreciate the vote of confidence, Mrs. Pollack."

Zack had remained fixated on his iPhone screen, the worry line between his eyebrows growing deeper as the security video continued to play. I decided not to interrupt him. Zack was one of the only men I knew capable of multitasking. I was certain he'd listened with at least one ear to every word of the conversation between Spader and his officer.

At that moment, one of the crime scene techs called to Spader. He told us to wait as he walked behind the garage. He returned shortly, a grim expression covering his face. "You no longer need to worry about Cormac Murphy, Mrs. Pollack. Someone took care of that problem for you."

My head spun. "If Murphy had Doyle killed, who killed Murphy?"

"That's what our investigation will reveal."

"Hopefully," I said.

"Hopefully," echoed Spader.

"Was he killed here?" asked Zack.

"Looks that way."

"How can you tell," I asked.

"His head was bashed in. The techs found a bloody brick buried with him. There's a brick missing from your flowerbed edging along the patio."

"I get that Murphy had plenty of enemies," I said, "and any number of them might have killed him. But why here? Murphy left Doyle's body in an SUV on my driveway to send us a message. What message is this killer sending? And now that Murphy is dead, can we be sure he was responsible for Doyle's murder? We have nothing to do with any turf wars in Boston. I haven't even been to Boston in more than a decade."

"The bigger question," said Zack, "is why were Murphy and one of his goons here last night?"

He showed us the video on his phone. "After Doyle's murder," he continued, "I installed another surveillance camera, one that would capture more of the street in front of the house."

Zack tapped the play button, and Spader and I watched as an SUV pulled into the driveway and parked. Two men exited the vehicle. Although he kept his head down, I recognized Murphy by his old-fashioned fedora and the cigar stub jutting from the corner of his mouth. The driver pulled a shovel from the back of the SUV, and the two men proceeded down the driveway to the back of the house and garage.

"I don't suppose you have video from behind the garage," said Spader.

"Afraid not," said Zack, "but the camera at the back door captured this." He brought up a second video that showed the man who had entered the house earlier leaving through the back door, grabbing a brick from the flowerbed around the patio, and stealthily making his way toward the back of the garage.

THIRTEEN

"That's not all," said Zack. He fast-forwarded the feed from the new camera. A few minutes later, it showed the driver racing down the driveway, jumping into the SUV, and peeling out into the street.

"Send me the feed," said Spader. "I'll run the plate, but I'm willing to bet we're dealing with another stolen vehicle."

"Keep watching," said Zack.

"There's more?" I asked.

"Oh, yeah, and it's quite odd."

Spader and I continued to watch the video. "Is that someone hiding behind the tree across the street?" I asked, squinting at what appeared to be a head peering out from behind the large maple.

Zack nodded. "Watch what happens next."

Someone dressed in a three-quarter-length parka with fur-trimmed hood stepped from behind the tree and darted across the street, running down our driveway and into the backyard. The way the person was dressed, including a muffler that partially covered the lower half of the face, made it impossible to determine whether we were looking at a burly man or a heavyset woman.

I gasped. "A lookout?"

Zack held up a finger. "Wait."

We continued watching as a dark SUV drove slowly down the street, parked across from the driveway, and cut its lights. The driver remained inside the car.

Zack fast-forwarded the feed. Half an hour later, the person who had run down the driveway reappeared with the man who had entered our house earlier that night. He carried a shovel.

They walked down the driveway, turned right at the sidewalk, and continued down the street.

The driver's side door of the SUV that had parked across from the driveway opened. A slight woman dressed only in jeans and an oversized hoodie that fell over her forehead bounded out, hurried across the street, and confronted the other two people. The man in the puffer coat and ski mask grabbed her arm and pulled her behind a row of waist-high hedges that bordered the property next door to us.

"It's difficult to tell what's happening," I said.

"At least they're not attacking her," said Spader, canting his head and squinting at the screen.

"Not physically," said Zack, "but from their body language, I'm guessing the three of them know each other and are in the middle of a huge fight."

"Amazing that none of the neighbors heard," I said. "Then again, scratch that. We weren't home, the McMansion across the street is empty, and the people on either side of us are extremely elderly and hard of hearing. They also probably turn in by eight o'clock each night."

A few minutes later, the woman stepped from behind the shrubbery. The lookout held onto her arm. When they crossed the street, the young woman climbed into the passenger seat of the SUV, the lookout behind the wheel, and they drove off. We watched as the man in the puffer coat continued down the street until he was out of view.

"He's no longer carrying the shovel," I said.

"No, he's not," said Spader. "Good eye, Mrs. Pollack."

Spader called Officer Eastman over again. "Looks like the perp ditched the shovel in the bushes next door."

"On it, sir." Officer Eastman jogged off, returning a few minutes later, his latex-gloved hand holding a dirt-encrusted shovel.

"Maybe forensics will get lucky," said Spader.

I had my doubts. If we were dealing with mobsters, they'd know to wear gloves or wipe their prints from anything they touched. I'm sure Spader knew that better than anyone. Maybe he was just trying to offer us some hope.

An officer headed toward us from the driveway. "Anyone missing a kid with a dog? He's out front. Claims he lives here, that he discovered the body."

"Nick," I said. "My son."

"Let him into the house," said Spader. "I'll talk to him there. I don't want the dog near the crime scene."

"Yes, sir." The officer headed back toward the front of the house. I noticed another uniformed officer questioning Jesse at one corner of the patio. His crew stood at the opposite corner, presumably waiting their turns.

Spader signaled to Zack and me. "You two are free to go back into the house."

~*~

Eventually Cormac Murphy's body was bagged and removed, and the crime scene unit finished processing the yard. Spader spoke briefly with Nick but didn't bother questioning Lucille. "No point," he said. "We spoke with her at the hospital this morning. She remembers nothing of her attack, and she was tied up and unconscious in the closet during whatever went down in the backyard afterwards."

Nick had taken Leonard and decamped to the apartment without a single word to me regarding his discovery of the body. He knew I'd stumbled across more than my fair share of murders since his father's death, and it scared him. On more than one occasion, he'd pleaded with me to stop investigating. I'd tried my best to honor his wishes, but the universe continued to work against me.

Nick didn't let much faze him normally, but beginning with Karl's death, he'd often had uncharacteristic bursts of anger. My boys had dealt with far too much since learning of their father's duplicity. Add getting permanently stuck with Lucille and their mother's proclivity for finding those dead bodies, and it was more than enough stress for the average adult, much less two teenage boys.

Cormac Murphy's murder had to have impacted Nick. Whether he wanted to or not, we needed to talk about it. Armed with a truckload of concern my son, I headed for the apartment.

I found Nick playing with Leonard in the living room. It suddenly hit me that my son had taken his psychological wellbeing into his own hands, whether he realized it or not. Leonard had become his therapy dog. Still, except for Ralph, pets don't hold up their end of a conversation.

I sat on the floor next to him and draped my arm around his shoulder. "Want to talk about it?"

He shrugged. "Not really." He looked up. "I'm assuming we're going to talk anyway?"

"We are," I said. "However, I'll give you a choice—me, Zack, or a therapist."

"I talk with Alex and Sophie."

"I'm sure you do, but that wasn't one of the options."

"I don't need a shrink."

"That leaves Zack or me."

I thought he'd opt to speak with Zack, figuring male bonding would trump maternal concern. However, much to my surprise, Nick began spilling out a rollercoaster of emotions he'd kept locked deep inside him for the past fifteen months. I listened, commiserated, and comforted.

When he had finally unburdened himself of all his emotional baggage, he heaved a huge sigh, then wrapped me in a bear hug that lasted longer than any hug since his diaper days. "Thanks, Mom. I guess I did need to let it all out. You were right."

"Mothers usually are."

He pulled away and looked at me doubtfully. "Even Grandmother Lucille? She's a mother, too."

"I'll admit, there are exceptions to every rule."

His stomach grumbled in reply.

I chuckled. "Are you telling me I'd better figure out something for dinner?"

He nodded. "Want some help?"

"Only if I can't convince Zack to order take-out. Go back to playing with Leonard."

When I arrived back in the house, Zack asked, "Nick okay?"

"I think so." I told Zack about our conversation and my revelation about Leonard.

"You think Nick would also like to talk to me?"

"Maybe. I'm sure there are things he still hasn't told me."

"Things a guy would never tell his mother?"

"Exactly. Besides, one talk is only a beginning. We should encourage him to confide more in us. Alex, too."

"Agreed, assuming we can pry him away from Sophie."

"There is that."

The sounds of yet another one of Lucille's reality TV shows blared from the den. I suppose she enjoyed them because arguing was her preferred form of discourse, and that's all that seemed to occur between the participants on most of those shows.

If she'd heard the sirens earlier or any of the police activity in the backyard, she chose to ignore all of it. Zack and I decided not to say anything to her unless she brought up the subject.

"What about Mama?" I asked.

Zack had released Ralph from his cage. The bird flapped his wings and took a spin around the house before returning and landing on Zack's shoulder. Ralph lowered his beak into Zack's shirt pocket in search of a sunflower seed.

"What about Flora?" asked Zack.

"How long do you want to foot the bill for her hotel stay?"

Zack settled Ralph on top of one of the cartons of dishes and cookware stacked in the dining room and placed a few more sunflower seeds within the bird's easy reach. Then he drew me into his arms. "Don't worry about the money. As I overheard you telling Lucille earlier, I have plenty of money, and I'm happy to pay until the repairs on your mother's condo are completed."

Ralph finished gobbling up the seeds and squawked, "*But, by the Lord, lads, I am glad you have the money. Henry IV, Part I.* Act Two, Scene Four."

"See," said Zack, nodding toward the African Grey. "Even Ralph is glad I'm paying for Flora's hotel room."

I eyed Ralph before responding to Zack. "I don't know what I'd do without you."

He laughed. "Don't think my decision is entirely altruistic. One less person in the house alleviates a huge amount of the stress around this place. Besides, with your mother gone, the boys get their bedroom back, and we once again get the apartment all to ourselves."

"So, your decision stems entirely from selfishness?"

"You have a problem with that?"

"Not at all." Smiling, I went to kiss him, but the kiss was cut short when my phone dinged with a text from Alex. "You'll be happy to hear we'll have even one less person for a few hours. Shane invited Alex to stay for dinner."

Zack raised a questioning eyebrow. "Shane or Sophie?"

"I'm sure it was Sophie's idea."

Before I had a chance to suggest we order take-out for dinner, Zack said, "Given the day we've had, let's order in pizzas for dinner."

While we waited for the delivery, he headed out the back door to grab a bottle of wine from the apartment, and I pulled veggies from the refrigerator to toss together a salad.

As I chopped, my mind raced, trying to comprehend the events of the past week. No matter where the various threads led, the only explanation that made sense was that everything was somehow intertwined. And I wondered if the key that unlocked the mystery was the box of jewelry Jesse Konopka had discovered in the attic.

Zack returned from the apartment. "Nick said to text him when the pizzas arrive."

I nodded. "I've been thinking."

"Good thoughts, I hope."

"Not really. I want to bounce a few ideas off you."

"Bounce away."

I added the cucumber I'd finished slicing into the salad bowl and offered Ralph a scrap before placing the bowl in the refrigerator. "What if Murphy showed up here because he either knew or suspected Johnnie Doyle had the jewelry from the burglary Murphy and Garrett Quinn pulled off years ago?"

"How would he have found out?" asked Zack as he uncorked the bottle.

"From the Gangster Grapevine and by putting two and two together."

He grabbed two wine glasses and filled both halfway. "I had no idea you lurked on the Gangster Grapevine. I'm all ears."

I landed a playful punch on his bicep. "Not me. Murphy."

He grinned as he handed me my wine. "Some people just can't take a joke. Please, continue."

I took a sip of the pinot noir, then headed into the living room and settled onto the sofa before explaining. "Murphy and Garrett Quinn burglarized one or more jewelry stores. Sometime later, Johnnie Doyle cut that deal with the Feds, Murphy wound up back in prison, and Doyle went into Witness Protection, along with his sister, her husband, and their young son."

"Well-established facts," said Zack. He grabbed the bottle of wine and joined me on the sofa. Ralph followed, landed on the back of the sofa, and climbed onto Zack's shoulder.

I held up a finger. "Bear with me. Murphy and Quinn would either have stashed the jewelry somewhere safe until they could fence it, or Quinn had possession of it. However, by the time Murphy was released from prison this time, Quinn was dead."

"As was his wife Colleen," said Zack.

"Right. But Murphy must have known about the raid on the Quinn farm and the story about the locket with the Rembrandt etching. Either he read about it in the newspaper at the time or heard about it from one of his mobster associates."

"Such as Lochlin Fitzgerald?"

"Exactly. Murphy knew Johnnie periodically holed up in New Jersey with his sister and her family. He would have known Colleen Quinn and Shauna Gallagher were sisters. Since he knew the FBI never found Colleen's locket with the Rembrandt—"

"How would he know that?"

I rolled my eyes. "If the FBI had recovered one of the pieces stolen in the largest art heist in history, don't you think the story would have made international headlines? Prisoners are allowed access to newspapers and television, aren't they?"

Zack's eyes twinkled as he drained his glass. "Just checking." He waved his hand. "Go on."

"If the FBI never found Colleen's locket," I reiterated, "Murphy had to assume they also didn't find the pieces from the jewelry store heist."

"Why would he assume that?"

"Are you testing me?"

His mouth quirked upward. "Maybe."

"Stop distracting me." I leveled one of my classic Mom Looks at him. "Because, as you well know, the FBI had a search warrant for the locket. Logically, the first place they'd look would be wherever Colleen kept her jewelry. They would have recognized the pieces taken during the jewelry store heist, especially since they had previously questioned both Murphy and Quinn after the burglary."

When Zack nodded, I began to believe he was taking me seriously. "Not only would Murphy have heard if the FBI found the jewelry, but he would also have been questioned again and most likely charged in connection with the burglary. Murphy then must have concluded that Colleen sent Shauna the locket, along with the jewelry from the heist, after the FBI showed up with that first warrant for the weapons."

Zack rose from the sofa, his expression thoughtful. He began pacing the living room as he said, "But given his connections, Murphy had to know Shauna was no longer living here. And therefore, Johnnie Doyle wouldn't be here."

I sipped my wine before answering. "Murphy knew that."

"Then why show up here?"

"I think he wanted to scope out the house, see who was living here, and what he'd be up against in order to formulate a plan to get his hands on the jewelry."

"Why would he think the jewelry was still here, if it ever was?"

"Because Johnnie Doyle told him."

"Except that Rosalie said Shauna didn't tell anyone else about the jewelry."

"Just because Shauna never told her brother she was in possession of the jewelry doesn't mean Johnnie didn't find out about it." I drained my glass and handed it to him for a refill.

As he poured two more glasses, he said, "You have a theory about that, too, I presume?"

"I do." Zack returned to the sofa and handed over my refilled glass. "Before Johnnie Doyle cut his deal with the Feds, he was working as a bagman for Murphy. Suppose he was also the getaway driver for the jewelry store burglary?"

Ralph interrupted. "*Flat burglary as ever was committed. Much Ado about Nothing.* Act Four, Scene Two."

I glanced at the parrot. "Thank you for adding your two cents, Ralph. Mind if I continue?"

When he squawked, I resumed. "Johnnie also may have put two and two together and figured Colleen sent the jewelry to Shauna."

I peered into my glass. Two bodies found on my property in five days is two bodies too many. I needed to figure out what was going on before the body count increased. Maybe I was grasping at those proverbial straws, but there had to be something that connected everything, and finding that something would put an end to this madness.

"Maybe Johnnie searched the house at some point when Shauna wasn't home," I said, "but when he went up into the attic, he only looked through all the old furniture and other items stored there, not thinking to check under the insulation stuffed into the eaves. At which point, he figured she had either stashed the jewelry in a bank safety deposit box, had already fenced the pieces, or had never had them in the first place."

"That still doesn't explain Johnnie Doyle's body winding up in an SUV parked in the driveway," said Zack.

"It does if Murphy caught up with him, and Johnnie was trying to save his own neck. Remember, Johnnie was on the run. He was probably depending on former connections to fix him up with false IDs and anything else he'd need to evade the cops. Someone had to have ratted him out to Murphy. Why else would Murphy and his henchman show up at the house with a shovel? Johnnie must have lied and told him Shauna buried the jewelry somewhere on the property."

"Doyle would have known Murphy was going to kill him anyway," said Zack.

"Of course. But Johnnie had to buy himself time. He would have said he didn't know where in the backyard the box was buried. He probably hoped to escape before Murphy returned."

"Your theory has a few holes," said Zack.

"Such as?"

"For starters, Johnnie Doyle's body showed up four days ago. If you were a mob boss who had abducted the guy who ratted you out to the Feds, wouldn't you check out his story *before* you killed him?"

I frowned. "That's certainly a huge hole."

"There's more," said Zack. "You're forgetting about the guy who entered the house last night, not to mention the lookout behind the tree and the young woman in the car. Where do they fit into your theory?"

I mulled over his question. "You think he was also looking for the jewelry?"

"Could be."

"But there was no evidence of him searching the house. If that's the case, he had to know where Shauna hid the jewelry."

A queasy feeling settled in my stomach, and it wasn't from the wine. "You don't think Rosalie told someone about the jewelry, do you? She wouldn't have known Shauna left the box behind in the attic, not until I told her today, after we'd turned the jewelry over to Ledbetter."

"I don't think Rosalie had anything to do with what happened last night," said Zack.

The queasiness subsided somewhat but still lingered. "Can we be sure?"

"No, but I find it highly unlikely that Rosalie is involved in any way, don't you?"

I thought back to my conversation with Rosalie Schneider. She'd wanted to see the jewelry, but that was purely out of curiosity, wasn't it? I heaved a huge sigh and shook my head. "If Rosalie suspected the jewelry was still hidden in the attic after all these years, why would she have waited so long to tell someone? Or if she'd told someone years ago, why would he have waited until last night to try to steal it? That's a coincidence that stretches credulity."

"So how do you explain the man who entered the house last night?" asked Zack.

"A loose thread. But I think we can assume the person lurking across the street was his lookout. We couldn't tell if it was a man or woman. Let's suppose it was not only a woman but his girlfriend. And what if the woman in the car was his wife? A wife catching her cheating husband and his girlfriend would explain the confrontation."

He nodded. "That's the most obvious explanation for the person across the street, assuming it was a woman. Either way, the lookout alerted him when the car carrying Murphy pulled into the driveway. As for the other woman? You could be right there, as well."

"But why wouldn't he have hightailed it out of the house when he learned someone had pulled into the driveway? He took a huge risk going into the backyard, not knowing who was back there and what they were up to."

Zack narrowed his gaze. "Unless he did know and figured the element of surprise was on his side."

"So, who is he?" My voice trembled with frustration and fear. I set my empty glass on the coffee table and pounded my thighs with my fists. "And how did he learn about the jewelry?"

"Stop before you hurt yourself." He placed a hand over my fists. "That's what we still don't know and what you're going to let the police find out."

I relaxed my hands, lacing my fingers through his hand. Staring at our intertwined fingers, I heaved a shuddering sigh, then looked up at him. "I'm just trying to connect the dots. Finding dead bodies, is one thing. Finding them on my own property rises to a far more frightening level."

He placed his other hand on top of mine. "I know."

"Our lives are at stake—my sons, yours, mine, Lucille's. Look what's already happened to her. I promise you, Zack, I'm not about to tangle with some unknown mob goon."

He took me in his arms. "Good. I plan to hold you to that promise."

Zack was about to kiss me when the moment was interrupted by my mother-in-law. Lucille usually galumphs into a room, her cane pounding on the floor, but neither Zack nor I heard her enter the living room until she bellowed, "Are you both conspiring to starve me?"

"Why would we do that?" asked Zack.

"I know you want to get rid of me." She then turned to me and said, "It's nearly seven-thirty. Where's my dinner?"

I clenched my jaw and gritted my teeth before pasting a smile on my face. Somewhere deep inside me I dredged up the strength to answer her in a soft, modulated voice. "A bowl of salad is in the refrigerator if you can't wait. The pizzas should arrive shortly."

The doorbell punctuated the end of my sentence. Zack rose to accept the delivery while I texted Nick.

~*~

Later that evening, I received a group text addressed to all Trimedia employees at the Morris County location. The tech gurus had solved the computer problem.

We were all expected to report to work tomorrow morning at the usual time.

FOURTEEN

After dealing with two murders and an attempted murder so far this week, dragging myself out of bed the next morning required Herculean strength, something I'm not known for on a normal morning. My body would require massive amounts of caffeine and sugar to get me through the day.

A protein-rich breakfast wouldn't hurt, either. Should I drag myself out of bed in time to eat one before rushing off to sit in rush hour traffic? Or should I roll over and grab a few extra precious minutes of shuteye before queuing up in the daily traffic jam?

Opting for shuteye, I pulled the quilt over my head. Surely Cloris would bring enough baked goodies to keep me going until quitting time, especially if they contained nuts, a fine source of protein. Cloris rarely let me down.

Unfortunately, Zack had other ideas. "Rise and shine, Sleeping Beauty."

"I'm not sleeping," I mumbled from under the quilt, "and I

know I don't look anything like a beauty at the moment." Who does, first thing in the morning? I always woke with bed head, puffy eyes, and pillow wrinkles covering my face. It's a wonder Zack didn't run for the hills. "Go away. I might frighten you."

"Not going to happen." He stripped the quilt off my body. "Go shower. Breakfast in ten minutes."

I pried one eye open and tried to focus on his fuzzy image. "It's not fair."

"What's not fair?"

I waved a hand in his direction. "That you look like that first thing in the morning, and I look like death warmed over." The man certainly lucked out in the gene lottery.

He glanced at the alarm clock. "I've been up for two hours."

I groaned. "Twist the knife, why don't you?"

Zack shrugged. "I had no choice. My book proposal is due today, and with everything that's been going on here, I never finished finalizing it yesterday."

"Proposal?" Why did that word ring a bell? Then it hit me. "Proposal!" I leapt out of bed. "What day is it?"

"Friday, why?"

"Yikes! Our monthly planning meeting is Monday. I haven't even started my proposal for the next issue." I raced into the bathroom, stripping off my pajamas as I ran.

Behind me, I heard him chuckle.

Showered and dressed, ten minutes later I arrived in the dining room. Zack had cooked bacon and eggs in the apartment and transferred them into the microwave in the dining room to keep warm while he toasted English muffins. I slapped together a breakfast sandwich, wrapped it in foil, and poured a to-go cup of coffee, adding a splash of half-and-half. "Thanks." I kissed him goodbye. "I'll eat in the car."

I donned a jacket, opened the front door, then thought better of it. Turning around, I headed back to the dining room table and grabbed a napkin and three extra slices of bacon. Then I raced out of the house.

Behind me, Zack laughed again.

"I live to amuse," I shouted over my shoulder as I closed the door behind me.

I hit bumper-to-bumper traffic the moment I turned onto Rt. 78. Time for breakfast. I unwrapped my bacon and egg sandwich. As I ate, I mulled over craft ideas for the next issue, but my brain kept detouring into the realm of mobsters and murder.

I wondered if Agent Smanski had made any progress in determining the authenticity of the Rembrandt etching. How wonderful if one of the stolen artworks once again hung in its rightful place within the Isabella Stewart Gardner Museum.

Of course, the etching was the smallest of the stolen artworks and a rather insignificant Rembrandt compared to the missing Rembrandt paintings, especially his only known seascape. The masterpiece *Christ in the Storm on the Sea of Galilee* had stood more than five feet tall.

Nevertheless, the return of *Rembrandt Aux Trois Moustaches* would mean one less empty frame hanging on the walls of the museum. Progress always starts with one step. Perhaps this one etching, no bigger than a postage stamp or a thumbprint, would finally provide the clue that led investigators to the recovery of the remaining missing artworks. No more empty picture frames in the various galleries to indicate where masterpieces had once hung.

And just like that, my musings about a decades' old art heist led to an idea for my magazine spread. Amazing how the human brain works.

Traffic started inching forward, slowly picking up speed until I glanced down at my speedometer and realized I was driving at the speed limit, a true unicorn occurrence during morning drive time in New Jersey.

Perhaps today might turn out better than I'd anticipated when I woke up this morning.

I arrived at work with enough time to make my daily morning pilgrimage to the break room. I found Cloris preparing a pot of coffee. A large bakery box sat on the table. I peeked inside. Cloris's baked goods always looked picture perfect and delicious. These looked downright weird. I wrinkled my nose. "What are they?"

"Cream puffs."

Not any cream puffs I'd ever seen. "Why do they look like brains? Did something go wrong in the bake?"

She laughed. "That's craquelin, a circle of cookie dough you place on top of the choux pastry before baking. It provides added crunchiness."

I grabbed one and stared warily before taking a bite. I needn't have worried. When it comes to baked goods, Cloris is never wrong. The addition of the craquelin had indeed added an extra crunchiness to the shell and raised Cloris's creampuffs to a higher level of perfection, if such a thing were possible. "Okay, you've sold me. They may look like brains, but they taste like heaven."

"Glad you approve," she said. "I thought I'd do an article on demystifying pâte à choux pastry dough. Do you think it's too advanced for our readership?"

I plopped the remainder of the cream puff into my mouth, closed my eyes, and savored the combination of delicate pastry and silky-smooth raspberry cream filling. "Pâte à choux by any other name is simply a cream puff," I said. "Call it pâte à choux, and you might intimidate our readers. Call it cream puff dough, and you'll have them grabbing their spatulas and heading for their stand mixers."

"Good idea."

"You should bring a box of these to our staff meeting Monday."

Cloris winked. "That was the plan." The coffee pot now full, she reached for two mugs and filled them, handing one to me.

"Although," I added, "maybe you should hold off until the October issue and call them brain puffs."

Of course, I was joking, but Cloris took me seriously. "Hmm...not a bad idea. I'll discuss it with Naomi. Regular cream puffs for this upcoming issue, brain puffs for October. Maybe with a drizzle of red glaze to simulate blood."

"Ugh!"

"What? I'll bet they'd be a big hit for Halloween parties."

"I'm sure they would, but you know my aversion to Halloween." The holiday was my least favorite, stemming from an unpleasant childhood experience involving raw eggs. My dislike had only grown as I dealt with more than my share of real-life scariness.

"What about you?" she asked, passing me the half-and-half. "Did you come up with an idea for the next issue?"

I took a sip of coffee before answering. "Finally on my way in this morning, thanks to the Gardner heist."

She quirked an eyebrow. "How so?"

"Thinking about all the empty frames hanging in the museum where the stolen art once hung. I'm going to do a spread on taking plain, inexpensive wooden picture frames and transforming them into one-of-a-kind works of art for displaying family photos."

"Great idea. Picture frames are so expensive."

Out in the hallway we heard some of our fellow editors and support staff arriving. "Time to get to work," I said.

Cloris grabbed two napkins, handing one to me. "Help yourself to a few more brain puffs before they disappear." She snatched two out of the box. I did the same before we exited the break room and headed down the hall to our cubicles.

Now that I had an idea for the craft section of the next issue, I set about working up my presentation for Monday's staff meeting. I perused Pinterest and Etsy, looking at various trends, then downloaded images to use as examples of what I had in mind. After printing them out, I created a vision board for a presentation.

We wouldn't nail down the theme of the issue until we'd all bandied about suggestions during Monday's meeting. Naomi Dreyfus, our editorial director, always had the final say regarding an issue's theme, but she valued input from all of us.

Except our fashion editor. Tessa Lisbon never stopped trying to change our third-rate women's magazine sold at supermarket checkouts into a publication that would compete with *Vogue*. If Naomi listened to Tessa, the entire staff would be out of jobs within a matter of months.

Because themes always coincided with the seasons and various holidays, all the editors had a general idea what Naomi might choose at the end of the planning session. For this upcoming issue, she'd most likely go with Back to School, End of Summer/Labor Day, Grandparents' Day, or the growing trend of Autumn Weddings. For that reason, I had to structure my idea as generically as possible for it to work with whichever theme Naomi picked. My decorative frames idea would work well with any of them.

Cloris had spent much of the morning downstairs in our photo studio, shooting video for a segment to air on our website and YouTube channel, along with stills for one of the issues currently in production. Shortly before lunch she arrived back upstairs, stepped into my cubicle, and casually asked, "Anything you want to tell me?"

I glanced up from my nearly completed vision board. "About?"

"Oh, I don't know. Maybe the dead body found in your backyard yesterday?"

"How did you—?"

"Find out? Are you kidding? It's all over the news this morning. I expected to find you fending off questions by everyone from the janitor to the CEO."

"No one has said a word to me."

"Maybe they're all too used to you finding dead bodies. Or scared it's contagious." She walked over to my computer and pulled up a local news feed.

With everything else on my mind, I'd completely blocked out the press. I knew they'd descended on our street within minutes of Zack calling in the body found buried behind our garage. Reporters monitor police scanners. They check police blotters. They hang around police departments and make friends with cops to scoop rival news outlets when big stories break. They constantly check social media feeds. They're so plugged in that sometimes they know about a breaking story before law enforcement.

The police had kept the press from coming onto my property during the investigation, but afterwards the gathered reporters would have pounced on Spader and other members of both the

Westfield and Union County departments, peppering them with questions and asking for statements.

Even though Zack hadn't mentioned anything, chances were, some more aggressive reporters had rung our doorbell while I was in the apartment with Nick. For all I knew, reporters had even accosted the pizza delivery guy.

I stared at the computer screen. With the release of the victim's name, the story had gone beyond local New Jersey news. The world now knew that Boston mob boss Cormac Murphy, suspected mastermind of the world's largest art heist, had been found buried behind my garage.

"Well?" said Cloris. "What am I? Chopped liver or your best friend?"

"I suppose that means you want to hear all the gory details."

"No, it means I know you better than you know yourself. You're the queen of keeping stuff bottled up inside you. We're going somewhere quiet for lunch, and you're going to dump on me."

I had said basically the same thing to Nick last night. I grabbed my jacket and purse. "Let's go."

~*~

Cloris drove us to an upscale burger restaurant a block off the main square in Morristown. Rollercoaster April had graced us with a sunny day today with temperatures hovering in the low seventies. We opted for outdoor seating and chose a table at the far end of the back patio to avoid any eavesdroppers. After the waiter had brought us coffee and we ordered, I caught Cloris up on the events that had occurred over the last few days.

"Let me get this straight," she said. "Since I last saw you at work Tuesday morning, first you found a cache of stolen jewelry in your attic and possibly one of the pieces of art taken from a Boston museum burglary more than thirty years ago?"

"Correct."

"But since your life is never that simple," she continued, "on the same day someone mugged Lucille?"

I nodded.

"Then, the next day Lucille was tied up and left for dead by someone who entered your house with a key?"

"Correct again. Most likely the mugger," I said.

"Anyone else in your family lose a key lately?"

"No."

"Okay, then most likely the mugger," she agreed, nodding. "I can buy that. But if that weren't enough, yesterday Nick found the body of a Boston crime boss buried in your backyard?"

"Cormac Murphy."

"And this Cormac Murphy was digging up your yard because he thought the jewelry was buried there?"

"That's my theory."

"And Murphy is the same guy who showed up at your house nearly two weeks ago looking for someone who hadn't lived there in a couple of decades, *and* Murphy is also one of the FBI's prime suspects in an unsolved major art theft in Boston but was never arrested and charged?"

"For lack of evidence and because he was in prison at the time of the heist."

"Right. Because we both know mob crime bosses never continue being mob crime bosses once they're incarcerated."

She stopped, inhaled a deep breath, then finally added, "Am I leaving anything out?"

"You forgot the dead guy in the Mercedes SUV last Sunday."

Cloris slapped the side of her head. "As if I could forget that recent tidbit of your crazy life."

"If you remember, that was Johnnie Doyle, the guy Cormac Murphy was looking for. I think Doyle lied to Murphy and told him he'd find the jewelry buried in my backyard."

Cloris executed an eye roll. "My mind is now officially blown. I have two things to say to you, Anastasia." She held up her thumb, "First, I'm glad I'm not you. And secondly..." Her index finger joined her thumb. "I hope this is the end of the story."

I shook my head. "I don't think so."

"Why not? Both Doyle and Murphy are dead."

"There are still too many worrisome loose ends."

"But the FBI has the jewelry and the locket with the etching. There's no longer any reason for the Boston mob to take an interest in you."

"The mystery man and his cohort don't know I'm no longer in possession of the jewelry." There was another niggle tugging at my brain. "Besides, we have no definitive evidence connecting Lucille's assailant with either the jewelry, the etching, or Murphy. However, if there's no connection, why was he in my house, and why did he confront Murphy and his goon in the backyard?"

"But why else would he have targeted your house?" asked Cloris. "You said he didn't ransack the place, and nothing was stolen. He must have known the jewelry was in the attic."

"But it no longer was," I reminded her.

She waved a dismissive hand. "He wouldn't have known that until he searched the attic and came up emptyhanded."

"You'd think at that point he would have rifled through the rest of the house," I said.

"Unless he was about to when the lookout called to alert him about the men headed into your backyard. Why sneak up on Murphy and his henchman if he didn't suspect they knew that either the jewelry or the etching was buried behind the garage? He ran the risk of one of them killing him."

"I agree, it's only logical to assume a connection," I said. "However, I've learned that logic and what appears to be conclusive evidence at first glance don't always go hand in hand."

Cloris took a sip of her coffee before asking, "Do you have any alternate theories, Sherlock?"

FIFTEEN

I noticed the waiter approaching with our lunch order and held up a hand to pause the discussion. He placed our plates in front of us, refilled our water glasses and coffee cups, and asked, "Is there anything else I can get for you ladies?"

I offered him a smile. "We're good. Thank you."

After he had walked out of earshot, Cloris repeated her question. "About those alternate theories, do you have any?"

"I did, but I don't."

She paused before taking a bite of her hamburger. "You need to explain that one."

"You know how Lucille tends to antagonize people."

Both of Cloris's eyebrows shot up, disappearing under her pixie bangs. "That's an understatement."

"At first, I thought the attack might be personal, that she'd ticked off the wrong person."

"That could still be the case."

"Then how do you explain why her assailant went into the

backyard?"

"I can't," she said. "Unless he's incredibly stupid. Or was stoned out of his mind."

I mulled over those possibilities as I dipped a French fry in ketchup and plopped it into my mouth. "A druggie would have tossed the house in search of money or anything easily pawnable. But if Lucille had tangled with someone experiencing major anger issues or suffering from a mental disorder—"

"He wouldn't be thinking clearly either way," said Cloris. She thought for a moment, then shook her head. "But you're right. Given the state of the house, it makes more sense that he came specifically either to harm Lucille or search the attic."

"If he was after Lucille and was experiencing a psychotic episode or suffering from delusions, it might explain the irrational act of confronting the guys in the backyard."

"Or if he was hopped up on meth," she said, "Those guys are bat-poop crazy. But even someone on weed might want to check out the 'dudes' in the backyard. Aren't stoners always looking for the next party? Maybe he thought the shovel was for digging a fire pit for a pot party."

I laughed.

"What?"

"Listen to us. Did you ever think in a million years we'd have such a conversation?"

"Not prior to Karl's death," she said, "but since then? When it comes to you, nothing surprises me anymore."

I frowned before biting into my hamburger. "Conversations about illegal drugs are the least of the strange twists my life has taken post-Karl."

Cloris raised her water glass. "Here's hoping your life becomes total Dullsville once you and Zack finally tie the knot."

"*Total* Dullsville?" I scrunched my face. "I don't like the sound of that."

"In every way except one."

"Better." I clinked my water glass against hers. "Which way did you have in mind, though?"

She winked. "I think you can figure that one out for yourself, Nancy Drew."

"You've officially veered into TMI territory."

"Not according to the BFF Code. No topic is off limits."

"Hmm...I'll have to find my copy to verify that."

Her eyes twinkled as she reached for another French fry. "Or you can take my word for it."

"I'll consider it."

We both worked on our burgers for a few minutes before I heaved a sigh.

Cloris raised an eyebrow. "What was that for?"

"Lucille's attacker. I'm still obsessing."

"He's definitely the missing puzzle piece."

"It's more like the puzzle is finished, but the last remaining piece doesn't fit."

Cloris pushed her empty plate aside and reached for her coffee cup. "I'm getting whiplash. Are we now ruling out that the guy stole her key because he wanted to search the attic?"

I shook my head. "Whoever he is, how would he know about the jewelry?"

Cloris leaned back in her chair and thought for a moment. "Would Johnnie Doyle have told him?"

"Why would he do that? If he knew Shauna had hidden the jewelry in the attic, he would have stolen it himself when his sister still lived here. Given her level of discomfort over receiving it, she never would have known it was missing."

"Unless she told him at some point after they had gone into Witness Protection."

"If so, Johnnie would have come back to steal the jewelry long ago. Why wait nearly two decades?"

Cloris knit her brows together and scowled into her coffee cup. "Don't you think it's mega-coincidental that both Lucille's attacker and Murphy showed up on the same night?"

"Of course, but I don't think we can rule out coincidence. Stranger things have happened."

"In your life?" Cloris snorted. "On a daily basis. But in this case, it made for one very deadly coincidence for Cormac Murphy."

"You don't sound convinced."

She raised an eyebrow. "Neither do you."

I sighed. "I'm not. I'm still trying to understand why the guy went into the backyard instead of leaving through the front door to avoid a confrontation."

I twirled the last French fry on my plate in the dregs of ketchup as I tried to make sense of what made no sense. I'd learned from my time spent stumbling across dead bodies that nothing is ever what it seems. Whenever I've gotten cocky and thought I had the answer to a mystery, I'd find myself confronted with another twist. Nothing is ever cut and dry, which is why it often takes law enforcement so long to solve cases. And why some cases are never solved.

But Cloris and I weren't in the middle of some esoteric discussion about criminology. These crimes involved me. My family. My home. Which is why I found it hard to step away and let the professionals do their job. I needed answers, not a cold case that could last decades before some armchair detective featured it on a podcast.

"What if I'm approaching this all wrong?" I asked, looking up.

"What do you mean?"

"I'm not sure, but I need to get into the assailant's head. Let's suppose for the moment that he did know about the jewelry and had come to search the attic. If I had searched the attic and come up empty, then saw two guys digging in the backyard, I'd logically assume they knew where the jewelry was hidden and had come for it."

"Time out," said Cloris, signaling with her hands. "If we're now back to Lucille's assailant knowing about the jewelry hidden in the attic, who besides Zack and the FBI knew you found it?"

"Rosalie Schneider but she certainly didn't attack Lucille. She's in her mid-eighties and half Lucille's size."

Cloris nodded. "I think we can safely rule Rosalie out."

"Then there's Jesse Konopka, our contractor. He found the box while running new electrical wiring."

Cloris's eyes bugged out. "You don't think—?"

I knew where she was going and stopped her. "Jesse didn't assault Lucille. He didn't know the contents of the box. Had he suspected it contained something valuable, he could have kept it and never told me he'd found it."

"What about his crew?"

"They weren't even in the house at the time. Jesse had to finish the electrical work before they could install the drywall. Jesse was alone in the attic."

"Are you certain he didn't say anything to anyone?"

"No, but I doubt he would."

"Color me skeptical," said Cloris.

"I caught the guy who tried to kill him," I explained. "He's so grateful, he's renovating my kitchen for free."

"Then it sounds like you're leaning toward the guy coming to harm Lucille and *not* knowing anything about the jewelry or the etching. We're caught in an endless loop."

"So now let's suppose that's the case," I said. "Which brings us back to why, assuming he wasn't high on drugs, he'd jeopardize his life by confronting two complete strangers who were obviously up to no good."

We both grew silent for a moment until Cloris said, "What if his lookout had goaded him? If she told him one of the guys was quite elderly, and the other had a shovel, they may have figured he could overpower them and steal whatever they had planned to dig up."

I snapped my fingers. "Or what they planned to *bury*. People don't plant pansies in their gardens late at night. Lucille's assailant might have thought this was his lucky break. He figured whatever they were up to, it had to be something nefarious that required the cover of darkness. Which meant they were either digging up something of value or hiding something valuable."

"Like drugs or money."

"Exactly. After all, this is New Jersey. We've got crime bosses and their minions living among us. Our mystery man wouldn't know who else lived in the house with Lucille. For all he knew, he'd stumbled on the home of a skimming bagman."

"Isn't that the reason you said Doyle ratted out Murphy?"

I nodded. "He cut a deal with the Feds. I'm sure Doyle wasn't the only bagman who ever helped himself to some of the protection money he collected for his crime boss."

"That makes more sense," she said, "but wouldn't both mobsters have guns? Why didn't they just shoot the guy?"

"Firing a gun risked a neighbor calling the police. If the assailant came up behind Murphy and bashed him in the head with the brick, the guy with the shovel might have decided it was in his own best interest to get the heck out of there."

"But he wouldn't have known if Murphy was dead or only knocked unconscious," said Cloris. "Would he? From what you've told me about Murphy, if he had survived, the guy with the shovel was as good as dead."

"Murphy wouldn't have survived," I said. "His cohort knew the assailant would make sure of that before he left."

"How would he know that?"

"Because that's what he would do. Mobsters and murders go hand in hand."

"Think like the bad guy." She tilted her head, her expression growing thoughtful. "I like this scenario. You don't have to worry about the guy returning to dig up your backyard in search of something that's not there."

I frowned into my coffee cup. "Only if he thought Murphy's associate ran off with whatever they had come to bury or dig up."

Cloris returned my frown with one of her own. "True."

I heaved a sigh. "The problem, though, is that I have no way of knowing if this scenario is fact or fiction. Until Lucille's unknown assailant is caught and locked up, we're not safe."

Cloris's eyes widened. "Tell me you're not planning to take matters into your own hands."

"I'm not, but not knowing why he was in my home means I don't know if he plans to come back."

"What are the cops doing?"

I shrugged. "Investigating as much as they can. If we're lucky, the guy left some DNA on the shovel, but unlike on television, lab results don't come back overnight. They take weeks. Or longer."

"In that case," said Cloris, waving over the waiter, "we may as well order dessert."

I laughed. "Why? Because you expect us to sit here until the results come in?"

"Heck, no. I plan to ply you with sweets to take your mind off the wait."

I glanced down at my stomach and hips. "And what's your plan for the calories?"

"Hey, you can't expect me to solve all your problems!"

"Except we haven't solved anything," I reminded her.

The conversation had gone around in circles of supposition with little making sense because we had so few facts. However, if nothing else, this recent episode in my life as a reluctant amateur sleuth had given me a greater understanding of the almost daily frustrations experienced by Detective Spader and all law enforcement.

The waiter arrived with the dessert menus. Cloris chose a gooey brownie topped with a scoop of fried vanilla ice cream and garnished with whipped cream and a drizzle of caramel sauce.

I choked back a gasp when I noted the number of calories on the menu. "I'll have a small dish of raspberry sorbet," I told the waiter.

"Really?" The corners of Cloris's mouth dipped down. "That's hardly dessert. After the week you've had, you deserve to indulge your sweet tooth."

"Only if you can prove to me this morning's cream puffs were made from celery stalks. Shopping for a wedding dress is still on my to-do list." I was already regretting the lack of willpower that caused me to order a burger and fries instead of a salad for lunch.

~*~

With my caloric consumption for the day still weighing heavily on both my body and my mind, I called Zack on my way home from work. "Have you started dinner?"

"I'm stuck on the train between Union and Roselle Park."

"Do you know why?"

"Some sort of police activity."

"That's not good. I don't suppose they told you what kind of police activity."

"A fire. The conductor either didn't have details or wasn't interested in sharing them. He hasn't walked through the car since."

"Did you check your phone?"

"Earlier. Nothing popped up. A brush fire near the tracks is a commuter nightmare but hardly breaking news."

"Any chance they'll let you off the train? I can pick you up."

"I already asked. Figured I could call an Uber. The conductor told me to sit back and shut up."

"He didn't!"

"Not in those exact words but the meaning was clear. I'll keep you posted."

"I'll stop to pick up the makings of a chef salad for dinner."

"Good idea. No telling how much longer I'll be. We haven't moved an inch in nearly an hour."

Once I hung up from Zack, I switched on 1010WINS, the all-news radio station. After listening to sports, weather, and financial news updates, the newscaster announced a lengthy recap of the day's top stories. Along with local New York City and metro area news, these included national and international headlines.

Twenty minutes later, the broadcaster finally announced, "This just in. We take you to Jody Tanis with an update on this afternoon's daring armed robbery at Hamill Savings and Loan Bank in Union, New Jersey. Jody, what can you tell us?"

"Thanks, Pete. According to police, the armed suspect, who was wearing a rubber Freddy Kruger Halloween mask, entered Hamill Savings and Loan in Union Center shortly before five o'clock. He grabbed a hostage as she was leaving the bank, then handed the teller a clear plastic bag and demanded he fill it with money."

The newscaster interrupted. "A *clear* plastic bag? That's certainly not typical of bank robbers."

"I suppose he wanted to make sure the teller didn't add a dye packet," said the reporter.

"Makes sense. Go on, Jody. What happened next?"

"The suspect dragged his hostage out of the bank, shoved her to the pavement, and jumped into a black SUV that had pulled up to the curb. A short time later, the SUV was found abandoned and on fire on the train tracks between the Union and Roselle Park train stations. A source with the Hudson County police tells me the vehicle was reported carjacked at gunpoint from the parking lot of the Walmart in Bayonne last night."

"And what can you tell us about the suspects?" asked the newscaster.

"Only that they're still at large and considered armed and dangerous. Bank video of the robber is up at our 1010WINS website but won't prove very helpful, given the mask. Union County Police are asking anyone with information to contact them.

"This has been Jody Tanis reporting from outside Hamill Savings and Loan on Stuyvesant Avenue in Union, New Jersey."

I turned off the radio and placed another call to Zack. When it went directly to voicemail, I left a message. "Not a simple brush fire. Check the 1010 website."

~*~

Half an hour later, I was unpacking the groceries I'd picked up at Trader Joe's when I noticed a piece of paper clinging to the side of a gallon container of milk. I peeled off the damp paper, adding it to the pile of junk mail on the dining room table.

Later, after I'd finished tossing together a chef's salad for dinner and slicing a baguette of French bread, I reached for the junk mail as I headed into the mud room. I had assumed the piece of paper stuck to the gallon of milk was another shopper's grocery list, accidently dropped as she reached for something in the dairy case. But as I glanced down at the pile of papers and envelopes in my hand, I suddenly realized what I held was no shopping list.

SIXTEEN

Although always jammed with shoppers, on Friday nights and throughout the weekend, the Westfield Trader Joe's always turns into a zoo. Not any run-of-the-mill zoo, though. A zoo during the debut of twin baby pandas. Traffic backs up in each direction down both Elm and Prospect Streets with cars waiting to enter the parking lot from either entrance. A continual crowd of cart-pushing shoppers, often with children pushing mini-carts, stream in and out of the store, clogging the aisles, and queuing up a dozen deep at each of the checkout lines. Any one of those customers may have slapped that piece of paper to the side of my milk container as I shopped or dropped it into one of my shopping bags while I loaded my groceries into my cart or hauled the bags into my car. I never would have noticed.

I removed the note from the pile before tossing the junk mail into the recycling bucket. My hand trembled as I stared at it. *Give it up before someone else gets hurt.*

The message, written in blue ink, now blurred from the

condensation on the milk jug, frightened me enough, but what ratcheted up my fear to extreme levels was the realization that someone had tailed me throughout the day. Someone knew where I worked and had followed me from the office to Trader Joe's. How long had this person shadowed me? Days? Weeks? And why hadn't I noticed? Was he parked outside right now?

I walked into the living room and glanced out the window but saw nothing unusual. No loitering strangers. Not a single car parked on either side of the street.

I checked the security app on my phone, scanning through the recorded video from this morning, starting with when the boys left for school. I watched myself leaving for work, Jesse and his crew arriving, and Zack heading out for his meeting in the city. I saw the mailman delivering the day's mail, my sons arriving home, and the workmen leaving for the day. In-between, a few delivery trucks had pulled up to the curb, their drivers jumping out to deposit packages at neighbors' front doors before they hurried back to their trucks and drove away. All activity on the street appeared completely normal.

Headlights shone down the street as a car turned onto Central Avenue. The headlights grew brighter as the vehicle approached. I stepped out of view behind the drapes but breathed a sigh of relief when I recognized Zack's Boxster pulling into the driveway.

Having no intention of springing this latest development on him the moment he entered the house, I darted back toward the dining room, grabbed a sandwich bag, and placed the paper inside. Then I dropped the bag into one of the drawers of the china cabinet. I'd show him the note later after Lucille had decamped to the den for her nightly reality television binge and the boys were buried in homework.

I returned to the foyer and greeted Zack at the door by wrapping my arms around his neck and kissing him in a way that I hoped masked the worry consuming me. "You're in time to join us for dinner," I said.

He returned my kiss. "As long as it comes with a shot of bourbon. Have I ever mentioned how much I hate bureaucracy?"

Did that mean Zack really wasn't secretly working for one of the alphabet agencies? I thought of posing the question but decided against it. Instead, I said, "Not that I recall."

"There was absolutely no reason for all of us to sit on that train for so long, but the conductor refused to unlock the doors."

"How far away was the car fire?"

"More than a mile down the tracks."

"But you had to wait until they removed the remains of the vehicle. That takes specialized equipment, doesn't it?"

"The car is still there. It's an active crime scene."

"Then how did you get home?"

Zack laughed. "You're not going to believe this."

"Try me."

"I ran into Bert Levy on the train."

"The state senator? I didn't realize you knew him."

"We first met years ago at a charity auction. Our paths cross every so often. He finally got so annoyed that he called the governor. Five minutes later, the doors opened, and we were allowed to leave the train. Five minutes after that, one of Bert's aides arrived to pick him up. He offered me a ride back to the train station parking lot to pick up my car."

"Good thing he was on the train. Otherwise, you and everyone else might have had to spend the night."

Zack shook his head. "No way. Bert or no Bert, a rebellion was brewing."

"I'm glad it didn't come to that. I already have one family member constantly fomenting rebellion." I then changed the subject. "How was your meeting?"

"Proposal accepted. How about your day?"

I hesitated for a split second before saying, "I came up with an idea for my presentation Monday."

The corners of Zack's mouth tipped downward. "Anything else?"

"Cloris and I went out to lunch," I added, then cringed at the forced brightness I heard in my own voice.

From the sober expression on Zack's face, I knew he wasn't buying what I was working too hard to sell. "And?"

I sighed. No way would I have made it as a member of one of the alphabet agencies. No matter how much I tried otherwise, I not only wore my emotions on my sleeve, but on my face and every square inch of my body. "I'll tell you the rest later. Meanwhile, I suggest you make that bourbon a double."

Zack said nothing, only shook his head as he made his way toward the apartment. By the time he returned, carrying two tumblers, each filled with ice and a splash of bourbon, Lucille and the boys had taken their seats at the dining room table.

When Zack handed me one of the glasses before joining us, Lucille glared at me as she grunted, then mumbled something under her breath that questioned my character. I ignored her.

I couldn't ignore my sons, though. Their mother rarely drank hard liquor except in girly umbrella drinks loaded with fruit juice and garnished with pineapple wedges and maraschino cherries. Otherwise, I drank wine.

Both Alex and Nick cast furtive, worried glances in my

direction. I offered them a smile of reassurance I didn't feel. Hopefully, my ability to pull the wool over their eyes worked better than my attempt at fooling Zack.

Even Ralph and Leonard seemed to pick up on the tension in the room, Leonard taking a protective stance, inches from the side of Nick's chair, while Ralph silently surveyed the situation from his perch atop the china cabinet.

After Lucille pushed away from the table and harrumphed her way toward the den, Alex said, "Whatever's going on with you two, Nick and I will clean up so you can deal with it."

"Hey, speak for yourself," said Nick. "I don't like being in the dark." With worry plastered across his features, he turned to me and asked, "You're not breaking up, are you?"

"We're not breaking up," I said. "And nothing's going on."

Alex stared pointedly at both Zack and me. "Could've fooled us," he said. "We'll clean up anyway, won't we, Nick?"

Nick tossed him a scowl. "Sure." He then turned to me and Zack. "But afterwards, I want to know whatever's not going on."

"Your mother and I will discuss it," said Zack. "Privately." He placed his hand at the small of my back, urging me toward the back door. Ralph took flight and landed on Zack's shoulder. As we passed the china cabinet, I stopped, opened the drawer, and grabbed the plastic bag with the note that had sent me into a tailspin. Zack eyed the bag but said nothing until we had arrived in the apartment.

He closed the door behind us and asked, "Am I to assume, this conversation involves whatever is inside that plastic bag clenched in your hand?"

When I nodded, he continued, "And would this conversation require more bourbon?"

I handed him the bag with the note. "You be the judge."

While Zack concentrated on the blurred message, Ralph flew off his shoulder, perched on the arm of the sofa, and squawked once before saying, "*In this I'll be impartial; be you judge of your own cause. Measure for Measure*, Act Five, Scene One."

Still staring at the note, Zack reached into his shirt pocket and presented Ralph with a sunflower seed. Then he asked, "Where did you find this?"

"In one of my grocery bags. It was stuck to a gallon of milk." I sighed as I sank onto the sofa. "I keep trying to come up with an explanation that has nothing to do with us and what happened last night, but I'm at a complete loss."

"Have you called Spader?"

"Not yet. I only found the note shortly before you arrived home."

Zack pulled out his phone and placed the call.

~*~

Spader arrived a short time later. He took one look at me, shook his head and said, "Just when I think I'm in for a relatively quiet night, I can always count on you to liven things up, Mrs. Pollack."

"Should I take that as a compliment, Detective?"

"Only if it helps solve these murders."

I pointed to the coffee table where Zack had placed the bag with the note. "Someone dropped that threat in one of my grocery bags earlier this evening."

Spader scooped up the bag and read the note. "Why does the paper look like it landed in a puddle?"

I explained how I came to find the note. "I thought it was a shopping list someone had dropped. I was about to toss it in recycling."

"Meaning I can expect your fingerprints are all over it?" he asked.

"Guilty," I said, "but in my defense, I thought it was trash."

Spader grimaced. "If this keeps up, I suggest from now on you travel with a set of rubber gloves in your purse."

"I keep hoping this new and unwelcome gig *doesn't* keep up, Detective. I never asked to morph into Nancy Drew." He opened his mouth to say something, but before he uttered a single word, I threw my hands onto my hips and added, "And if you say I'm too old to be Nancy Drew, you might have to arrest me for assaulting an officer."

Spader let loose a belly laugh. "I refuse to answer under the grounds that it may incriminate me."

He then sobered and changed the subject. "I'll see if we can get a hit off the note, and I'll have our techs go over the security camera footage at Trader Joe's. Maybe we'll get lucky. Meanwhile, keep your eyes open, and call me if something or someone looks suspicious."

As soon as Spader left the apartment, I collapsed into Zack's arms. "What makes me a mobster magnet?"

Zack leaned his chin on my head and said, "When I find the answer to that, I'll let you know."

"Don't take too long. This has grown really old. I want it to end."

"That makes two of us. But first we have a more pressing issue."

I stepped out of his arms, stared up at him, and said, "I know. Alex and Nick. I hate worrying them further, but we need to tell them for their own safety."

"Don't forget Lucille," said Zack.

I groaned. "One step at a time." I pulled my phone out of my pocket and texted the boys to join us in the apartment. "We'll deal with Lucille afterwards."

The boys had gotten so accustomed to close encounters of the murderous kind that hearing about the note didn't faze them. Or if it did, they'd inherited their ability to mask their emotions from their father. That bothered me almost as much as receiving the note. My kids should neither have to accept murder and mayhem as a normal part of their lives, nor bottle up their emotions for fear of worrying their mother.

Zack and I followed the boys out of the apartment and into the house. I girded my loins for the expected confrontation with my mother-in-law.

After I explained the situation to her, Lucille, in typical Lucille fashion, blamed Zack and me for everything. I had promised myself I wouldn't let her rile me. Instead, I reminded her no one was forcing her to remain in my home. "You're free to leave at any time."

"You'd both like that, wouldn't you?" she said.

Frankly, yes, but I bit another hole in my tongue rather than allow her to bait me.

As we left the den, she said, "I wouldn't be surprised to learn you've concocted all of this nonsense about mobsters and murders to force me out of my son's home."

"If only that were true," I muttered under my breath.

Before we got into bed, Zack said, "I armed the security system to send an alert to my phone if anyone walks onto the property, not just if someone opens a door or window."

"Are you expecting that will help me sleep tonight?"

"It's part of the plan. I have a few other tricks up my sleeve as well."

Unfortunately for Zack, I was so emotionally drained from the events of the last two days, that I fell asleep the moment I snuggled into his arms.

~*~

Three hours later, I was startled awake by the sound of the security notification on Zack's phone. Disoriented and with adrenalin pounding through my veins, I groped for the lamp on the nightstand.

Zack reached over and grabbed my hand before I found the switch. "Don't turn the light on," he whispered. He was sitting up in bed, staring at his phone. "Look." He held the phone out toward me.

I pulled myself into a sitting position and blinked my eyes into focus. Two men, both with shovels, had entered the backyard. We watched as they split up, one heading toward the plantings behind the house, the other toward the side of the garage under the staircase. "Do you think one of them is the guy who was with Murphy Wednesday night?"

"Makes sense. Looks like he's come back to find what Murphy was after, and he's brought help."

"Wouldn't he figure the guy who killed Murphy had already found the jewelry?"

"Only if it had been buried behind the garage, which it wasn't."

"It wasn't buried anywhere," I reminded him.

"But Murphy's henchman doesn't know that."

"Right. Assuming Doyle told Murphy about the jewelry to buy himself time, he would have only said it was buried *somewhere* in the yard. Not that it helped him since Murphy killed him anyway."

"We don't know exactly what happened to Doyle," said Zack. "Remember, his body showed up in the Mercedes last Sunday, three days before Murphy and his henchman arrived to dig in the backyard. We don't know what led Murphy to believe the jewelry was buried on the property."

While we continued to watch the video, Zack placed a 911 call. Then we both dressed in the dark to wait for the police.

Unfortunately, we hadn't accounted for my mother-in-law. We watched in horror as she exited the house through the back door. Brandishing her cane, she screamed at both men. "Get off my son's property!"

I gasped. "She's going to get herself killed."

Zack reached for his gun as the two men dropped their shovels, pulled guns, and raced toward Lucille. One of them tackled her to the ground, then forced her to her feet and back into the house.

"Now what?" I whispered.

"We play it by ear and bide our time until the cops arrive."

"What if the boys wake up?"

"We hope they're a heck of a lot smarter than their grandmother."

"That's a given, but it's not much of a plan."

He grimaced. "It's all I've got right now, sweetheart." He placed a whispered call to the police, alerting them to the changed circumstances.

From the living room we heard one of the men say, "Sit down and shut up."

"What gives you the right?" demanded Lucille. A sane octogenarian would have complied, realizing her life was in danger. Not my mother-in-law.

"This gives me the right, lady. Now tell me where the jewelry is buried, or I'll put a bullet between your eyes."

"Go play pirates somewhere else. I don't know anything about any buried jewelry. You have the wrong house."

"You're lying. I know the jewelry is here. I was with Cormac Murphy the night someone offed him while we were digging for it."

"I don't know any Cormac Murphy."

"You don't have to know him. He's dead. Which is what's going to happen to you if you don't tell me what I want to know."

"Maybe she's got that Al Heimer Disease," said the other guy, speaking for the first time.

"Alzheimer's," said the first guy. "Jeez, don't you know nothing?"

"I know I shouldn't have let you talk me into this wild goose chase."

"You didn't think it was such a wild goose chase when you thought you were in for a fifty-fifty cut."

"I'm just saying maybe the broad's right. Why would jewelry from a Boston heist years ago be buried in a New Jersey backyard?"

"Because Johnnie Doyle said it was."

"And you believed him?"

"Murphy believed him."

"Maybe Murphy *wanted* to believe him. You got proof?"

"Doyle's sister used to live here."

"So?"

"Murphy pulled off a series of jewelry heists in Boston with Garrett Quinn. Quinn was married to one of Doyle's sisters. The other sister lived here years ago before Doyle ratted out Murphy."

"Still don't make no sense, Vinnie. Doyle was just trying to keep Murphy from whacking him."

"Exactly. Do you think Murphy would've spared him if he discovered Doyle had lied to him?"

189

"He didn't spare him."

"That's beside the point, Bozo."

"What if there are other people sleeping in the house?"

"They better keep sleeping. I'll stay with granny here. You go back outside and dig."

"You're the boss."

"Yeah, and don't you forget it."

A few seconds later, Vinnie spoke to Lucille again. "How many other people are here?"

"If my son were still alive, he wouldn't let you get away with this."

"I'm not interested in dead people, lady."

"I'm not telling you anything."

"We'll see about that. Let me introduce you to Mr. Griptilian."

"What's that?" I whispered to Zack.

"A lethal folding knife."

I gasped. "We can't let him torture her."

"Stay here." He slipped from the room. A moment later I heard him say, "Drop the knife."

I grabbed one of Zack's other guns and crept along the wall down the darkened foyer. Ahead of me, light bled into the foyer where it met the living room.

"You and what army's gonna make me?" asked Vinnie. "It's two against one, cowboy. My gun and knife to your gun. Odds are, I'm the one walking out of here alive. And with the jewelry."

I inhaled a deep breath before stepping from the foyer into the living room and pointing Zack's gun at the intruder. "I just changed those odds."

Lucille sat cowering in the corner of the sofa. Vinnie stood over her, one foot planted on the floor, his other knee pressing into her thigh. In one hand he held a deadly looking knife, the point of the blade disappearing into the folds of my mother-in-law's neck. With his other hand, he pointed a gun at Zack.

From the sound of his voice, a gruff bass, I had envisioned Vinnie as a stereotypical bar bouncer type with an acne-pocked complexion and tattoos covering muscular arms, a barrel chest, and a thick neck. Instead, with his wiry frame, oil-slicked hair, and pencil mustache, he bore a striking resemblance to the weasel characters in *Who Framed Roger Rabbit?*

Vinnie sneered. "You'd have me quaking in my boots if I believed you even knew how to use that gun."

I cocked an eyebrow. "You willing to try me?"

"I wouldn't bet against her," said Spader, stepping in from the kitchen. "Now, drop the gun and knife before I drop you."

SEVENTEEN

Two officers who had followed behind Spader cuffed Vinnie while I handed Zack's gun back to him. "Daring move," he whispered. "What would you have done if he'd called your bluff?"

"Relied on your expert marksmanship."

With a tilt of his head, he drew my attention to the gun he'd taken from me. "You do realize this isn't loaded?"

"I do."

He stared at me for a long moment before he finally said, "Don't pull a stunt like that again. You aged me ten years in ten seconds."

"You aged me twenty." A girl's gotta do what a girl's gotta do. I'd acted solely on instinct and adrenalin, a mama bear protecting her sleeping cubs and standing by her man. But before that rush of adrenalin ebbed, I had one more act of bravery inside me.

I stepped over to where one of the officers was reading Vinnie his rights. Now that he stood upright, I saw that he was only an inch or two taller than Lucille, although she outweighed him by at least fifty pounds.

Under different circumstances I suspect she would have clobbered him upside his head with her cane, but a cane is no match for a gun and a knife. At least she showed some common sense tonight. Too bad it was after she confronted two mobsters in the backyard.

When the officer had finished Mirandizing Vinnie, I stood directly in front of the now sullen-looking goon and said, "You were right about one thing, Vinnie. The jewelry was here."

When he snarled in response, I continued, "But it was never buried in the yard. It was hidden in the attic, and the FBI has had it ever since we found it."

"You think I was born yesterday, lady? No one's that stupid. You've got it stashed somewhere, or you've already fenced it."

I shrugged. "You'll have no choice but to believe me once the pieces are entered into evidence at your trial."

I then turned to the two officers, each holding onto one of Vinnie's skinny arms, and said, "Would you gentlemen kindly remove this scumbag from my house?"

As they led Vinnie toward the back door, he aimed a parting shot at me. "This ain't over, lady."

Unfortunately, I had already come to the same conclusion.

Across the room, Zack and Spader were engrossed in a tete-a-tete. Lucille hadn't moved from the sofa. I walked over and sat beside her, visually examining the side of her neck but saw no indication that Vinnie had punctured her skin. "Are you okay, Lucille?"

She speared me with a double evil-eyed glare. "No thanks to you."

Why do I bother? Without saying another word, I stood and

joined Zack and Spader. Zack looped his arm around my shoulders. My body released an involuntary shudder as I hugged his waist.

I knew we'd only closed the book on one chapter in this ongoing drama. We hadn't yet reached the end. I doubted either Vinnie or his sidekick had dropped that menacing note in my grocery bag earlier today. Subtlety is not a hallmark of the Mafia. They're far more direct with their threats.

"What about the second guy?" I asked Spader.

"Frankie Fallon. This one is Vinnie Monaghan."

"You know them?"

"Both have a long list of priors. We ran into Fallon—literally—as he was hightailing it out of your yard. We were in the process of surrounding the house on all sides."

"Vinnie had sent him back outside to keep digging," I said.

"The only digging he was doing was digging tracks through the azalea bushes into Mrs. Schneider's backyard."

"Interesting."

"How so?" asked Spader.

"Wednesday night Vinnie Monaghan ran out on Murphy. Now tonight, Frankie Fallon runs out on Vinnie. I suppose it proves one thing."

"What's that?" asked Zack.

"That there's no honor among thieves."

Spader chuckled. "I'm glad to see you haven't lost your sense of humor, Mrs. Pollack."

I glanced at my mother-in-law, still ensconced on the sofa. Her arms crossed, her lips tight, she glared daggers at the three of us. "It's what keeps me going, Detective."

~*~

The next morning, I woke to the aroma of fresh coffee and something that smelled suspiciously like baked goods, but Zack wasn't cooking breakfast. His arm was draped over me, spooning my body into his. I pried open one eye. Light streamed into the room from the cracks between the blinds. I checked the time and nearly panicked before realizing it was Saturday. After the horrors of last night, I wanted to remain snuggled under the quilt, wrapped in Zack's arms.

My bladder had other ideas.

"Where are you going?" he mumbled as I gently wormed my way loose from his embrace.

"Nature calls."

"Let it go to voicemail."

If only bodily functions worked that way. I grabbed my robe and headed into the bathroom to take care of business. By the time I returned to the bedroom, Zack had fallen soundly back to sleep. The scent of dark roast lured me into the dining room.

I found Alex and Nick scarfing down thick slabs of banana bread drizzled with maple syrup. When they saw me, Alex jumped up to pour me a cup of coffee while Nick sawed off a frozen slice of bread and popped it in the toaster oven for me.

I kissed them good morning. "Don't the two of you have to leave for work?"

Alex checked his phone. "We have time."

"Enough time for you to tell us what was going on here last night," said Nick.

I sighed. "And here I thought both of you had slept through it."

Nick glanced toward his new best friend, currently sprawled at his feet. "Leonard woke me. He jumped on the bed and started whimpering."

I glanced down at the dog. "I didn't hear him."

"When we realized what was happening, I calmed him."

"I listened at the door," said Alex, "but decided you'd want us to stay in the bedroom."

Nick glared at his brother. "You decided. I wanted to help."

"Alex was right," I said. At least one of my sons showed some common sense.

"How did they get in the house?" asked Alex. "Weren't the doors locked?"

I explained what had happened. Neither seemed surprised that their grandmother was responsible for the home invasion.

"Did one of those guys write that note you found yesterday?" asked Nick.

"I don't think so."

Alex gave voice to my deepest worry. "Which means this still isn't over."

"Not yet, I'm afraid." I reached across the table and clasped each of their hands. "That's why the two of you need to be super careful and let Zack or me know if you see or hear anything strange or suspicious."

"We will," said Alex.

"Nick?" I asked.

"Definitely." Then he added, "Would you have shot that guy, Mom?"

"To protect both of you? Absolutely."

Nick's eyes grew wide. "Wow, Mom, you've turned into such a badass. I didn't even know you knew how to use a gun."

"She doesn't," said Zack, striding into the dining room. "But maybe it's time she learned."

"What about us?" asked Nick.

Zack and I exchanged a long look before he said, "Your mother and I will discuss it."

I hate guns. I don't like having them in my house, and I don't want my sons going anywhere near them. That had always been my stance. However, the advent of mobsters, murders, and a multitude of mayhem in our lives now forced me to confront my greatest fears and objections.

After more than a year of deadly encounters, perhaps the time had come to rethink my position. The next time I reach for a gun, I may have to use it. And if so, I'd better know how to load it, fire it, *and* hit my target.

Zack poured himself a cup of coffee and joined us at the table. "Don't forget Jesse or someone from his crew is grouting the tile backsplash today."

"Right. I'd better shower and get dressed." I kissed Alex and Nick goodbye and hurried to the bedroom.

After hearing countless renovation nightmares from coworkers, I had dreaded the work on my home dragging on for months. I wouldn't have thought it possible to install a new kitchen in six days. It helped that all the finishes and appliances we'd picked had been in stock.

Jesse employed only licensed tradesmen, all of whom arrived promptly each morning and put in ten-hour workdays. Only the countertops involved a subcontractor. They were measured once the cabinets were installed and arrived the next day.

When the crew had needed to wait for spackling or paint to dry or the countertops to arrive, they had turned their attention to the foyer, replacing the tiles with new pre-finished hardwood that perfectly matched the existing floors.

Of course, it had helped that along with discovering the like-new flooring under the wall-to-wall carpets, Jesse had also found hardwood in equally good condition under the kitchen linoleum, which someone had nailed down instead of gluing and added toe molding around the perimeter to hide the nails. Not having to deal with asbestos removal or install new flooring had significantly cut the time Jesse had allotted for the kitchen phase of the reno.

Even a dead body on the property hadn't significantly altered his timeline. All that was left after grouting the tile backsplash were the appliances, scheduled to arrive later this afternoon. Monday morning the crew would start work on the master bathroom.

If only the rest of my life worked with such clockwork precision...and without dead bodies.

~*~

After showering, I opened my bedroom door to find my mother-in-law standing on the other side of the door. "I need you to drive me to Harriet's apartment."

I'd learned from Detective Spader that a judge had ordered Harriet Kleinhample placed under house arrest for the next month. If he hoped to teach her a lesson, he was in for a shock. Harriet and my mother-in-law were the original Thelma and Louise. The moment the court removed Harriet's ankle monitor, she'd find new wheels, and the two curmudgeonly commies, along with the eleven other members of the Daughters of the October Revolution, would be up to their usual antics.

"I have an appointment this morning," I said. "I can drop you off beforehand."

"I'm ready to leave now."

"I'm not."

"The world revolves around you, doesn't it, Anastasia?"

Did she really expect me to hop in the car while still dressed in my bathrobe and slippers? This time I didn't bite back the sarcasm on the tip of my tongue. "Absolutely, Lucille. Can't you tell?"

She pounded her cane on the floor, turned her back on me, and clomped out of the bedroom. A moment later the den in the TV began blaring an episode of some hair-pulling, trash-talking reality TV show.

Before we left the house, Denny arrived to grout the tile. "I'll be out of your hair in a few hours, Mrs. Pollack."

"No rush," I said. "I'm taking my hair out for a much-needed trim. Mr. Barnes is working in the apartment above the garage. Let him know before you leave."

Denny's eyes grew wide as he focused on something over my left shoulder. I turned my head to find Lucille standing in the doorway, one hand white knuckling her cane, the other planted on her hip. Her lips pursed tightly as she stepped into the kitchen and slowly took in the renovation, as if this were her first look, which I doubted.

Her eyes narrowed into slits as her gaze landed on Denny. "Who are you?" she demanded.

Denny cowered like a kid caught cheating on a test. His mouth flapped open and closed several times, but no words came out. Lucille's ability to intimidate people who meet her for the first time is legendary. Denny was no exception, despite the image he projected with his muscular physique and tiger tattoos.

"This is Denny, Lucille. He works for the contractor."

She hmphed before aiming her wrath at me. "My poor Karl is turning over in his grave the way you waste his hard-earned money."

Second verse, same as the first. Ignoring her, I added another puncture wound to my tongue before speaking to Denny. "We'll get out of your way."

He offered me what I could only interpret as a sympathetic smile. "Enjoy your morning, Mrs. Pollack."

"Thank you, Denny." Then, as I stepped into the dining room, I said, "I'm leaving if you want that ride, Lucille."

Once in my Jetta, my mother-in-law sat in stone-faced silence for the fifteen-minute trip to Harriet Kleinhample's apartment. When I pulled to the curb in front of the building, she hauled herself out of the car without so much as a thank-you. I remained until she had lumbered up the stairs and was buzzed into the lobby. As I pulled away, I wondered how she expected to get home.

I executed a U-turn and drove back to Westfield. My hair salon was less than a mile from my home. By driving thirty minutes roundtrip out of my way to do Lucille a favor, I'd lost half an hour of my precious weekend. Was it too much to ask that she show a little appreciation?

When I arrived at the salon, I settled into the chair by the wash basin, closed my eyes, and tried to relax. The scalp massage helped but not enough to keep me from dwelling on Lucille's behavior.

Always a difficult woman and never a fan of her son's choice for a wife, she'd grown increasingly more hostile since Karl's death. The minor stroke she'd suffered last summer had exacerbated her belligerent behavior toward me and anyone connected to me. I feared she'd only get worse with each passing year.

Sooner or later, I'd be forced to consider permanent assisted living for her. Lucille had bridled over her short stay at Sunnyside of Westfield, a facility considered one of the premier assisted living and rehab centers in the state. She'd go ballistic when she saw the less-than-ideal facilities Social Security, her paltry pension, and Medicaid would cover for long-term assisted living, and no matter what she believed to the contrary, thanks to her son, I had nothing to kick in to supplement her meager income.

I was still deep in the weeds of my thoughts when I left the salon. As I beeped my car unlocked, someone grabbed my arm and jabbed a gun into my back.

I froze. As a pair of nails dug into my upper arm, a gravel-voiced woman spoke into my ear. "Don't try anything stupid, and you won't get hurt."

EIGHTEEN

Although downtown Westfield always bustled with shoppers on Saturday mornings, the few people currently in the parking lot were too far from where I had parked. Not a single person looked in our direction. Even if someone had, no one was close enough to realize a madwoman held me at gunpoint.

My assailant shoved me into the backseat of my Jetta and scrambled in next to me. I stole a quick look at her, surprised to find a woman about my mother's age. However, unlike Mama, this aging baby boomer hadn't held up well. She had a weathered, careworn look about her. Her dulled copper hair was streaked with gray and in dire need of a stylist. Her skin sagged around her jowls and neck. Rolls of fat bulged from under a too tight olive green ribbed knit cardigan sweater that had seen better days a decade ago.

Someone shut the back passenger door, then climbed behind the wheel. I realized it was a second woman, much younger and extremely skinny. Stringy, blonde hair in need of a washing fell below her shoulders. Without turning around, she held her hand over the seatback, palm up.

"Give her your keys," said the woman who had grabbed me.

The sleeve of her hoodie had hiked up her outstretched arm. As I placed my keys in her hand, I noticed the remnants of a bruise circling her wrist. When she checked the rearview mirror while backing out of the parking space, I took note of her eyes, empty-looking, as if she were operating on autopilot. I couldn't see enough of her face to discern a physical similarity between her and the woman holding a gun to me, but I wondered if my kidnappers were a mother/daughter duo.

"Give me your purse," said the gun-toter.

After I complied, she rifled through it. "Where's your phone?"

"In my jacket pocket."

"Hand it over."

After I gave her the phone, she powered it down. "We wouldn't want anyone tracking us," she said. The smile she offered me sent chills up and down my spine.

"Look, if it's my car and money you want, take them. Just let me out and drive off."

She laughed. "I want a lot more than this piece of junk and the few dollars in your wallet."

"Like what?" Although the answer began to dawn on me. Somehow this woman knew about the jewelry Shauna Gallagher had hidden in my attic all those years ago. And if so, why were so many lowlifes suddenly coming out of the woodwork in search of a box hidden away at least two decades ago?

Maybe Cloris had been right about Jesse. Perhaps, he'd assumed the box he found in my attic contained something of value and was too good a story not to mention to friends and family. He didn't know we'd handed over the jewelry to the Feds.

However, I found it hard to believe the woman seated beside me and her cohort traveled in the same circles as Jesse and Robyn Konopka. Someone else had talked, most likely one of Murphy's underlings. Was this woman the wife of one of them?

"Someone hid a box in your attic years ago," she said, confirming my thoughts. "I want the jewelry that was in that box."

"I don't have it."

She waved the gun in my face. "Don't lie to me!"

I pressed myself into the corner of the seat against the back door. "I'm not lying."

She inched closer and held the gun to my temple. "Don't think I won't use this."

"I believe you, but you have to believe me, I no longer have what you want."

"Where is it?"

"We turned it over to the FBI."

My statement hit her like the proverbial ton of bricks. Shock, disbelief, then finally anger scrolled across her face within a split second before she said, "Are you really that stupid, or do you think I am?"

The woman driving the car barked out a laugh. "That's just great. I told you this was a stupid idea. Now what do we do?"

"She's lying. Shut up and drive."

A moment later, the driver swerved and braked hard to avoid a truck that had run a red light. I flew sideways into my abductor. She lost her grip on the gun. It dropped to the floorboard and went off.

The driver screamed.

"Keep driving!" shouted the older woman as she pushed me off her, then leaned down to scoop up the gun from where it had landed on the floorboard. "You could have gotten us killed."

"Would you have preferred I let that truck broadside us? Come to think of it, maybe I should have let him hit us. I would have loved to see how you'd talk your way out of this situation when the cops arrived."

"Keep it up, and you'll be sorry."

"I'm already sorry. Sorry I let you drag us—"

She swung the gun away from me, leaned forward against the back of the front seat, and placed the barrel against the driver's neck. Through gritted teeth, she said, "Not another word! Do I make myself clear?"

When the driver nodded, the woman leaned back and once more aimed the gun at me.

I don't know which pounded harder and louder, my heart from my surging adrenalin or my eardrums from the gun's thunderous discharge. I had no idea where the bullet had lodged. All I knew was it hadn't hit me or either of the two women. Under the circumstances, I would have preferred otherwise. If one of them had been wounded, I may have had a chance to escape.

As I tried to ignore the gun pointed at my head, I took a deep breath, both to calm my nerves and sniff out any telltale odor of gasoline or smoke. Finding myself at the mercy of a couple of deranged kidnappers was bad enough. I really didn't want my day—and my life—ending in an explosive conflagration. But not detecting any foreboding odors, I figured I was at least safe from that fate.

We drove in silence for a few minutes. The driver had taken us through Westfield, into Scotch Plains, and onto Rt. 22. Eventually, the woman with the gun said, "Get down on the floor and face the door."

I hesitated.

"Now!" she screamed.

I lowered myself into the small space between the seats and crouched, facing the door. Did she plan to open the door and push me out into traffic? That was my last thought before the world turned black.

~*~

I found myself balled up with one side of my face pressed against a scratchy carpet that reeked of mold and mildew. I had no idea how much time had passed. Tamping down the panic that threatened to overwhelm me, I concentrated on the fact I was still alive. I had no idea where I was, but at least my kidnapper hadn't kicked me out into oncoming traffic at sixty-five miles an hour as I'd earlier anticipated.

I tried to raise my head, but pain and dizziness quickly forced me to give up that idea. My mouth and throat felt like I'd swallowed shards of glass. I ran a sandpaper tongue around my parched lips and pried open the eye not embedded in the carpet. The darkness remained.

My muscles refused to move without torturing me, leading me to believe I'd remained in this cramped position for several hours, if not longer. At least my captors hadn't bothered to bind my arms and legs, whether through negligence, stupidity, or cockiness. Perhaps it was a mistake I could use to my advantage.

Staying still, I waited for the cobwebs to clear from my brain. As much as it hurt to move, I finally raised my arm and gingerly probed my head with my fingers. I found no goose eggs or sticky blood residue from a gash.

If my assailant hadn't knocked me unconscious with her gun,

had she somehow drugged me? I thought back to the moments before I blacked out but couldn't remember seeing a syringe. Was it possible to sustain a concussion without feeling even a localized sore spot? My head ached all over, one area no worse than another.

Eventually, my eye adjusted to the darkness. At first, I had feared I was locked in the trunk of a car, but I now saw that I was in what appeared to be a small closet. When I tried to raise my head again and turned slightly, I saw a thin sliver of light flooding in from under the door.

I also heard voices. Although too muffled and distant for me to make out any part of the conversation, the tone sounded far from friendly. I couldn't tell how many people were involved, but it was more than the two women who had abducted me. I could only conclude the people on the other side of the door were arguing over what to do with me.

A short time later I heard a door slam. Within seconds the closet door swung open, flooding the small compartment with light. "Get up," said the older woman.

I squinted from the shock of the blinding brightness and cringed at the menace in her voice. Through slitted eyelids, I reached for the door jamb and tried to hoist myself to my feet. My legs had other ideas. Halfway up, they morphed into overcooked linguine, and I collapsed backwards into the closet, hitting my head on the wall. The impact caused a lone wooden hanger to tumble from a shelf above my head. It smacked me in the face, gashing my cheek, causing my nose to bleed, and splitting open my lip.

The woman rattled off a litany of curses as she grabbed my arm and dragged me from the closet, then yanked me to my feet. Her age and flab certainly belied her strength. When she let go of my arm, I fell to my hands and knees. She uttered a few more choice words as she kicked me once, and I face-planted into the shag carpeting.

"What good will it do to knock her out again?" asked the younger woman.

"If you don't want to be next, get over here and help me."

The two of them each grabbed one of my arms. I screamed as the older woman wrenched so hard, she nearly dislocated my shoulder. They hauled me to my feet and deposited me on a chair in the corner of the room.

The older woman bent over me and said, "Scream again, and it'll be your last." She turned to the younger woman and said, "Keep an eye on her," before she crossed the room.

Hugging her chest, the younger woman stood a few feet from me, staring at her feet. I sucked in a lungful of musty air and took in my surroundings, a sleazy motel room that probably rented by the hour, if not the minute.

The older woman returned. She carried the gun and my iPhone. "We all decided you're lying. So here's what's going to happen. We're going to make a trade, your life for the jewelry that was in the box."

I choked back a whimper. "I told you, I don't have the jewelry."

She pointed the gun at me. "I'm giving you one more chance to tell the truth."

Staring into her eyes, I knew if I tried once more to convince her I didn't have the jewelry, she'd pull the trigger. I held out my hand for the phone.

She dropped it onto my lap. "You're going to do exactly what I tell you." She pulled a folded piece of paper from her jeans pocket. "Take it."

I reached for the paper.

"Facetime your boyfriend. Read him exactly what's written on that paper. Don't say another word. No hello. Nothing. Got it?"

I unfolded the sheet of crumbled yellow copy paper advertising a yard sale that had taken place weeks ago. After a moment of puzzlement, I flipped over the paper, scanned the handwritten message on the back, and nodded.

"After you read those words," she continued, "you're going to disconnect the call. Just so you both know I mean business, I'll be just out of camera range, but my friend here won't." She then placed the barrel of the gun against my temple. "Now make the call."

She had powered up my phone before handing it to me. I input my password. The screen showed a slew of missed calls and text messages, all from Zack. According to the clock, six hours had elapsed since I'd left the hair salon.

Zack answered on the first ring. The gun pointed at my head told him everything he needed to know about the situation. My hand shook and my voice quavered as I read what my captor had written. When I had finished, he opened his mouth to speak, but the woman pressed the gun more forcefully against my temple. Tears filled my eyes as I disconnected the call.

She grabbed the phone from my hand, powered it down, and slipped it into her back jeans pocket. Then she unplugged two of the lamps and ripped out the cords, tossing them to the younger woman. "Tie her up."

The older woman stood with the gun pointed at me as the younger woman crouched in front of the chair and trussed me like a turkey. "Tighter," she said.

"I'm pulling it as tight as I can. Any tighter and I'll cut off her circulation."

The woman hauled off and smacked her upside her head, knocking her to the floor. "I don't care. I said tight."

The younger woman scrambled back into position and resumed binding me. As she pulled tighter, the electrical cord cut into my wrists. I inhaled sharply, biting back the pain.

She cut her eyes up toward me for the briefest of moments before returning to her task. In that split second when our eyes met, I had seen the pain in them. This young woman was not a willing participant. Could I somehow convince her to help me?

When I was tied up to the older woman's satisfaction, she spoke to the younger woman. "You're staying here with her while I pick up the jewelry. I'll call you once I'm back at the motel."

"What about her?" she asked, nodding toward me.

"Leave her. Someone will find her eventually. They probably clean this dump at least once a month." She grabbed both her purse and mine off the bed.

"You're leaving now?" asked the younger woman. "He won't be there for two hours."

"It's not like the drop is around the corner. Besides, I have to eat dinner, don't I?

"What about me?"

"What about you?"

"When do I get dinner?"

She shrugged. "You can eat once you get back to the motel."

"And her?"

The older woman rolled her eyes. "Seriously?" She slammed the door behind her as she left.

"You know she's crazy," I said after we heard the car pull away. She exhaled a long, shaky sigh before mumbling, "Tell me something I don't know."

"Is she your mother?"

She shook her head.

"Did she force you to help her?"

She nodded.

"If you help me, I can help you."

She glanced at the door, as if afraid the older woman would walk back through it at any moment.

"If you don't help me, you're an accessory to a kidnapping. Do you know what that means?"

When she nodded again, I saw tears running down her cheeks. "I never wanted any of this. I had no idea what they had planned. They said we were going on a vacation." She began to sob.

"What's your name?"

She blubbered, her name flying out on a hiccup. "Gigi."

"Gigi what?"

Her eyes widened. "I can't tell you that."

"Fair enough. My name is Anastasia. Anastasia Pollack. You said 'they' before. How many other people are involved in this?"

"No!" She shook her head violently, terror written across her face. "Don't ask me about them. If they find out I told you anything, they'll kill me."

"I promise. No more questions about them." I held up my bound wrists. "If you untie me, I can get us out of here."

She hesitated. "They'll find me and kill me."

"I know people who will protect you."

"What kind of people?"

"Law enforcement."

She eyed my wrists and took a step closer to me. "Did you really turn the jewelry over to the FBI?"

I stared directly into her eyes. "Yes."

"How did you know it was stolen?"

I told her about my conversation with my neighbor Rosalie, the research I'd done on the Internet, and the connection between the suspects in the museum heist and the Boston jewelry store robberies. I ended by saying, "Two Boston mobsters are already dead, including a high-ranking crime boss. These people you're protecting are playing with fire."

"I'm not protecting them," she said, new tears spilling from her eyes. "I'm terrified they'll kill me."

"Gigi, do you really think they're going to let you live after what you've seen?"

She buried her head in her hands and sank to her knees. Apparently, the reality of her situation hadn't sunk in until this moment. "What am I going to do?"

"You're going to untie me, and we're going to get out of here."

Between her shaky hands and continuing tears, Gigi worked for at least ten minutes before she managed to release my wrists, then my ankles. I tried standing, but although not as severe, the dizziness persisted, and my legs still wobbled. "Did she drug me?"

Gigi lowered her head and stared at her shoes. "When you were crouched on the floor of the car."

"Do you know what she used?"

She shook her head.

"I'm guessing she took your phone?"

"And my wallet."

"Then how is she going to call you?"

"I suppose on that." She pointed to a rotary dial landline on the nightstand separating the two double beds.

I wouldn't count on it but didn't voice my skepticism. I needed

Gigi to stay focused on escaping, not break down and become useless, especially since *useless* aptly described my present physical condition. However, more than likely, the plan had included someone returning to eliminate both of us.

With Gigi's help, I made it to the bathroom before my bladder gave out. Then I gulped down mouthfuls of water at the sink. When I lifted my head and stared into the small mirror hanging above the sink, I barely recognized myself. Thanks to the coat hanger and the drugs still in my system, I looked considerably worse than Lucille had after her recent run-ins with the carjacker/burglar.

I glanced around the small bathroom but found neither a sliver of soap nor so much as a paper towel. Using only my fingers and the hem of my T-shirt, I did what I could to clean the dried blood from my face. If I ever learned the name of this place, I'd give it a no-star rating on Yelp.

Afterwards, I asked Gigi to help me to the window. I pulled back a corner of the drapes to ascertain our location. I had expected to look out onto a motel parking lot on Rt. 22. Instead, I found us in the middle of a wooded area dotted with a handful of dilapidated cabins.

And no vehicle parked in front of 'our' cabin.

My heart plummeted. "We have no transportation." I knew I wasn't in any condition to hike back to civilization. I glanced at the landline. Not knowing when someone would show up to finish us off, I didn't want to wait around in the cabin for a rescue. However, I saw little choice.

I took a few tentative steps toward the phone. Gigi grabbed onto my arm, but I waved her off. "Let me try on my own."

She followed a step behind me. The aisle between the two beds wasn't wide enough for us to walk abreast, but if I felt my legs giving out from under me, I'd be able to twist my torso to direct my fall onto one of the beds. Telling myself progress is often one small step at a time, I slowly made my way to the nightstand and managed to arrive still on my feet.

The phone looked like it predated my birth. I couldn't remember ever having used a rotary dial phone, only push-button. I picked up the receiver and held it to my ear before sinking onto the bed. No dial tone. "The phone is dead."

NINETEEN

Gigi's eyes again welled up with tears that spilled down her cheeks. For a moment, I thought we were doomed, but then her eyes widened, and she said, "I don't remember her taking your keys from me."

She began fishing around in her various pockets, finally removing a set of keys—my keys—from a pocket in the dingy pale pink hoodie she'd worn earlier, and which was now draped over the arm of the only other chair in the room. She held up the keys, smiling as she jingled them. The clinking metal became my new favorite piece of music.

"The car has to be around here somewhere," she said. "Maybe Na—" She caught herself, then continued, "Maybe one of them pushed the car out of view around to the side or the back of the cabin."

"Let's hope so." I grabbed her arm for support. "Come on. It's time to get out of here." She started to hand me the keys. "You're driving. I'm still wonky from whatever drug she used on me."

We found the car on the side of the cabin, behind a huge rhododendron bush and out of view of the other cabins, not that the precaution seemed necessary. From all indications, none of the other cabins appeared occupied.

"How did you know about this place?" I asked as Gigi slowly navigated downhill along an unmarked dirt road.

"I didn't. They did."

I looked around as she drove. "Is there an office?"

"Not that I saw."

"How did they get the key?"

"The door was unlocked when we arrived. I guess they made arrangements earlier."

Eventually, the dirt road ended at a second dirt road. That one took us to a gravel road which finally brought us to a paved road. The woods thinned out, then segued into rolling fields, but so far, we came to no crossroads that might bring us to a farmhouse or other inhabited structure. Nowhere along the way had I seen any signs or other dwellings.

I never cared for all the bells and whistles of upgraded automobiles. My only two requirements in a vehicle were safety and reliability. For the first time, though, I wished my Jetta had included all those bells and whistles—especially a built-in navigation system. "It's a good thing you know where you're going," I said.

Gigi worried her lower lip and darted a quick look in my direction. "Actually, I don't. I think we're headed back to the main highway, but I'm not sure."

"We're driving down the mountain, at least. That's a good sign."

"That's what I'd hoped."

I wish I knew what Zack planned to do. He couldn't deliver jewelry he didn't have, and he certainly wouldn't risk showing up at the drop point without it, not when he had no idea where I was. The ransom note I'd read to him made no mention of my captors turning me over to him on the spot. His only direction was to come alone to the parking lot of a boarded-up motel off Rt. 9 in Jersey City and leave the box of jewelry on the floor of the skeleton of an abandoned car he'd find at the back of the building.

I knew he'd alert Spader and Ledbetter. Between the cops and the FBI, they'd have worked out some sort of plan. Zack was too smart to show up alone and walk into a trap.

I needed to get to a phone to let him know I'd escaped. So far, though, we hadn't come across any civilization, and since I had no clue where we were, I didn't know when we'd find a convenience store, gas station, or even a home with a sympathetic resident who would allow me to place a call.

Something else niggled at the corner of my mind, but I couldn't grasp hold of it. My brain was still too drug-fogged.

I glanced at the gas gauge. At least we had nearly half a tank of gas. The topography suggested we were somewhere in northwestern New Jersey, most likely Sussex County. But we could just as easily be in upstate New York or northeastern Pennsylvania, hopefully not too far beyond state lines. Neither of us had any money nor credit cards. Running out of fuel would really suck.

Gigi sighed.

"What's wrong?"

"I don't remember driving this long through the middle of nowhere. Maybe I should have turned in the opposite direction when we came to the paved road."

219

"Do you remember these fields?"

She shrank into herself, as if anticipating that I'd yell at her. Or worse. "Not really."

I tamped down my angst and frustration, forced a lightness into my voice, and said, "That's okay. Let's drive for another two miles. If we don't come upon a gas station or a main road, we'll turn around."

Her voice trembled. "You're not upset with me?"

"Gigi, I couldn't do this without you." I flashed her a smile. "We're a team. Don't forget that."

Her shoulders relaxed as she returned my smile. "Thank you."

"No, thank you," I said. "I really mean that."

We drove along in silence for another few minutes. Finally, she said. "I think we should turn around."

"Wait, I think I see something up ahead."

She hunched over the steering wheel and squinted. "Where? I don't see anything."

I pointed. "Behind that clump of trees in the distance on the right. I see something silver. It could be the tin roof of a building."

She nodded and continued to drive. Sure enough, a mile down the road we came to an unmarked gravel road, turned in, and after a few hundred yards arrived at a barn with a silver pickup truck parked near the open doors. A herd of black and white dairy cows grazed on a hillside in the distance.

"Will you be okay if I wait in the car?" asked Gigi.

She couldn't mask the fear emanating from her entire body. I don't know what the older woman and the others had done to her, but I had a feeling it paled in comparison to what I had experienced. "I'm feeling much stronger. Kill the engine, though. We can't afford to waste gas."

As soon as she'd turned off the car, I stepped out and took a few tentative steps. My legs held. I filled my lungs with fresh air and made my way across the gravel to the open barn doors. As I drew closer, the odor of manure and livestock became nearly overpowering. I switched to mouth-breathing to keep from gagging on the stench.

At the entrance to the barn, I called, "Hello? Is anybody here?"

"That you, Katie?"

"No, sir. My name is Anastasia. You don't know me, but I need your help, please."

"What kind of help? I'm kinda busy right now. I've got a breeched calf."

I didn't know the first thing about animal husbandry, but I assumed a breeched calf was like a breeched baby. If so, the man really did have his hands full—literally.

With time a luxury neither of us had, I opted for the most condensed version of the day's events. "I was attacked. I'd like to use your phone to let my fiancé know I'm okay and on my way home."

That's when the fog lifted, and the brain niggle formed into a coherent thought. When I was told to FaceTime Zack, the woman with the gun had referred to him as my boyfriend. How had she known about him?

"Attacked?" asked the man, pulling me back to the present. "By whom?"

"I don't know."

"You escaped?"

"With some help. Look, it's a long story, and I'd be happy to tell you all about it, but please, it's important I make that call. You're the first person I've come across after driving for nearly half an hour."

"Come on back. Fourth stall on the left."

I slowly made my way down the dark barn to the one stall flooded by an incandescent bulb. A gray-haired man, well past middle-age, hunched over the rear of a cow in obvious distress, his hands shoved up inside the cow's body.

He turned his head to look at me over his shoulder, staring for a long moment at my face. "You weren't kidding. He really did a number on you."

"She," I said, "and you're looking at the cleaned-up version."

He squinted at me. "Another woman did that to you?"

"Indirectly." Again, time was of the essence, and I didn't want to go into a longwinded explanation. "An extremely strong and crazy woman with a gun."

"Phone's over there," he tilted his head toward a black medical bag. "I'm Doc Bradley, the local vet. Anything broken?"

I wiggled the bridge of my nose to be sure. "I don't think so."

"I'd take a look, but I've got to get this calf turned around before it's too late."

"I understand. I'll be all right."

He nodded. "Make your call. Passcode is 838362, VETDOC. Let him know you're okay and where you are."

"Where am I exactly?"

"Sussex County. Not far from Rt. 206. I'll give you directions. You good from there?"

"Definitely. I wasn't sure I was still in New Jersey."

The cow bellowed her distress, and the vet turned his attention back to his patient.

I found the phone sitting on top of various items in the open medical bag. Zack answered with a cautious, "Yes?"

"I'm okay," I said. "I escaped."

"Are they looking for you?"

"No, they have no idea."

"Where are you?"

"In a barn in Sussex County, watching a very nice veterinarian coaxing a breeched calf to turn around."

He laughed despite the seriousness of the situation. "Sorry. Only you."

"I know. My life is bizarre."

"Your face—"

"Will heal. No permanent damage. I'm alive, Zack. I'm safe, and I'm—" I gasped.

Doc Bradley stood and smiled at me as we both watched the little calf struggle to its feet. He made it on the second attempt and immediately searched out his mama's udder.

"What? What's going on?"

I started laughing. "I just watched a miracle. Who would have thought this day would end with the birth of a baby cow?"

"It's not over yet," he said, crashing me back down to reality.

"I know. Be careful."

"Don't worry. I have plenty of backup."

As I knew he would. I disconnected the call and returned the phone to the medical bag. "Thank you, Doctor."

He was cleaning his hands at a nearby sink. "Give me a minute, and I'll write down those directions for you."

After he'd dried his hands, he returned and pulled out a prescription pad and pen from his bag and a tube, which he handed to me. "Rub some of this antibiotic ointment on those cuts."

"I won't start mooing, will I?"

He chuckled. "I hope not."

After jotting down directions, he ripped the sheet from the pad and handed it to me. "You sure you'll be okay? You look shaky. Wasn't from watching me, was it?"

"No, it's the aftermath of whatever drug they used on me." I finished dabbing the ointment on my cuts, capped the tube, and held it out to him.

"Keep it," he said, dismissing the tube with a wave of his hand. "But you shouldn't drive."

"I'm not. The young woman who helped me escape is waiting outside."

"Before you go…" He reached into his back pocket, pulled out his wallet, and grabbed a few bills. "Stop and get yourself something to eat and drink. You look like you need it."

I shook my head as I took a step away from him. "I can't take money from you."

He grabbed my hand, placed the bills in my palm, then curled my fingers around them. "I insist."

I stared at my hand, unsure what to do. Finally, I said, "I'll pay you back."

"Not necessary. All I ask is that you call me when you're safely home." He pulled a business card from his wallet and wedged it under my thumb. "Otherwise, I won't sleep tonight. You wouldn't keep an old man awake all night, would you?"

"Absolutely not," I said, shoving the bills and card into my pocket. "Thank you again."

I left the barn and climbed back into my Jetta.

"I was getting worried," said Gigi. "You were gone longer than I expected."

"The owner of the pickup was busy birthing a calf."

She nodded as if this were an everyday occurrence in her normal world. Maybe it was. Gigi had offered no personal information about herself, and I hadn't asked for fear of spooking her.

"You made your call?" she asked.

"Yes, and I have directions to get us back to the highway. Turn right when you get out to the main road."

"That's the direction we were going."

"We're only a few miles from the highway."

Gigi scrunched up her face. "Why did it seem so much longer this time?"

"We've been on a local road that parallels Rt. 206. You were probably correct in thinking we had driven in the wrong direction. We'll pick up the highway at a different place from where you exited." My stomach rumbled loudly, reminding me I hadn't eaten since breakfast.

Gigi glanced at me. "I'm hungry, too."

"Once we turn onto Rt. 206, we'll find a place to stop to get some food."

"We have no money."

"We do now. The vet lent me a few dollars." *Lent* being the operative word. No matter what he had said, I had every intention of reimbursing him for his kindness and generosity.

Once we exited onto Rt. 206, we drove for about ten minutes before the rural landscape began yielding to an occasional strip mall with a handful of stores, none of which sold food unless we wanted cannabis-infused edibles. We passed several of those, along with multiple gyms, yoga studios, adult bookstores, and laundromats.

As we continued driving, the strip malls multiplied until they took over the roadway. The variety of businesses expanded to include tax prep, veterinary clinics, pool supplies, and gardening centers. Finally, I spotted an iconic New Jersey image and said, "I see a diner up ahead on the right."

A moment later Gigi turned off the highway, pulled into a spot in the half-full parking lot, and parked my Jetta. Then we hiked the short distance to the entrance.

We entered through a set of double-glass doors. The hostess took one look at me and gasped.

"It looks much worse than it feels," I assured her, which was pretty much a lie at that point.

"If you say so, but I'm happy to bring you some ice for those bruises."

"I'd appreciate that."

She hesitated for a moment. I think she expected me to explain why I looked like a walking, talking punching bag, but when I said nothing further, she led us to a booth at the rear of the diner and handed us menus.

"You look really bad," said Gigi.

"I feel worse," I said.

"But you—"

"Didn't want to get into it with a total stranger."

She nodded and turned her attention to her menu. A moment later, the hostess returned with a bowl of ice, a towel, and a travel packet of Motrin. "Thought you might have use for this," she said, handing me the pills.

"Thank you," I said.

As soon as she walked back to the hostess stand, a waitress arrived with glasses of water and took our order. Even though it was closer to dinnertime than breakfast, Gigi and I both settled on the all-day breakfast special of two eggs, bacon, hash browns, toast, orange juice, and coffee.

My lip on one side of my mouth had mushroomed to twice its normal size, thanks to the attack of the wooden coat hanger. I wrapped some ice in the towel and held it to the swollen area. With a straw inserted into the opposite side of my mouth, I washed down the Motrin.

Our food was in front of us in under five minutes. I zeroed in on the orange juice. As hungry as I was, my body craved a sugar rush. I transferred the straw from the water glass to the juice. As I sipped, I took care to avoid any citrus coming in contact with my split lip. Once I'd drained the glass, I attacked the plate of food as best I could, eating only on the good side of my mouth.

We ate in silence, but halfway through the meal, I took a sip of coffee, then asked, "I know you don't want to mention names, Gigi. I understand your fear and will respect your decision, but how did you wind up involved with that awful woman?"

She ignored me at first as she grabbed three packets of sugar substitute. Concentrating on her task, one by one she tore open the packets, dumping the contents of each into her coffee. Before stirring, she added enough cream to transform the black coffee to near ivory in color.

I had just about given up hope of hearing an answer to my question when she finally mumbled, "I guess you could blame it on hormones." Then she finally raised her head and with a sheepish expression, met my gaze.

When I raised an eyebrow, she explained. "I ignored my mother's advice and ran off with an older guy who claimed to love me." Gigi shook her head and added, "Mom says I have daddy issues because my father walked out on us years ago. I guess she's right. He's old enough to be my father."

I had assumed Gigi was in her twenties, but I'd come to suspect I may have overestimated her age. She'd now confirmed my suspicion. "How old are you, Gigi?"

"Sixteen."

"Did you sleep with him?"

She blushed. "Does it matter?"

"If you did, it's an additional crime he's committed."

"But I consented."

"Doesn't matter. Transporting a minor over state lines for the purpose of having sex is a federal offense. It's called the Mann Act, and it's been a law for more than a hundred years. Where is he now?"

"I guess he's with his...with her...on his way to pick up the jewelry."

Was she about to identify him as the woman's brother? Son? Husband? I ignored the slip, not wanting to raise her defenses, and pressed on. "How did they even know about the jewelry?"

Gigi chewed on a slice of buttered toast. "Beats me. I thought we were headed to New York City. She was always nice to me from when I first met her. When she suggested a road trip, I was excited to join them. At first, we had fun."

"But?"

"We never got to New York. Next thing I know, we're in a sleazy motel on some busy highway. Prior to that, we'd stayed in nice places, not dives. Once we arrived, they'd take off for hours at a time, leaving me stuck with nothing to do except watch TV, and that dump didn't even have cable."

"For how long?"

"Nearly a week."

"Why didn't you leave?" Although, even as I asked the question, I suspected I knew the answer—Stockholm Syndrome.

"They threatened to track me down and kill me if I did. Besides, they took my wallet and phone. Where was I going to go without money?" She looked up at me and sighed. "And that was before things got really crazy."

"In what way?"

She speared me with one of those *duh* looks I find so annoying coming from my sons. "Today?"

"You didn't know she planned to kidnap me?"

"Not until she waved a gun in my face this morning and told me I'd better cooperate—or else."

"How did she know where to find me?"

"We followed you."

"You knew where I live?"

Gigi shrugged. "They knew the house where the jewelry was hidden."

"How?"

"I don't know. Like I said, I thought we were going to do the tourist thing in New York." She offered me a rueful smile. "Guess that's not happening anytime soon."

"Probably not."

I picked up the remaining strip of bacon on my plate and took a bite as I puzzled through what I'd learned. The logistics bothered me. "There were only two people involved? The man and woman?"

She nodded.

"And you traveled here together?"

When she nodded again, I continued, "But only two of you kidnapped me. She left by herself to get the jewelry. Did they rent a second car after arriving? One she left in the parking lot where she grabbed me?"

If I could get word to Zack about the make and model of a rental, the police would be able to identify my abductor or her accomplice, either from the rental agreement or through fingerprinting the vehicle. I had full faith in whatever Zack had cooked up with Spader and Ledbetter, but it was always a good idea to have a Plan B. I'd learned from my past experiences that when dealing with criminals, situations often veered sideways.

Gigi shook her head. "Every few days they'd steal a car, then switch the plates."

"Did they steal plates off other cars?"

"I don't think so."

"Why not?"

"Too risky. Stolen plates would be in the system. You can buy old license plates at flea markets and junk stores."

Who knew? Certainly not me, but I wondered how a sixteen-year-old came by this knowledge. I sighed as I scooped up the remains of my scrambled eggs. So much for Plan B.

Instead, I changed the subject slightly and asked, "What will you do once they're captured?"

Gigi stared down at her empty plate. "Call my mom to apologize."

"And then?"

She shrugged. "Go home, assuming she sends me money for a ticket."

"Is there any possibility she won't?"

She looked up at me and grinned. "I sure hope not. Otherwise, you're stuck with me."

I studied her over the rim of my coffee cup. Was she fishing for an invitation to avoid returning home? "You'd have to share a room with my communist mother-in-law."

Gigi's eyes bugged out, and she sputtered into her coffee. "Mom better come through."

TWENTY

By the time we'd finished eating, my wooziness and the cobwebs clogging my brain had finally dissipated. When Gigi and I returned to the car, I said, "I'm feeling up to driving if you'd like me to take over."

"You sure?"

"If I find myself tiring or losing focus, I'll pull over, and we'll switch back."

She handed me the keys. "I never realized how exhausting it is to sit behind the wheel of a car. This is the most I've driven since getting my license a few months ago."

Given her state of mind and what she must have endured, I found it surprising she was a novice driver. "No one would ever know," I said. "You're a natural." However, I was glad I'd heard her admission *after* she handed over the keys and not at the beginning of our journey toward freedom.

I settled into the driver's seat, started the car, and pulled back onto Rt. 206. At one point I glanced over at Gigi and saw her picking pill balls from her oversized pink hoodie. Suddenly my brain cells shifted into abacus mode, added two and two together, and came up with *why hadn't I figured this out earlier?*

Once the shock of my *duh* moment wore off, I asked, "Gigi, did you drive into Westfield by yourself Wednesday night?"

She turned to stare at me, her mouth agape. "How did you know about that?"

I explained what we had seen on the surveillance camera. "The young woman who confronted the two people exiting my backyard was wearing a light-colored hoodie. That was you, wasn't it? You followed them to my house that night, didn't you?"

She inhaled a ragged breath. "And paid for it afterwards. Big time."

"How did you get a car?"

"It was one of the stolen vehicles I told you about. They made the mistake of leaving the keys in the motel when they left that night."

"But wouldn't they have driven off before you could leave without them seeing you? How did you know where they went?"

"I watched them from the window. They got into his SUV and drove across the parking lot to the bar next to the motel. I figured if they were just going to get some beers, they would've walked. It wasn't more than a few yards away. Once they'd entered the bar, I snuck downstairs and hid in the car, watching until they left the bar and drove off. Then I followed them, making sure to stay far enough behind so they wouldn't see me."

"Why confront them? Why not leave at that point?"

She hesitated for a moment, staring into her lap as her hands fidgeted with the hem of her hoodie. "Because I was pissed. I wanted to know what was going on, why I was stuck in that fleabag motel, and why we hadn't gone to New York like they'd promised." She glanced up at me, chagrin written across her face. "Stupid, right?"

Definitely. But my own experience with sixteen-year-olds had taught me they were often less than rational creatures. Instead of agreeing with her, I reached across the seat and squeezed her hand. "Sometimes things happen for a reason."

"What do you mean?"

"If you had driven off Wednesday night, I might be dead by now."

Her eyes widened. "You think it was divine intervention?"

I thought about that for a moment. Was it? "I don't know," I finally answered. "But what I do know is that my chances of survival increased dramatically because you chose to follow them rather than take off Wednesday night."

Her brow furrowed. "I hadn't thought of it that way."

Now that I had solved one mystery, I turned my thoughts to the man who had mugged Lucille and broken into my home, the perverted creep who had also seduced an impressionable and needy sixteen-year-old. As I hit the replay button in my brain and considered the timeline of events that had occurred over the last two weeks, I discovered his identity.

I glanced over at Gigi. She had returned to her nervous preoccupation of picking the fabric pills from her hoodie. At least she wasn't dropping the fuzz balls on the floor of my car. Instead, she carefully deposited them in the hoodie's kangaroo pocket.

For the time being, I'd keep my second aha moment to myself. One huge question still loomed. How did he know about the box of jewelry in my attic?

We arrived home to a darkened house. I wasn't surprised. Zack wouldn't have wanted Alex and Nick home alone during the drop and had probably sent them to stay with Shane and Sophie. Since Lucille had no other transportation, if she hadn't called a cab, she was still at Harriet's apartment. With any luck, she'd stay overnight. For all I knew, my mother-in-law had previously moved some of her clothes into Harriet's closet.

Once inside the house, I resisted the urge to use the landline to contact Zack. Not knowing what was going down, I didn't want to risk screwing up whatever operation he, Spader, and Ledbetter had coordinated to nab my abductors. I did check for messages, though, and found several, each one more increasingly irate, from my mother-in-law.

I deleted Lucille's nasty voicemails. Afterwards, I headed down the hall to my bedroom. Gigi followed me like a puppy dog. I pulled some clean clothes from my dresser and handed them to her. "If you need them, I'll get you some safety pins."

"What for?"

"The sweatpants have an elastic waistband," I said, "but you're much thinner than I am. If they don't stay up, you can use the safety pins to cinch them."

I then pulled a towel and new bar of soap from the linen closet and led her back to the hall bathroom. "You'll find shampoo and conditioner on the shelf in the shower. Take as much time as you want. I'll be using the other bathroom."

"You have kids?" she asked as we passed Alex and Nick's bedroom.

"Two boys. One your age, one two years older."

"They're very lucky to have such a cool mom."

I stopped her as she turned to head into the bathroom. "Gigi, I'm sure your mother is worried sick about you. After you shower, you should call her."

She bit down on her lower lip. Huge worry lines settled across her forehead. "What if she won't let me come home?"

"Would you like me to speak with her first?"

The desperation left her face and she brightened. "Would you?"

"Absolutely. She should know what a brave daughter she's raised."

Tears filled her eyes. Before they spilled down her cheeks, she dashed into the bathroom and closed the door. A moment later, I heard the shower and headed for my own bathroom.

While the shower water heated up, I stood in front of the mirror and stared at the mess that stared back at me. Ignoring the cuts and bruises, I concentrated on the tangled mass on my head. So much for treating myself to a salon styling. I could never get my hair to look as good as it did after a professional blowout. Now, only hours after dropping nearly a hundred dollars, my hair resembled a rat's nest. I ran a brush through it to deal with the knots, then stripped off my clothes and stepped into the shower.

I was rinsing the conditioner from my hair when I heard the bathroom door creak open. My heart pounded as a blurry figure stepped into view and I recognized the silhouette on the other side of the steam-covered glass.

~*~

Zack stripped off his clothes and joined me. "It's over," he said, pulling me into his arms. He studied my face for a moment, then gently kissed my injuries.

I heaved a huge sigh of relief as I clung to him. "Even when I don't get involved, I wind up involved." I lifted my head off his chest and craned my neck to look at him. "When will the murder and mayhem end?"

"I wish I had the answer to that."

"That makes two of us."

We shared a look of longing, but with unspoken agreement decided now was not the time. Instead, I finished rinsing the conditioner from my hair, and we exited the shower.

As we dressed, Zack said, "You'll never guess who was behind this."

"Bet I can. It was Denny, wasn't it?"

He cocked his head toward the bedroom door. "Did the young woman currently camped out in our living room tell you?"

"She was too scared to name names. I figured it out as we drove back to the house." I explained how Gigi's pink hoodie led me to connect the dots.

I then explained how I backtracked over the timeline of events from the last few weeks. "Only one person was on the periphery at every point."

I ran through the series of events. "Last Monday night we surprised a Dumpster diver who had an accomplice waiting in a car at the curb. My guess is that guy wasn't interested in copper as you originally suggested."

"What else of value could he possibly find in a construction Dumpster?"

"Information."

Zack contemplated for a moment, then said, "I hadn't thought about that. When people have a Dumpster on their property, they often take the opportunity to toss items they no longer need or want. Not everyone bothers to shred personal documents."

"Exactly. He didn't find anything like that, but he realized we were starting a major renovation. The next day Denny showed up looking for a job. How many unemployed construction workers troll for work by driving around residential neighborhoods?"

"I'm guessing very few. They'd have better luck hanging around the contractors' entrance at building supply centers."

I continued explaining my theory. "When Jesse told him he didn't have any openings, the guy asked if he could leave his references and contact information just in case Jesse had an opening in the future. Later that afternoon Lucille was mugged and her purse with her house key taken."

"I'm beginning to see where you're going with this," said Zack. "But how would this guy have known about Lucille?"

"Gigi said he and his accomplice stole a series of cars and changed the plates, giving them a second set of wheels. My guess is she followed Lucille. After he left our house, he called her. She told him about Lucille, and they hatched the plan to steal her purse."

"As far-fetched as it sounds, it's all very plausible," said Zack.

"And of course, the very next day, Jesse found himself short-staffed after Roscoe's accident. Sound suspicious?"

"You're suggesting the accident wasn't an accident."

"Let's just say enquiring minds want to know."

"And the next night," said Zack, following my lead, "someone used a key to break into the house, assaulted Lucille, and killed Cormac Murphy."

"Although Gigi doesn't know Denny's responsible for Murphy's murder, she did admit that our mystery man is the older guy she ran off with, and his lookout was the woman who kidnapped me."

Zack raised an eyebrow. "Older man? Denny is in his thirties."

"To a sixteen-year-old someone in his thirties is an older man."

"And the woman? How is she connected to him?"

"Gigi wouldn't say, but she did nearly slip at one point, leading me to believe they're related. She could be an older sister, an aunt, a cousin, even his mother."

Zack nodded. "I think she's in her sixties, but she could be younger. However, none of this is proof. It's all circumstantial evidence."

"But there's more. Denny overheard me reminding Mama about the science fair and what time we needed to leave. He knew we'd be out until late Wednesday night. He also knew I was going to the salon this morning and dropping off Lucille at Harriet's before my appointment. I'm betting he called his accomplice as soon as I left."

"You think she was loitering down the street, constantly watching the house?"

"Sometimes but not this time because she needed to bring Gigi with her to drive while she held me at gunpoint."

Zack scowled. "What about the other times? Where was Gigi? Are you sure she wasn't also an accomplice and has decided to turn on them to save herself?"

I could understand how Zack would think that. I told him how Gigi said they'd leave her stuck in the motel with no phone and no money and threatened her if she tried to leave. "That kid is terrified of them, Zack."

"But she left the motel last Wednesday night," he reminded me, "and followed them here."

I explained how the woman had left the keys to the second vehicle in the motel the night Gigi followed them. "I asked her why she didn't just take off at that point."

"And?"

"She's a kid, Zack. A misguided sixteen-year-old who was

promised a vacation in New York by a man who convinced her he loved her. She was pissed, and like many sixteen-year-olds, she wasn't thinking clearly."

His brow wrinkled. "I'm not sure I buy that, but let's move on. How would the woman know which salon you went to?"

"She didn't have to know. All she had to do was drive around downtown until she spotted where I'd parked my car and wait for me to return. There are only so many parking lots in downtown Westfield."

He grew silent for a moment, and I could sense he was mulling over everything I'd laid out. Finally, he said, "Okay, let's say everything is fact and nothing is conjecture. If so, we're still missing a huge puzzle piece."

I sighed. "I know. We still don't know which one of them knew about the jewelry and how they found out."

"Any theories?"

"I'm thinking the older woman is the wife of one of Murphy's goons, either Vinnie Monaghan or Frankie Fallon."

"It's possible, but I have another theory."

"I'm all ears."

"She's Cormac Murphy's daughter."

TWENTY-ONE

My jaw dropped to my toes. "I never considered that. She'd be about the right age. Did Cormac Murphy have any daughters?"

"Three, according to Ledbetter. And two sons. All in the family business."

"If not a daughter, she might be a daughter-in-law."

"Another possibility. We'll know more later. Right now, neither of them is talking, and they've both lawyered up."

"Have they been charged?"

"Not yet, but Ledbetter assured me they won't be released anytime soon. He was waiting for a hit from fingerprints and facial recognition. The woman won't even tell them her name. I wanted to get back to make sure you were okay."

Zack laced the fingers of his right hand through my left hand. Before we headed into the living room, I turned to face him and asked, "Are the boys at Shane's?"

He nodded. "They know you're safe. Shane offered to keep them overnight."

"Good. I think that's best with Gigi here. She's skittish enough as it is."

"Plus, Ledbetter still needs to get statements from the two of you. He'll be here within the next hour or so. By then he also may have more answers for us."

We found Gigi huddled in the corner of the sofa, her arms wrapped around her knees. Leonard crouched with his head in his paws a short distance away. He silently eyed Gigi. I couldn't tell if he was guarding her or thought he was guarding us from her.

With her ultra-thin body lost in my way-too-big-for-her New York Mets sweatshirt and sweatpants, she looked even younger than her sixteen years. She ignored Leonard and stared warily at Zack.

I took a seat beside her, placed my hand on her forearm, and asked, "How about a cup of hot cocoa?"

When she nodded, Zack smiled at her and said, "Hot cocoa coming up. I'll bet you like marshmallows."

Some of the fear faded from her eyes. The corners of her mouth curled up slightly, and she nodded.

As Zack made his way into the dining room, Gigi whispered, "Is that your boyfriend?"

"Fiancé."

She glanced down at my ring. "I didn't notice before. It's very pretty."

I chuckled. "You're forgiven. We were kind of busy."

Gigi turned her head to watch Zack in the dining room while he prepared the cocoa. As I followed her gaze, for the first time I noticed the dining room was no longer as crowded as when I left the house this morning. Although cartons of food and dishes still filled the floor, the refrigerator and microwave were missing, as was the coffeemaker. I'd completely forgotten the new appliances had been scheduled for delivery this afternoon.

Cup in hand, Zack strode into the kitchen. A moment later I heard the new microwave nuking the cocoa.

"He's kinda cute," said Gigi, dragging my attention back to her.

"And taken. You need to start dating guys your own age."

Her eyes grew wide. "I didn't...I meant no..."

"Hey, it's okay." I placed a calming palm on her knee and smiled at her. "I was kidding."

"Oh." She heaved a deep sigh. "I guess you're right, though. You *and* my mom." Her eyes pleaded with me. "You'll still call her for me, won't you?"

"Of course. There's someone coming to the house to take our statements. I'll phone her once he leaves."

Gigi's expression grew anxious. "What kind of statement?"

With Ralph perched on his shoulder, Zack returned to the living room. He held the mug of hot cocoa in one hand, an ice pack in the other. "For your bruises," he said, handing me the ice pack before passing the hot cocoa to Gigi.

Gigi stared wide-eyed at Ralph, her mouth agape.

"He won't hurt you," I assured her. "Ralph is very friendly."

"And smart," added Zack.

"Ralph, huh?"

I shrugged. "He belonged to my great-aunt. I inherited him when she died."

"Can I pet him?"

Zack handed Gigi the mug and reached into his shirt pocket for a sunflower seed. "Offer him this."

She placed the sunflower seed between her thumb and forefinger and tentatively raised her arm until the treat was within

Ralph's reach. He dipped his head and grabbed it with his beak. Gigi giggled.

Afterward, she turned back to me, her expression once again wary. "You didn't answer my question about the statement."

"About what happened to us," I said. "Our statements will help law enforcement determine the extent of the crimes Denny and that woman committed."

Gigi gripped the mug with both hands as she stared at us, puzzlement written across her face. "Who's Denny?"

Zack and I shared a quick look before I refocused on Gigi. "The man you ran off with. Dennis Clancy?"

She shook her head. "I don't know anyone by that name."

I placed my hand on her shoulder. "Gigi, you don't have to be scared anymore. They're both in police custody. They can't hurt you. You can tell us the truth."

"I am telling you the truth," she said, growing defensive. "I don't know anyone named Dennis or Denny Clancy. I swear."

Zack whipped out his phone and brought up the surveillance video from this morning when Denny arrived to grout the backsplash. He turned the phone so Gigi could see the screen. "Do you know him?"

"That's Nathan. Nathan Curtis."

Or not. Considering Zack's theory that my kidnappers were related to Cormac Murphy, they both might use multiple aliases. "He told us his name was Dennis Clancy."

Gigi's eyes grew wide, and her lower lip trembled. "You met him? What was he doing here?"

"Working for our contractor," said Zack, taking a seat in one of the wingback chairs across from the sofa.

Gigi blew a ragged breath into her mug, took a sip, then shook her head before saying, "That make no sense."

"Why is that?" I asked.

"Why would he be working for a contractor? We're supposed to be on a vacation. Besides, they're super-rich. Nathan always took me shopping and to concerts and out to expensive restaurants. That's why I didn't understand why we were staying in such a crappy motel."

Zack's forehead wrinkled, a sure sign the wheels in his brain were furiously spinning. "Did he charge things or pay cash?" he asked.

"Cash. Always. Why?"

"No reason," said Zack. "Just curious."

I had an idea where his thoughts were leading. I offered a bread crumb along the path. "Gigi mentioned Nathan and the woman would carjack vehicles, then switch out the license plates to avoid detection."

When he locked eyes with me and offered a near imperceptible shake of his head, I knew we were both thinking about yesterday's bank robbery in Union, the one committed with a carjacked SUV abandoned on the railroad tracks.

Gigi wrinkled her brow. "What's that got to do with paying cash instead of using credit cards?" she asked.

"Nothing," I said. "Just something you told me that I thought I should mention."

"People go to ATMs to withdraw money all the time, don't they?"

"Of course, they do," I assured her. I then changed the subject. "Gigi, do you now feel comfortable enough to tell us your last name?"

"I guess." She balanced the cocoa mug between her knees and

stared into it as she answered. "It's Abbott."

"And the name of the woman with Nathan?" asked Zack.

As Gigi concentrated on fishing a mini marshmallow from the mug, she sucked in her lower lip. Neither Zack nor I pressed. Finally, she plucked a marshmallow from the mug, sucked it into her mouth, and said, "Maeve."

"Is Maeve related to Nathan?" I asked.

"His mother." Then she ducked her head and mumbled, her voice ragged, "I don't know what I did wrong. They were both always so nice to me before we arrived here."

"You didn't do anything wrong," Zack assured her.

Her head whipped up, and she focused on him. "How do you know?" she asked, revealing typical teenage angst. "You weren't there."

This wasn't the time to explain to Gigi that she had been groomed, that Maeve and Nathan were predators. Hopefully, her mother would get her the help she'd need to move on from her harrowing experience. Instead, I said, "I think what Zack means is that sometimes people don't show us their true nature when we're first getting to know them."

Ralph squawked. "*There the action lies in his true nature. Hamlet.* Act Three, Scene Three."

Gigi's eyes bugged out. "He knows Shakespeare?"

Zack rewarded Ralph with another sunflower seed and said, "I told you he was smart."

"Weird." She returned to sipping her cocoa and after a minute said, "It's like Maeve and Nathan became different people after we arrived in New Jersey. Like that story about Dr. Jekyll and Mr. Hyde but without the murders." Her eyes grew wide again, and she said, "Or maybe not."

I saw comprehension slowly dawning in her eyes. "Do you really think they were going to kill us, or did you say that to get me to help you?"

"I believe they would have killed us."

She shook her head. Even after all she'd gone through, I knew she didn't want to believe me. "If you're right," she finally said, "how can you ever trust anyone you meet?"

"You take your time," I said. "You don't rush into anything."

"Like running off with people you've only known for a month?"

"Like that," I said. "And trusting your gut instead of your hormones."

A tear trickled down her cheek. She swiped at it with the back of her hand and said, "Life was a lot simpler when all I wanted was a Barbie Dream House. Maybe I should become a nun."

I laughed. "There are many options besides Barbie's Dream House and the convent. You'll figure it out, Gigi. You're a smart kid."

She snorted. "If I'm so smart, how come I was so stupid?"

A sixteen-year-old with a knowledge of Shakespeare and *Dr. Jekyll and Mr. Hyde* wasn't stupid. Perhaps too sheltered, but I had high hopes that Gigi would move on from this ordeal and not let it define the remainder of her life.

"Everyone makes stupid mistakes," said Zack. "Smart people learn from them and don't make them again."

Gigi offered up a rueful grin. "I guess I still have lots to learn."

With Gigi feeling more comfortable around Zack, I said, "If you'll both excuse me for a moment, I promised the veterinarian I'd call to let him know we arrived home safely.

~*~

Special Agent Aloysius Ledbetter arrived a few minutes later. I was pleasantly surprised to see Detective Spader with him, given the possessive nature of law enforcement when it came to cases that crossed jurisdictions. The detective took one look at me, shook his head, then handed me my purse and said, "Let me know if anything's missing."

After I introduced the two men to Gigi, Spader pulled a phone and wallet from his pocket and handed them to her. "Same for you, Miss Abbott. Let me know if anything is missing."

Agent Ledbetter then said, "We'd like to interview Miss Abbott first, then you, Mrs. Pollack. I know everyone has questions. We'll answer as many as we can after we get your statements about what happened."

"Anastasia and I will be in the den while you speak with Gigi," said Zack, "unless you'd rather we head up to the apartment."

"The den will suffice," said Ledbetter.

As Zack and I began to leave the living room, Gigi latched onto my arm. "Can she stay with me?"

The two men conferred for a moment before Ledbetter nodded his consent. "Mrs. Pollack may stay, but she's not allowed to offer any input. You can't confer with her in any way before answering our questions. Do you understand, Miss Abbott?"

"Yes," said Gigi. She heaved a sigh of relief. "Thank you."

Gigi and I reclaimed our seats on the sofa. She tucked her legs beneath her and continued to hold onto my arm. Ledbetter and Spader each settled into one of the wingback chairs opposite us. Both men whipped out pens and notepads, but Spader remained silent while Ledbetter questioned Gigi.

By this point, Gigi had already told me enough that when Ledbetter's questioning ended nearly half an hour later, I hadn't learned anything new other than she came from a small town outside of Atlanta, Georgia. So much for Denny—or Nathan—traveling from New Mexico to New Jersey in search of a construction job. That, too, was a lie.

Gigi answered every question posed to her except for those which she didn't know the answer to, such as how Maeve and Denny knew about the jewelry or the cabin in Sussex County. Throughout the questioning, her answers were consistent with what she'd earlier related to me.

Ledbetter turned to Spader. "Anything I've missed?"

Spader flipped his notepad closed. "I think you've covered it all." He turned to Gigi and said, "Thank you for your cooperation, Miss Abbott."

Gigi's eyes darted between both men. "Anastasia...Mrs. Pollack said you'd protect me. What happens if they get out on bail?"

"They won't," said Ledbetter. "Between what you've provided us and other evidence we've collected, we have more than enough for indictments. Those two are going away for a long time."

"What other evidence?" she asked.

"We'll explain that after we speak to Mrs. Pollack, okay?"

Gigi reluctantly stood. Leonard followed her as she headed toward the hallway. Once at the foyer, she hesitated and glanced back over her shoulder. "We won't be long," I assured her.

She nodded and headed down the hallway toward the den, Leonard at her heels.

Once we heard Gigi enter the den and the door closed, Spader asked me, "You believe her?"

His question surprised me. "Don't you, Detective?"

"I'd like to, but I also know she could be a darned good actress.

I've seen it before." He tilted his head toward Ledbetter. "We both have."

"You're wrong. I've spent enough time with Gigi today to know otherwise. She's as much a victim as I am. Maybe more so."

"Meaning?"

"I used to be a teacher, Agent Ledbetter. I'm trained to spot child abuse."

"Explain," he said.

"In my opinion, this is classic manipulation of a young girl coaxed into a situation, believing she's found love. She was manipulated and physically abused when she didn't do as she was told. I saw it with my own eyes. The only thing that child is guilty of is being naïve and impressionable. Don't expect me to testify against her if you decide to charge her as an accessory to kidnapping and this goes to trial."

Ledbetter eyed Spader, then flipped his notepad to a fresh page. "Let's move on for now. Tell us what happened today."

By the time I'd finished, another half hour had passed. I was emotionally drained, physically exhausted, and once again ravenously hungry.

Ledbetter stood and stretched. "Need a break?"

"What I need is a beach vacation with an endless supply of umbrella drinks. You offering?"

He snorted. "Unfortunately, I think Uncle Sam would balk if I tried to expense that. Try this guy," he said tilting his head toward Spader.

The detective laughed. "Sorry, Mrs. Pollack. That's way above my pay grade."

I sighed. "You guys are no help."

"We do have some information that might interest you,

though," said Ledbetter. He pulled out his phone and shot off a text. A moment later Zack and Gigi returned to the living room, Ralph on his customary perch of Zack's shoulder and Leonard following closely behind.

I suggested we move to the kitchen. "I don't know about the rest of you, but I need to eat something. You can all help us inaugurate our new kitchen."

Without waiting for an answer, I strode through the dining room and into the kitchen where I stopped short and soaked up the view. Zack came up behind me, wrapped his arms around me, and rested his chin on my head. "Well?"

"No peeling linoleum? No chipped Formica? No cabinets from another century?" I turned to face him, threw my arms around his neck and kissed him. "What's not to love?"

"Does that mean my standing as head chef is in jeopardy?"

"Heck, no. I'm quite happy to remain your sous chef for life."

I pulled cheese, crudites, hummus, a bowl of grapes, and an assortment of beverages from the new refrigerator while Zack placed Ralph back in his cage. Then he grabbed crackers, plates, glasses, and utensils from the boxes in the dining room.

Once we were all settled on stools around the new kitchen island, except for Leonard, who took up a position near Gigi's stool, Ledbetter said, "We're still in the early stages of investigating, but we now know we're dealing with Shauna Doyle Gallagher and Aiden Gallagher."

TWENTY-TWO

I gasped, nearly choking on the grape I'd popped into my mouth. "That's how she knew about the jewelry." Then I turned to Spader. "I guess you were wrong. Murphy didn't order a hit on the Gallaghers. They've been alive all this time."

"What can I say?" He shrugged and offered me a sheepish grin. "I'm only semi-perfect."

"That's not all," said Ledbetter, as he spread hummus on a cracker. "They're throwing each other under the bus. Each claiming to be an unwilling participant of the other's scheme."

"And once again," I said, "we have an example of no honor among thieves. But what about Kellen Gallagher? Where does he fit in all of this?"

"Turns out Kellen died years ago," said Ledbetter.

"How?" asked Zack.

"Hit and run."

"Let me guess," I said, "The vehicle was stolen, and they never caught the driver."

"Give that lady a bubble gum cigar," said Spader, winking at me from across the island.

Gigi's head had whipped back and forth throughout the discussion, often wide-eyed with her mouth hanging open. Finally, she said, "Time out, guys. Who are these people you're talking about, and what do they have to do with Maeve and Nathan?"

"The Gallaghers were the former owners of this house," explained Zack.

"Maeve and Nathan Curtis are really Shauna Doyle Gallagher and her son Aiden," said Ledbetter. "They have multiple connections to organized crime, including several high-profile unsolved cases."

Gigi's mouth gaped open. She turned to me. "The ones you told me about? The robberies at the museum and the jewelry stores in Boston?" She shook her head. "Nathan couldn't be involved in those. You said the museum was robbed more than thirty years ago. He would've been a little kid."

"Tangentially involved," said Ledbetter.

Confusion spread across Gigi's face. "Tange—what?"

"Indirectly," he said for the first time smiling at her. "The FBI suspected Shauna's brother-in-law Garrett Quinn was involved in the museum and the jewelry store robberies, but they never had enough evidence to charge him. An informant admitted to seeing Colleen Quinn, who was Garrett's wife and Shauna's sister, with one of the stolen items. However, before the FBI could search her property, Colleen mailed Shauna that item along with others, asking her to keep them safe."

"Shauna hid the jewelry under a pile of insulation in the corner of my attic," I said. "But sometime later, Shauna, her husband, their young son, and Shauna's brother went into Witness Protection."

"What's that?" asked Gigi.

"It's when the government gives people new identities and moves them to a different part of the country," explained Ledbetter.

"Why would they do that?"

"To protect them after they testify in a court case," I said. "Shauna's brother testified against a Boston mob boss."

"The same Boston mob boss," added Spader, "that we suspect Aiden—or Nathan, as you know him—murdered and buried behind Mrs. Pollack's garage Wednesday night when he came to search the attic for the jewelry."

Gigi's eyes grew wide, and her voice climbed several octaves. "That's what they were doing here? He killed someone?"

"And nearly killed my mother-in-law," I added.

Gigi began to shake with such force, she nearly tipped over the glass of apple cider she held clenched between her two hands. She turned to me and said, "I'm glad I listened to you. I wasn't sure whether to believe you at first, but hearing this, I now know for sure. You were right. They really would have killed us."

She turned to Ledbetter. "Will my mom and I have to go into this Witness program?"

"The program is voluntary," he said, "and in your case, I don't think it will be necessary. We've connected those two to enough crimes that they'll never see freedom again."

"More than what you've said?" she asked.

"Much more," said Spader, "For starters, it's looking like we can tie them to a series of carjackings and bank robberies across the country dating back more than ten years."

"What about the one in Union?" asked Zack.

Spader nodded. "Among others. Our modern-day Ma Barker and her criminal spawn have been busy."

"But why didn't Maeve take the jewelry with her when she moved?" asked Gigi.

"That's a different branch of the Justice Department," said Ledbetter. "I'm assuming the Gallaghers were whisked away by the U.S. Marshals in the dead of night. They wouldn't have been allowed to take anything with them."

Gigi's jaw dropped. "They had to leave all their stuff?"

Ledbetter nodded. "Everything. The most innocuous item might tie them to their former life and jeopardize their safety should the wrong person notice it. As for the jewelry," he added, "if she had been allowed to take her belongings, how would she have explained being in possession of stolen property?"

Gigi considered that for a moment. "I guess that would've been a problem."

"A huge one," said Spader. "But under the circumstances, it's also possible the hidden jewelry didn't cross her mind at the time if she was running for her life."

"Although," I said, "given Johnnie Doyle's ties to Cormac Murphy, doesn't it seem odd the house wasn't thoroughly searched by law enforcement, either before the Gallaghers entered Witness Protection or afterwards?"

"It should have been searched," said Ledbetter, "but again, not my branch of government."

"We don't know that the house wasn't searched," said Zack, "Maybe whoever was assigned the attic didn't check under the insulation as thoroughly as he should have."

"If he had," I said, "he would've found the jewelry, and we

wouldn't be sitting here discussing it right now."

My family and I also wouldn't have had to deal with two murders, a mugging, an attempted murder, and a kidnapping, but I kept that comment to myself. Neither Spader nor Ledbetter were responsible for what had or hadn't occurred all those years ago.

"Anyway," said Spader. "Since there were never any reports that the stolen items were recovered, Shauna Gallagher rightly assumed the jewelry was still hidden in the attic."

"That still doesn't explain why she waited so long to retrieve the box," said Zack.

"That's not something we can explain," said Ledbetter. "At least not yet. Possibly, it had something to do with Kellen Gallagher's death."

"How?" I asked.

"From what we've determined," said Ledbetter, "Shauna and Aiden embarked on their life of crime shortly after the hit and run."

"Another possibility," added Spader, "is that the delay in trying to recover the jewelry somehow involved Shauna's brother Johnnie Doyle. We hope to learn more as the investigation proceeds."

As I munched on a cube of cheddar atop a cracker, I mulled over everything I'd heard so far. Something niggled at the back of my brain. I thought about my initial conversation with Rosalie and suddenly landed on the part of the story that didn't make sense to me. "I don't get it," I said.

"What part?" asked Ledbetter.

"Shauna told my neighbor Rosalie Schneider about the jewelry Colleen sent her. Rosalie said Shauna was freaked out because she knew Colleen's husband Garrett was in the mob and suspected the jewelry was stolen. She wanted no part of it, but she was too scared to contact the police, fearing they'd arrest Colleen. That's why she hid the box in the attic. Rosalie said not even Shauna's husband knew about the jewelry and especially not Shauna's mob-connected brother Johnnie."

"Is there a question?" asked Spader.

"A good one," I said. "What changed? What suddenly turned a supposedly law-abiding housewife into a vicious criminal?"

"Perhaps, she never was a law-abiding housewife," suggested Zack. "We only know what Rosalie told you. How do we know Shauna didn't have some ulterior motive for what she told Rosalie?"

"Like what?" I asked.

"Who knows?" he said. "Perhaps to cover up what was really going on back then."

"Interesting theory," said Ledbetter. "We'll have to pay a call on Mrs. Schneider."

"I don't think so," I said. "If that were the case, why tell Rosalie anything about the jewelry? How does it help Shauna in any way to admit she suspects she's in possession of stolen property?"

"Valid point," said Spader.

Ledbetter stood. "Rest assured, we'll get to the bottom of this. For now, it's time to call it a night." He nodded to Gigi and me. "Mrs. Pollack, Miss Abbott, I realize it's been a long day. I'll contact Social Services to find accommodations for Miss Abbott."

"That won't be necessary," I said. "Gigi can stay with us. I plan to call her mother as soon as you leave."

Ledbetter turned to Zack. "You okay with this?"

Zack eyed Gigi. Hearing Social Services, she had grown

terrified and grabbed onto my arm. He turned back to Ledbetter and nodded.

"As long as you accept responsibility," said Ledbetter. He thanked Gigi and me for our statements, then turned to Zack, adding, "And for your assistance."

Zack cut me a side-eye. "Let's hope it's the last time it's necessary."

"Speaking of which," I said, pointedly staring at all three men, "other than telling us you caught Shauna and Aiden, you failed to mention how."

Ledbetter tilted his head toward Zack. "I'll leave that to this guy." He placed his hand on Spader's shoulder. "Like I said, it's been a long day."

Taking his cue from Agent Ledbetter, Detective Spader popped one last grape into his mouth and sidled off his stool. "Once again, thank you both for your hospitality," he said, nodding to me and Zack.

"The two of you are always welcome," I said, "either together or separately."

"But next time," added Zack, "let's make it purely a social call."

Both Spader and Ledbetter laughed.

"Before you leave," I said, "I have one more question."

Agent Ledbetter raised an eyebrow. "Yes, Mrs. Pollack?"

"Have you heard from Agent Smanski regarding the etching?"

"Not a word."

"Really? I wouldn't think it would take that long to authenticate."

"Not my area of expertise," he said. "I'll be in touch if I hear anything."

"What etching?" asked Gigi.

I told her about the miniature Rembrandt stolen from the museum. "The box of jewelry contained a locket with the same etching. We don't know if it's the original or a copy."

"A real Rembrandt?" Her eyes bugged out. "Wow! Do you think Shauna knew?"

"Probably not at first," I said, "but she may have found out about Colleen's connection to the etching the same way I did, from articles on the Internet."

"There's a huge reward for any information leading to the recovery of the missing artworks," said Zack. "Maybe that's why Shauna came back in search of the jewelry after all this time."

"That makes a lot of sense," I said. "Colleen is dead. Since the locket was costume jewelry, not one of the pieces from the jewelry store robberies, Shauna didn't have to worry about being charged with possession of stolen property. She could claim the locket was a gift from her sister."

"How would she explain the Rembrandt?" asked Spader.

"She could say she had no idea it was there all these years, that it was hidden behind a childhood photograph of the three Doyle siblings."

Ledbetter offered me a look of skepticism. "And she suddenly decided to remove the photograph after owning the locket for decades?"

"Exactly," I said.

"Why?" asked Spader.

"What if she said she saw one of the documentaries about the Isabella Stewart Gardner Museum? She suddenly realized the locket Colleen sent her might be the one Lochlin Fitzgerald claimed Colleen wore and contained the etching."

Agent Ledbetter's forehead furrowed as his brows knit

together. "You think she planned to turn the etching in to collect the reward money?"

"It's a theory," I said. "It would certainly explain why she waited so long to retrieve the jewelry."

"But what about the jewelry?" asked Ledbetter. How would she explain the rest of it?"

I grinned at him. "What jewelry, Agent Ledbetter?"

"The stolen—oh," Ledbetter grinned back at me. "I see where you're going with this, Mrs. Pollack. All Shauna had to say was Colleen never sent her a box of jewelry."

"What proof does anyone have that Colleen sent Shauna the stolen jewelry? Only the word of a neighbor who told me Shauna claimed to have received it from Colleen. That's hearsay, right?"

"Then how did the stolen jewelry get in your attic?" asked Gigi.

"Shauna could profess to not knowing about any jewelry hidden in the attic."

"But there was," said Spader.

"True," I said, "but there are other ways the jewelry might have wound up in the attic."

Spader raised an eyebrow. "Such as?"

"Shauna could place the blame on her brother. What if Johnnie stole the jewelry from Murphy and hid it in the attic? That would explain why Murphy came looking for him as soon as he got out of prison and why he insisted Johnnie had something of his. With both Johnnie and Murphy dead, who's to say that's not what really happened?"

I turned to Gigi. "That's why Shauna and Nathan would have killed us. For her plan to work, she couldn't have any witnesses to refute her claim about suddenly finding the Rembrandt in the locket."

"Mrs. Pollack," said Agent Ledbetter, "I think you may have connected all the dots for us."

"Now all you have to do is prove it," I said.

"You sure you're not interested in working for me, Mrs. Pollack?"

Zack looped his arm around my waist. "She's not. Stop asking."

Ledbetter shrugged. "Can't blame a guy for trying."

~*~

Once Detective Spader and Agent Ledbetter departed, I placed a call to Gigi's mother. She answered on the first ring. "Gigi, where are you? I've been worried sick."

"This isn't Gigi, Mrs. Abbott. My name is Anastasia Pollack. I'm calling from New Jersey."

"Who are you? Why do you have my daughter's phone?"

"She's fine, and she's safe, but she's had quite a harrowing experience."

I heard her breath catch. "What do you mean? What happened?"

"I'll let her explain that to you, but I want you to know you have a very brave daughter. You should be extremely proud of her."

"I don't understand. I should be proud of my daughter for running off with some creep old enough to be her father?"

"No, for saving my life."

Silence greeted my statement. Then, in a confused voice she asked, "Did you just say my daughter saved your life?"

"I did."

Mrs. Abbott burst into tears. "I was beside myself with worry, not knowing where she was. Her phone kept going to voicemail. I filed a missing person report with the police."

When I explained how Gigi hadn't been in possession of her phone until a short time ago, she asked, "Why are you calling me instead of my daughter?"

"She's afraid you won't forgive her for running off."

"Oh, for heaven's sake," she cried. "Of course, I forgive her. She's my daughter. I love her."

"I think that's all she needs to hear, Mrs. Abbott. Gigi is welcome to stay here until you can make arrangements to get her home." I then handed the phone to Gigi.

As I exited the room to give mother and daughter some privacy, I heard Gigi say, "Mom, I'm so sorry. You were right. I should have listened to you."

While Gigi spoke with her mother, I joined Zack in the den. "I want all the details," I said, settling next to him on the sofa. "Don't leave anything out."

He took my hand in his. "Not much to tell. The Feds had the place staked out before I arrived."

"Did they give you a bulletproof vest to wear?"

"Ahead of time. And a wire." He brought my hand to his lips and kissed it. "I was totally protected."

"Unless you took a bullet to the head," I muttered.

"They would have been taken out before they had a chance to get off a shot."

I twisted around and locked eyes with him. "By you or the Feds?"

"Both."

"I hope that's the truth. Then what happened?"

"Shauna and Aiden had parked in the shadows of the abandoned motel. When I placed the box in the burned-out shell of the car as directed, Shauna shouted at me to get back in my car and drive off. I asked where you were. She laughed and said she wasn't that stupid. They'd release you after they'd gotten safely away."

"But you knew they no longer held me."

"I did, but they didn't know that. I had to play along as if I thought they had you stashed somewhere."

I shook the cobwebs from my brain. "Of course. The Feds moved in after that?"

"They waited until the Gallaghers had grabbed the box and opened it."

"No jewelry?"

"Jewelry but not what they expected to find. One of Ledbetter's team had bought an assortment of cheap costume jewelry at one of the big box stores."

"Surprise, surprise." I snorted. "I hope the Feds captured that on tape."

"They did, but if it's ever publicly broadcast, the networks will have to bleep out every word of dialogue."

Gigi appeared at the entrance to the den, Leonard at her heels. "Sorry to interrupt," she said.

"You're not interrupting," I assured her.

"My mom's flying up first thing tomorrow morning."

"You patched things up with her?" I asked.

"Yeah," She stared at her feet as her fingers worried the hem of the sweatshirt I'd lent her. "I'm grounded for a month when I get back home, but that won't be until after we spend a few mother/daughter days together." She looked up and cracked a sheepish grin. "Looks like I'm getting that New York City vacation after all."

~*~

266

By late the next day, life had begun to return to normal. Gigi's mother had arrived mid-morning and whisked the teenager off to Manhattan. Alex and Nick returned home a few hours later. Zack and I had FaceTimed with them the night before to explain my injuries and assure them they hadn't occurred at the hands of my kidnappers. I'm not sure they believed my tale of the falling coat hanger, though. I haven't been hugged this much by my sons since they were toddlers.

Shortly before dinner Zack received a call from Agent Ledbetter. He had more information about the case. Zack had planned to grill steaks and invited him to join us. He arrived with a bottle of wine and a bouquet of spring flowers.

Zack took one look at the flowers Ledbetter handed me, frowned, and said, "The answer is still no, Al."

I raised both eyebrows. "You're not even going to wait until he asks a question?"

"I know the question," said Zack, "and I know how persistent Aloysius Ledbetter can get when he wants something."

I wondered if this was from Zack's own personal experience. Was the FBI the alphabet agency Zack claimed he didn't work for? I looked from one alpha male to the next and laughed. "You two want to take this outside? I think there may be some old boxing gloves in the garage."

"No need," said Ledbetter, "The flowers are a thank-you, nothing more."

Zack eyed him suspiciously. "For what?"

"Cracking our case." He turned to me. "You were right, Mrs. Pollack. Once again."

"About?" I asked.

"Your theory that Shauna and Aiden Gallagher returned for

the locket, hoping to find the etching and claim the reward."

"They confessed?" I asked.

"Eventually, when confronted with the lengthy list of charges they faced and the mandatory time they'd receive if found guilty. Their confessions might convince the Bureau of Prisons panel to shave off a few years, but they're both still going away for a long time. This also spares you and Gigi from testifying."

"I like the sound of that," I said. "I never want to see those two again for as long as I live."

Zack continued to eye Agent Ledbetter. "You sure you're not hiding any ulterior motive?"

"Not unless your fiancée is interested."

They both turned to look at me. "Absolutely, positively no way. Not interested. Never. Ever."

Ledbetter grinned. "I'd say that's a definite maybe."

"The lady has spoken," said Zack. "How do you like your steak?"

Over dinner Agent Ledbetter filled in more details about Shauna and Aiden's life of crime. "Shauna grew increasingly bitter over the years. Life in Witness Protection isn't easy. Kellen's death compounded the situation. Her brother's subsequent arrest and disappearance added to her stress."

I speared Ledbetter with a look of skepticism. "Are you suggesting Shauna and Aiden began robbing banks to relieve her stress?"

"In a manner of speaking," said Ledbetter. "They needed money. Shauna had no skills, and Aiden was a pampered loser. Ironically, they were good at it. If not for your kidnapping, we wouldn't have solved all those open cases."

"What about the cabin in Sussex County?" I asked. "How did

they know about it?"

"That was an old hunting camp owned by a private group," said Ledbetter. "Kellen used to take Aiden up there. Aiden remembered where the keys were hidden."

One more mystery solved. There was only one left. "What about the etching? Was it the original?"

Ledbetter shook his head. "Afraid not. But I do have some good news for you. There was a reward offered for the jewelry. You should receive a check from the insurance company in a few weeks."

EPILOGUE

Five Weeks Later

With my luck over the past sixteen months, I half-expected to awaken this morning to a category five hurricane, a freak June snowstorm, a corpse in my coral bells—or all three. Instead, the weather report called for a sunny day with only the hint of a breeze and highs in the mid-seventies. Perfect outdoor wedding weather.

Although, with my track record, there was still the possibility of a dead body. Last summer, in the middle of Mama's marriage to the late Lawrence Tuttnauer, the police had interrupted the ceremony, and it wasn't to offer their congratulations.

I'd had enough of dead bodies.

"Ready?" asked Alex.

My sons had drawn straws to determine which one would walk me down the makeshift aisle of strewn rose petals and which one would act as Zack's best man. I shook all thoughts of murder and mayhem from my brain and replaced them with the love I felt for my family and the man standing next to Nick across the yard under a floral arbor.

"Ready," I said, taking Alex's arm as Mama stood waiting on my other side.

"You look beautiful," she whispered.

Mama had insisted on taking me shopping for a full-blown wedding gown, complete with train and veil. After tense negotiations, I had convinced her that a simple white dress was far more appropriate for a forty-something widow walking down the aisle for the second time. I had chosen a white lace sheath with a scooped neck and cap sleeves. Instead of a veil, I wore a garland of white tea roses perched atop my head.

All physical remnants of my recent ordeal had disappeared. Cuts healed. Bruises faded. The emotional scars still haunted me, though. I knew those would take more time. They had joined a long list that began with the shock of Karl's betrayal and had snowballed ever since.

I caught Zack smiling at me from the end of the aisle and smiled back. Today was the first day of a new beginning.

When the Westfield High School string quartet struck up the first notes of Pachelbel's "Cannon in D," friends and family, seated in the rows of white chairs on either side of the aisle, stood and turned toward us.

As Alex, Mama, and I slowly walked down the aisle, I focused on Zack but couldn't help noticing the beaming faces on either side of the aisle. Every one of them meant so much to me. Old friends like my bestie Cloris McWerther, who'd insisted on catering the wedding luncheon as her gift to Zack and me. And newer friends like Tino Martinelli, and Shane and Sophie Lambert. Even my half-brother-in-law Ira Pollack. Annoying though he was, he always meant well. I hoped someday he'd find someone to love who would not only return his love but somehow find it in her heart to love his three spoiled kids.

Even Detective Spader had come, as well as Agent Aloysius Ledbetter and his wife, and Zack's ex-wife Patricia with her husband and their twins.

Only Lucille was missing. Although invited, she had refused to attend. Harriet Kleinhample's house arrest had ended. She had arrived early this morning in yet another Volkswagen minibus to pick up my mother-in-law. With any luck, they'd stay away until all our guests had departed.

We arrived at the makeshift altar. I handed Mama my bouquet of lilies, tea roses, and baby's breath, turned to face Zack, and placed both of my hands in his.

Life was good. Now, if it would only stay that way from this day forward.

ANASTASIA'S FRAME ART CRAFTS

Thinking about the empty frames hanging where stolen art once hung in the Isabella Stewart Gardner Museum gave Anastasia the idea for the craft projects for the latest issue of *American Woman*. These are some of the ideas she came up with for taking plain, inexpensive wooden picture frames and transforming them into one-of-a-kind works of art to display family photos from vacations, holidays, and special events.

Road Map Decoupaged Picture Frame

Nowadays we use the map apps on our phones, but it's still fun to buy maps of the places where we've travelled, or you may have some sitting around from pre-smart phone days.

Materials: unfinished wooden picture frame (available at craft stores), road map, craft stick (optional,) foam brush, scissors, decoupage medium, tweezers (optional).

1. Cut out sections of the map into manageable pieces, about 3" - 4" in length and wide enough to wrap around the frame.

2. Using the foam brush, apply decoupage medium to the wrong side of the map cut-outs.

3. Position a map cut-out on the frame, wrapping around to the inside and outside so that all exposed sections of the wooden frame are covered. Use the tweezers to aid in placement.

4. Eliminate wrinkles, air bubbles, and excess medium by gently pushing down on the map with your fingers or the craft stick, working from the center outward. Remove any excess decoupage medium with a damp cloth.

5. Glue the next section of map onto the frame, overlapping the first piece slightly. Repeat until entire frame is covered.

6. Allow decoupage to dry completely. Once dry, apply several coats of decoupage medium to the entire surface, allowing each coat to dry completely before applying the next coat.

Decorative Photo Mat

Any paper souvenir items, such as postcards, ticket stubs, maps, menus, programs, etc. will work for this project. For larger souvenir items, follow directions below. For smaller items, create a collage, gluing randomly around the mat. Follow directions below for finishing edges.

Materials: photo frame, pre-cut mat or cardboard the same size as frame, paper souvenir items, ruler, craft knife, glue stick, photo, photo tape.

1. If your frame didn't come with a pre-cut mat, create one by cutting an opening centered in the cardboard, slightly smaller than the photo you plan to use.

2. Cut larger souvenir items slightly larger than the mat.

3. Apply glue to the surface of the mat. Glue the souvenir to the mat. Allow glue to dry.

4. Turn the mat to wrong side. Using the craft knife, make angled cuts in the paper in each corner of the cutout. Trim the four sides of the paper to 1/2" from the interior opening of the mat.

5. Apply glue to paper, then fold edges around to wrong side of mat.

6. Trim the paper even with outer edges of mat.

7. Tape picture behind mat. Insert mat into frame.

Shabby Chic Picture Frame

This frame makes a wonderful Valentine's Day gift. You might want to frame a vintage Valentine rather than a photo. It also works as a frame for a wedding photo or a bridal shower gift with a photo of the lucky couple.

Materials: unfinished wooden photo frame (available at craft stores); white primer spray paint; assorted lace trims, ribbon, buttons, beads, and other accessories; fabric glue and jewelry glue.

1. Spray frame with light coat of primer. Leaving some of the wood grain showing through the paint will add to the antique look.

2. Position the lace trims and ribbons on the frame to form an appealing collage effect. Glue in place with the fabric glue.

3. Place the buttons, beads, and other accessories around and on top of the lace and ribbons. Glue in place with the jewelry glue.

Seashells, Buttons, Charms, or Beads Frame

Here's a way to make use of all those seashells you've collected at the beach or the spare buttons and beads you have sitting around in a drawer or closet.

Materials: wooden frame; assorted small seashells, buttons, charms, or beads; hot glue gun or jewelry glue.

1. Glue shells, buttons, charms, or beads in a grouping at one corner of the frame or randomly around the entire frame.

A NOTE FROM THE AUTHOR

Dear Readers,

In 1990, thirteen major artworks were stolen from Boston's Isabella Stewart Gardner Museum. The brazen theft has since become known as the greatest art heist in history. As of this writing, not a single piece of the stolen artworks has ever been recovered. No one was ever charged with the theft, and most of the suspects and persons of interest have since died.

I've been fascinated by this unsolved crime for decades and decided to use it as the inspiration behind *Guilty as Framed*, the eleventh full-length novel in my Anastasia Pollack Crafting Mystery series. My story incorporates actual events as gleaned through my research. However, for the purpose of storytelling, I've taken literary license to fictionalize these events, changed the names of suspects, and created new characters.

If you're interested in learning more about the robbery and investigation, there are many news reports and articles on the Internet as well as several books and documentaries that are available.

I hope you enjoyed *Guilty as Framed*. If so, please consider leaving a review at your favorite review site.

Happy reading!
Lois Winston

ABOUT THE AUTHOR

USA Today and Amazon bestselling author Lois Winston began her award-winning writing career with *Talk Gertie to Me*, a humorous fish-out-of-water novel about a small-town girl going off to the big city and the mother who had other ideas. That was followed by the romantic suspense *Love, Lies and a Double Shot of Deception*.

Then Lois's writing segued unexpectedly into the world of humorous amateur sleuth mysteries, thanks to a conversation her agent had with an editor looking for craft-themed mysteries. In her day job Lois was an award-winning craft and needlework designer, and although she'd never written a mystery—or had even thought about writing a mystery—her agent decided she was the perfect person to pen a series for this editor. Thus was born the Anastasia Pollack Crafting Mysteries, which *Kirkus Reviews* dubbed "North Jersey's more mature answer to Stephanie Plum." The series now includes eleven novels and three novellas. Lois also writes the Empty Nest Mysteries, currently at two novels, and one book so far in her Mom Squad Capers series.

To date, Lois has published twenty novels, five novellas, several short stories, one children's chapter book, and one nonfiction book on writing, inspired by her twelve years working as an associate at a literary agency.

To learn more about Lois and her books, visit her at www.loiswinston.com where you can sign up for her newsletter and follow her on various social media sites.

Made in United States
North Haven, CT
28 February 2023

33309677R00178